ADIOS PANTALONES

by
J. STERLING

Adios Pantalones
Copyright © 2018 J. Sterling
All Rights Reserved
Editing and Formatting:
Pam Berehulke
Bulletproof Editing
Cover Design:
Michelle Preast
Indie Book Covers
Cover Model:
Drew Leighty
Cover Photography:
@Dexterbrownfoto

Print Edition

No part of this book may be reproduced or transmitted in any form or by any means, electronic or mechanical, including photocopying, recording, or by any information storage and retrieval system without the written permission of the author, except for the use of brief quotations in a book review.

This is a work of fiction. Names, characters, businesses, places, events, and incidents are either the products of the author's imagination or used in a fictitious manner. Any resemblance to actual persons, living or dead, or actual events is purely coincidental.

ISBN-10: 1-945042-10-9
ISBN-13: 978-1-945042-10-2

Please visit the author's website
www.j-sterling.com
to find out where additional versions may be purchased.

Thank you for purchasing this book.

Please join my mailing list to get updates on new and upcoming releases, deals, bonus content, personal appearances, and other fun news.

http://tinyurl.com/pf6al6u

DEDICATION

This story is for everyone who found love with someone they thought couldn't give it. For the guys who changed our perspectives, who were better than we thought they were, who not only rose to the occasion but owned the whole mother 'effin thing. :)

FOUL MOOD
Ryan

SOMETHING WAS DEFINITELY wrong with me tonight. I was in a shitty mood, and for no good reason. At least, not one that I could pinpoint.

"Hey, Ryan," a female voice shouted at me from across Sam's, the bar my brothers and I owned, and I knew what was coming before I even turned to face her.

The fact that the woman shouting at me was a gorgeous brunette did nothing to improve my state of mind. Beautiful women were a dime a dozen in Los Angeles, and I got to see them every single night. Hell, most of them screamed my name and left me their phone numbers on their way out the door, each one hoping I'd call.

Part of me no longer wanted to indulge in this game of *let's get Ryan to take his shirt off*, but like a good fucking sheep, I did what was expected of me.

"Yeah, sweetheart?" I forced a grin, my teeth grinding together as I fought the urge to run.

She looked around at the bar, still packed even though it was closing time, and gave me a grin of her own. "Can I get an Adios . . ." Her lips pursed and her eyebrows raised seductively as she waited.

"Pantalones," the rest of the bar crowd sang out in unison.

So I did what I always did—took off my damn shirt and tossed it onto the register, screams and whistles filling my ears like we were at a strip club.

As I made the last drink of the night, I got lost in my own thoughts, my mind a scary place to be when I was in one of these rare moods.

I couldn't remember how this tradition got started in the first place, but I was fairly sure that I brought it on myself. You would think it would be every man's fantasy to have a roomful of women screaming his name each night. You would think that every guy on God's green earth would love to have women falling at his feet the way women seemed to fall at mine.

But if you thought that about me, then you didn't know me at all.

It wasn't that I didn't love the attention, because I did. I simply wanted more. I wanted to be more than the guy everyone claimed to be in love with, but no one really knew. I wanted to be the guy women brought home to their parents, not the one they brought home to their apartment for a one-night stand, or offered to suck off in the bathroom.

Some nights I felt cheap, like I was little more than a piece of meat, not worthy of having an actual conversation with.

Feelings like that weren't exclusive to women, although you'd swear women cornered the market on the notion. Women could be just as bad as guys, if not worse, when it came to ogling, catcalling, or treating someone like they were nothing but a hot body with a pretty face. I wasn't sure they always realized it, but sometimes they could make a guy feel about an inch big with the things that came out of their mouths.

Yeah, I know I sound like a fucking chick right now. If my older brother, Frank, knew what I was thinking, he'd make fun of me and call me a princess or some shit like that, but it doesn't change the way I feel.

I, Ryan Fisher, want to fall in love—true love, real love, authentic love. I want to fall in love like both my brothers did. Well, not *exactly* the same way that they did . . . because, hello, Drama 101.

But still . . .

Maybe that was my problem tonight. Maybe I was jealous that they'd both found the loves of their lives, and here I was, taking my damn shirt off night after night and going home alone. There was something fucked up about being adored, but knowing the feelings weren't based in anything real.

It didn't make you feel loved. It made you feel *lonely*.

"What's the matter with you tonight?" my younger brother, Nick, asked as he peered over his shoulder at me. His blue eyes matched mine in shape and color, and sometimes it really tripped me out to look at them.

When I shrugged but didn't respond, Frank grinned at me.

"Is it that time of the month?"

I glared at him, not amused at his joke.

Frank used to be a real stick-in-the-mud, the one Nick and I picked on, but now that he was with his girlfriend, he was a changed man. Frank was actually fun again and seemed truly happy, something that had been missing from his life for years. I hadn't realized how miserable my brother had been until I saw him come to life when he met her.

Looking across the bar, I spotted Frank and Ryan's girlfriends, Claudia and Jess, sitting together at a table as they waited for the bar to close.

I wanted that. I wanted my girl to be sitting there with them, talking, laughing, and waiting for me. The problem was, I had no idea where the hell *my* girl was, when I'd find her, or how. I spent the majority of my time here at Sam's, so if she never walked through those bar doors, how would I ever meet her? And how would I know that she was worth taking the risk for, when I'd all but decided to not date our customers anymore?

Speaking of, dating a customer had worked out for Frank, but I considered that a rarity, something you would expect to happen all the time in this business but usually never did. I honestly had no fucking idea where *my* girl was, but I definitely knew I wasn't currently looking at her.

"I'd love to go home with you tonight," the brunette purred as I handed her the drink she'd ordered.

"Sorry. Can't." Without further explanation, I turned my back and hurried away from her, couldn't get the fuck away quick enough.

Yeah, something was definitely wrong with me tonight.

In my defense, I'd quickly learned that dating the women who came into the bar wasn't necessarily the best idea. At first, I didn't see the harm in dating anyone who caught my eye, and before I knew it, I was going out with a different girl almost every night. Okay, *going out* probably wasn't the right term. But those women had all been wrong for me, and I knew it the second we left the party atmosphere of the bar.

Eventually, all the women I'd taken out started congregating at Sam's . . . on the same nights. They argued, fought for my attention, and tried to outdo one another in every way possible. It was only then that I realized I'd created a bit of a problem.

The thing was, these women all knew they could find me here at Sam's nearly every night, and as a bartender, I had to be friendly and accessible. I hadn't even considered that reality before it was too late. Frank had warned me that dating customers was a bad idea, but as usual, I hadn't listened.

None of the women seemed to take into account that the bar was my place of business. They saw it as a fun place where they could find me anytime they wanted, no strings attached. But the truth was that these women waltzed into my office and did whatever they wanted, without a second thought, and I had nowhere to hide when someone I once took out came in and refused to leave. To say that things got uncomfortable there for a while would be a serious understatement.

Looking back, I consider myself lucky that Frank hadn't murdered me.

RUNNING
Ryan

I LOVED TO run. Aside from bartending and creating new drinks, running was the only thing that made me feel alive. I loved the feel of my feet pounding against the pavement, my chest heaving as I sucked in each jagged breath. Nothing beat waking up to run along the beach path in Santa Monica just as most people were headed into the office.

I ran at the same time every morning, and the handful of faces that passed me on the path had become all too familiar. There was the man who always wore a neon-pink shirt, no matter what. And it wasn't the same shirt, so "pink guy" had a freaking collection of T-shirts in that color. A few weeks ago, he started waving at me each morning, so I guessed we were jogging friends now.

There was a group of guys who ran together, each of them trying to outrun the other. They were intensely competitive, always racing, and they knew me by name, shouting it one by one as they raced past. It never failed to make me laugh, hearing my name fly out of their mouths as they bolted past me.

The attractive brunette who ran with her twins should have been competing in an Olympic game the way she pushed that giant stroller without toppling it over. She smiled at me too as she maneuvered the beast past me.

And then there was Grant. He was an elderly man I slowed down for whenever I saw him, just so I could jog alongside him. He had the best stories, always talking to me about how romance used to be when he was a kid, and how times had changed. Then he usually called me some insulting name. He had told me on more than one occasion that I was born in the wrong era, and I agreed. We sometimes stopped and had coffee together after our run, him asking me about the bar, and me asking him about the love of his life. His whole face lit up whenever he talked about his wife, even though she was no longer here.

"Help! Someone help!" A woman's voice tore through the otherwise calm morning, her panicked tone making goose bumps rise on my skin.

I stopped and whirled around, searching for where the shouting was coming from. Swiveling my head, I couldn't see anything out of the ordinary.

"Help me!"

I zoned in and dashed toward the distressed cry, having no idea what exactly I was looking for. Spotting two people on the ground in the distance, I picked up the pace and pulled my cell phone from my pocket as I ran.

When I reached the woman, I recognized the man she held in her arms. My heart nearly stopped as I took in Grant's face, his expression pained and his eyes closed.

"What happened?"

The woman looked up at me. "I'm not sure. Heart attack, maybe? He clutched his chest before he fell to the ground. I don't think anyone else saw him because no one stopped." Her voice was shaking, her eyes brimming with unshed tears. Sunlight caught her hair, making her look angelic, not that she needed the help. She was fucking beautiful.

Without another word, I dropped to the ground on the other side of Grant and dialed 911.

"We need an ambulance at the running path near lifeguard station number twenty-three." I didn't need to look around to know exactly where I was. I had this stretch of beach memorized. "Male, I think he's about seventy. Good shape, jogs every morning." At the dispatcher's question, I leaned forward to bring my ear toward Grant's mouth and nose. "Yes, he's breathing, but it's shallow and sounds labored... Okay. Please hurry."

My eyes locked on the scared woman sitting in front of me, Grant's head cradled in her lap. I didn't recognize her, had never seen her running the path before. And trust me, I would have noticed her, with or without the halo that still framed her face.

"Are you okay?" I asked.

Her hazel eyes met mine, and she took me in for a beat before responding. "You know him?" she asked, not answering my question.

I nodded, fighting the urge to reach out and touch her. Golden-brown hair had fallen around her cheeks, and I wanted to tuck the strands behind her ear.

"Do you think he'll be okay?" she asked, her attention focused on Grant.

I forced a smile and looked down at the man I had come to respect and considered a friend. "He's tough. He'll pull through. Won't you, Grant?" I waited for him to nod, or move, or blink, but he did none of those things. He hadn't moved at all since I got there. He was as still as the woman holding him.

"I've never seen you before." The words were out of my mouth before I could stop them, my tone far more flirtatious than I'd intended.

"I usually run earlier," she said before stopping short, like she was uncomfortable divulging that bit of information to a perfect stranger.

I extended my hand. "I'm Ryan."

Her lips tightened as she stared at my hand, making no move to reach for it. "I know who you are."

That shocked me. It probably shouldn't have, but it still took me by surprise. "You do?"

"I've been to your bar," she said, then added, "Once." She leveled me with her steady gaze before focusing back on the old man.

I sat there, confused for a second at her attempt to blow me off.

Had I been rude to her at the bar? I couldn't imagine that could be true, but her pretending I didn't exist when I was sitting right across from her made me uncomfortable. Women didn't usually hate me without provocation, and I had no idea what I could have possibly done to her and not remember it.

"Are you going to tell me *your* name?" I decided to push her a little more, see what she might give me. It was a foolish move, so call me a damn fool if you want. I found myself staring at her and the halo around her head that made her look like a real-life angel.

"I told you my name the last time you asked. I'm sorry you don't remember it," she said, her tone anything but sorry.

For once in my life, I found myself unable to read a woman's eyes. She looked right at me, her expression shuttered, and I had no idea what she was thinking or feeling.

Based on her reaction, I was almost convinced she hated me. No, *hate* was too strong a word, but she definitely wasn't impressed with me, neither now nor the first time we met. The time I didn't remember.

The piercing shriek of a siren filled the air, and I looked up to see an ambulance headed in our direction. I jumped to my feet, waving my arms to draw their attention as they navigated off the road and toward the path where Grant still lay unresponsive. A small crowd had formed around us as the paramedics hopped out and ran forward, carrying a stabilizing board.

Two EMTs crouched down next to Grant. "Did you see what happened?" one of them asked.

The angel shook her head. "I only saw him clutch his chest before he fell."

"Has he said anything? Talked at all?"

"No," she said as they moved him carefully from her care. Her breathing quickened, her worry for Grant etched all over her face. She couldn't have hidden her concern if she tried, that much I could tell. I could practically see her heart on her sleeve, bleeding for a man she didn't even know.

I wrenched my gaze away from her and watched as the paramedics took Grant's vitals, spouting off directions and information to each other in a shorthand I didn't understand but desperately wanted to. They hooked him up to contraptions I couldn't name and strapped him onto the board. I'd never felt as helpless as I did in those moments when I wasn't sure if he was going to live or die. His face was so pale.

The paramedics wheeled him away and I followed behind.

"Can I go with him?" I shouted.

"Are you family?"

"A friend," I said, my racing heart pounding like a two-hundred-pound gorilla at the possibility of his refusal.

The paramedics loaded Grant into the back of the waiting ambulance, moving fluidly in concert as I stood there helplessly waiting for a response.

"Come on." He waved me inside, granting me access to the back of the vehicle, and I hopped in. "Sit there." He pointed, and I did as I was told.

"What hospital are you taking him to?" the angel called out, and I realized I'd almost forgotten all about her.

Almost.

"Saint Johns," the EMT said before the doors slammed shut, locking us in, and the ambulance took off without a chance for another word to be spoken.

This time, however, my angel's eyes didn't stray from mine as the vehicle pulled away. Her focus stayed locked on me, her eyes saying things I still couldn't understand.

It pissed me off, but I'd concentrate on finding her later, and would figure out what I'd done to make her dislike me so much. For now, I needed to make sure Grant was going to survive and live to see another day.

*

Unable to sit still, I paced back and forth in the hospital's waiting room while they did whatever they were doing to Grant, hoping like hell he'd pull through.

Bits of our conversations over the past few months played in my mind as I remembered the things he'd told me about life and love, always doling out advice like he was an expert on the subject. I considered him one, to be honest.

For me, he was a confidant of sorts, always giving me shit but encouraging me in the same breath. Grant claimed to understand my fairy-tale heart, telling me that I was born in the wrong time, surrounded by the wrong kind of women.

My lips twitched into a smile as I remembered the first time I met him.

After an extra-long run one morning, I found myself sitting alone at a small beachside café. Mumbling to himself, Grant sat at the table next to mine and pulled out a newspaper. He continued talking to himself under his breath, and when I glanced over my shoulder at him, he caught me.

"Was I talking out loud again?" he'd asked, looking sheepish.

Grinning at him, I said, "I didn't mind."

"Like I'd give a shit if you did anyway."

His blunt words caught me off guard, and I almost choked on my water. I laughed and immediately pulled my chair over to his table, settling in.

He raised one bushy gray eyebrow, giving me a stern look. "Did I invite you over here, son?"

"Nope. But I don't give a shit either," I fired back.

He'd laughed then, a big, hearty sound that made me smile as he smacked the table with the palm of his hand.

"All right, smartass. You can stay."

Our friendship began that morning.

I learned that both Grant and his wife, Carol, had been the youngest of all their siblings and were the only ones still living. At least, until his wife passed away a little over a year ago. Since they didn't have any kids, he was all alone.

Grant said life sucked without her, but every morning he kept waking up, so he guessed it wasn't his time to go. He'd started jogging out of sheer boredom, or that's what he always claimed. But the man was toned and wiry, built like a fucking racehorse, and that kind of thing didn't happen overnight. Especially not at his age.

A doctor holding a clipboard appeared in front of me, startling me out of my memories. "Are you with Grant Masterson?"

I nodded. "Is he okay?"

"He made it through surgery without any issues. We need to keep him here for the next few days for observation, and to make sure no infection sets in. But barring any complications, he should be able to go home Friday."

"That's great. Can I see him?"

"He's still in recovery, but I can have someone give you a call when he wakes up."

"Really? That would be amazing. Thank you." I jotted down my name and number on a pad of paper. "He doesn't have any family, so I really would appreciate that call."

The doctor nodded and took my note before walking away.

My mind flashed briefly to the angel from earlier, and I wondered if she'd be making an appearance at the hospital to check on Grant. My gut instinct told me that she definitely would, and I was tempted to camp out in the lobby until she showed up.

I quickly decided against it. If I was going to run into her "accidentally on purpose," then I wanted to be prepared for it. I wanted to catch her off guard by being completely on mine.

In the meantime, I called an Uber to come pick me up and take me to get my car. I'd already run enough for one day.

STUPID RYAN FISHER
Sofia

THE OLD MAN from this morning consumed my thoughts. I found myself thinking about him when I should have been focused on work. But one second my thoughts were on Grant, and the next, they were centered on Ryan Fisher.

Why did he have to be so good-looking? Even wearing workout clothes, Ryan still looked like a tanned god in running shoes.

The worst part was that he knew it. Ryan Fisher was completely aware of the effect he had on women, and I knew he assumed I'd be like all the rest of them the moment he jogged to my side. I refused to swoon at the attention he decided to toss my way, no matter how much my traitorous body had wanted me to.

I wasn't like the other women who frequented his bar. At least, that's what I tried to convince myself. I hadn't lied when I told him that I'd only been to his bar once. It was Sarin, my coworker and friend, who had insisted we go there, claiming that Sam's Bar had the best drinks and the hottest bartenders. Even the men in our group agreed, not about the hot-bartender part, but about the drinks. Not to mention the fact that we all worked for one of the social-media companies the bar featured on their wall, so it felt like going there was mixing business with pleasure.

I knew all about Sam's, couldn't have avoided the knowledge if I tried, but I'd never been there. I didn't usually go out, even though my coworkers asked all the time, and urging me to join them at their standing happy-hour Thursday date together. Being a single mom hadn't really afforded me the luxury of an active social life. Unless you counted Disney-channel movies with my eight-year-old as dates, which I totally did.

The second Sarin and I walked through the doors of the bar, I felt like I was in another world. The place was filled with so much life. All the patrons seemed genuinely happy and upbeat, chatting loudly and snapping pictures along the social-media wall that the youngest Fisher brother had dreamed up. It had been an odd thing to notice, all the smiles on people's faces, but it was hard to ignore the atmosphere of the place when it surrounded you and sucked you in.

And then I saw Ryan, with those ridiculously beautiful blue eyes and sandy-brown hair, and a part of me melted inside. I hadn't been attracted like that to a guy in what seemed like a thousand years.

When our eyes met, Ryan smiled at me and the rest of the bar disappeared. He had a way of making you feel like you were the only person in the room. He'd asked me my name that night, just like I told him. The only problem was that he asked *every* girl her name before committing it to memory—only for the night, apparently—and then proceeded to talk sweetly, dropping your name now and then to make you feel special.

And like a fool, I'd fallen for it . . . hook, line, and sinker. For all of about two minutes, until I noticed the way he interacted with every girl at the bar.

I hadn't been special.

I hadn't been anything.

I'd been a customer, a paying customer, and that was all.

Ryan had a job to do, and he did it well. I couldn't begrudge him that, so I think my annoyance stemmed more from the fact that not only had I stupidly thought he was genuinely flirting with me, but that I had actually wanted him to.

I had wanted Ryan Fisher, bar owner and custom drink-maker, to be into me. Even if it was purely ego based, I'd still wanted it.

I soon learned that I wasn't the only one. The majority of the women at the bar hoped Ryan would choose them that night. I'd overheard more than one girl talking about his sexual prowess and the things he liked to do in the bedroom, many claiming they were back at the bar for seconds. Even when I tried to block out the conversations, they swirled around me, never ceasing or lacking in sordid detail. It was almost a little embarrassing, to be honest, and I wondered if Ryan relished in that kind of attention, or if it made him uncomfortable.

I never got the chance to ask because my cell phone rang after I'd been there for about an hour. My son, Matson, had developed a sudden fever, so my night was cut short. My coworkers groaned but understood as I left some cash on the bar and hurried out into the still warm air. There was only one person in the world I'd drop anything for, and it was my son. Nothing and no one came before him.

Being a mom changed you. It had changed every single thing about me. Like a bad after-school special, I found out I was pregnant my senior year of high school. I'd been on the pill, but apparently I could now count myself in the unlucky two percent of women the pill didn't work for. My boyfriend of two years, Derek, bailed the second I told him. He'd already been accepted at one of the Ivy League colleges back east, and a baby wasn't in his plans.

Apparently, I hadn't been in his plans either, but I didn't know that at the time. I'd always thought we would stay together once he left for college, but Derek told me that day that he never planned to date me long distance. He said that college was a time for playing the field, not being locked down. Then he begged me to get an abortion, even offered to pay for it, saying that this could singlehandedly ruin his reputation.

I'd told him I'd think about it, just to get him to back off, but I hadn't meant it. I was keeping this baby whether he wanted me to or not.

One afternoon, Derek's father, Damian Huntington, showed up at school and approached me as I headed to my car. After introducing himself, he told me he knew that I was pregnant and also asked me not to have the baby. He claimed I was ruining both of our lives, and that I would thank them in the future if I got *rid of it*—his words, not mine. He foolishly assumed that I insisted on having the baby to keep Derek in my life, but it hadn't been about Derek at all.

I stood firm in my decision, telling him that they didn't need to be involved, and that I'd forget they ever existed. I never spoke to them again, not to Derek or his parents. None of them tried to reach out, not even after Matson was born. So about a year and a half later, I blocked all the Huntington family on every one of my social-media accounts. The last thing I wanted was them stalking me and seeing pictures of the child none of them had wanted me to have.

After her initial disappointment at my situation, my mom flipped her lid at the things Derek and his father had said to me. On some level, I believe she felt betrayed by them in the same way that I had. We'd done a lot of things with Derek's parents in the two years that he and I had dated, and I think Derek's family's reaction to the news surprised her.

Mom begged me to let her confront them.

I begged her to let it go.

My mom had a bit of a Latina temper that I loved because she was fiercely loyal and protective, but I knew her efforts would only make the situation worse. I promised both my parents that we would all be better off without the Huntingtons complicating our lives, and after a while, they begrudgingly agreed.

Even though my parents had initially been sad for me, wishing that I wasn't pregnant so young, their concerns faded away the second Matson arrived. It was no longer about how hard my life would be, and whether I was making the right decision. At that point, it became all about Matson and the joy he brought into our lives, a joy we hadn't realized we needed. An unexpected baby did that to a family sometimes, brought you light in the darkness.

I was fortunate that my mom worked from home, so she volunteered to watch Matson while I worked during the day part time and went to school at night. My parents wanted me to have a bright future, and they knew I needed their help to make it possible.

It took me longer than most people my age, but I finally got my bachelor's degree in online communications and ended up scoring a job at one of the biggest social-media companies in the world. I was the executive assistant to the vice president of development, and I loved my job.

Matson and I moved out of my parents' house a couple of years ago when a family friend decided to move overseas but hadn't wanted to sell their small three-bedroom bungalow in Santa Monica. They gave me an amazing deal on rent, claiming that I was helping them out more than they were helping me, and Matson and I had lived there ever since. I woke up each morning beyond grateful for my life, which most people might have found crazy, considering.

"Earth to Sofia."

A hand waved in front of my face, and it was only then that I realized I'd been completely lost in thought.

"Sarin, hi. Sorry, what were you saying?"

She rolled her brown eyes as she brushed her jet-black hair behind one ear. Sarin was Indian, and had the most beautiful features. Her eyes carried a depth most people never recognized, and she had the softest skin I'd ever laid eyes on.

"Who were you thinking about? I hope he was hot."

It was my turn to roll my eyes. "If you consider a seventy-something-year-old man hot, then sure."

"Didn't realize you liked them so much older, Sof. Is that why you're still single? Want to go play bingo at the senior center later?"

"Asshole," I muttered. "What do you want?"

"I need you to come with me. I have to pick up a shit-ton

of cupcakes for the office, and I told them I needed your help."

Sarin was an assistant as well, but she worked for the president of the company. He had three assistants in total, two in the office and one at his home. Sarin was the second-in-command at the office, which meant she could walk away from her desk for extended periods of time, unlike Jeanine, the first assistant.

"Okay. Let me tell Martin first," I said.

"Your boss already knows. Come on," she said, impatient.

"Let me at least tell him I'm leaving," I insisted. I never left my desk unattended without telling him first. The thought of Martin shouting at me from his office and not getting a response almost made me laugh out loud. It was unthinkable.

Sarin urged me to hurry. I had no idea what the rush was all about, but was grateful for the distraction. I needed to stop thinking about Ryan.

I'd already called the hospital the moment I arrived at the office and asked about visiting hours. They wouldn't give me any information about Grant's condition over the phone, no matter how hard I begged, so I had no idea if he'd pulled through or not.

I could have called the bar and asked Ryan if the old man was okay, but I planned to avoid him at all costs. The last thing I needed in my life was a man-whoring bartender who took home a different woman every night. That wasn't the kind of example I wanted to set for Matson, and it wasn't the kind of man I wanted in my life.

No, I'd find out if Grant pulled through on my own, by going to the hospital the minute I got off work.

FIGHTING OVER ANGELS
Ryan

I WALKED INTO the bar and sent our day-shift bartender home after settling in.

"Still in a pissy mood?" Frank asked when he spotted me.

"No, it's about my buddy Grant. You remember him, right?"

Frank nodded. "The old guy? Comes in here sometimes to give you shit?"

"Yeah." I grinned, thinking about the few times Grant had graced us with his presence. He gave each of us Fisher boys crap, but always me the most. "He had some sort of heart issue. He's in the hospital."

"Shit, is he okay? How'd you find out?"

"I saw him on the beach this morning." I shook my head to rid myself of the mental image of him lying there unconscious. "I went with him to the hospital. They said he made it through surgery, but I really want to see him."

"Go," Frank said. "I can handle this."

I shook my head. "He's not awake. They're going to call me as soon as he is," I said as I rinsed out a glass and set it on the rack to air dry.

Frank came over to stand next to me. "He doesn't have

any family, right?"

"No. Just him."

"He'll be okay," Frank said. "He's a tough old bastard."

I was thankful for his optimism but couldn't shake the antsy feeling that had been dogging me, and I knew it wasn't only because of Grant. The angel had me bugging out. I'd never so blatantly been hated by a woman before, and I wasn't exactly sure how to handle it. Not that I hadn't ever pissed off a female in the past, but I'd always known what I'd done to deserve it. When it came to this particular woman, I had no fucking clue, and it was ruining my ability to think about anything else.

"What else is eating at you?" Frank narrowed his green eyes on me, eyes that looked just like our mother's.

I sucked in a long breath, wondering if I should tell him or not. I figured I had nothing to lose except my pride, and that was a lost cause when it came to my older brother. If there was an opportunity to tease me, he took it.

"It's a girl." I shrugged, not knowing exactly what to say.

I braced for the insult I suspected was coming, but never did. Dating Claudia had changed Frank, softened him, which made my life a lot easier.

Instead of giving me shit, he just asked, "What girl?"

I shrugged. "I don't know. She was the one who found Grant, but she was ice-cold toward me and it's driving me crazy."

Frank's usually serious face broke into a grin. "I would have paid money to see that." He chuckled, shaking his head at the thought. "Did you know her?"

"She didn't look familiar, but she said she'd only been here one time."

"Only once?" Frank's tone was incredulous, and he wasn't off base for feeling that way. People usually didn't come into Sam's one time and then never again, not unless they were tourists.

"Maybe you flirted with her and then ditched her for someone else," he suggested, all serious again. "Or maybe she's one of the women who thought you really liked her when you were just being you."

Frank knew how often the latter part of his statement happened. After closing one night, he told me that women thought I was really into them and took my flirtatious nature to heart. He said that when they flirted back, they meant it, and maybe I should try to be a little less friendly.

I actually tried to take his advice for one night, but that lasted for all of about an hour. When I tried to tone things down, I hated how unnatural and uncomfortable I felt in my own skin. I was a nonsmiling, unfriendly version of myself in some stupid attempt to make sure our customers didn't think I wanted to spend the rest of my life with them. It was ridiculous, and I refused to be someone I wasn't.

The truth was that I wasn't even flirting, to be honest. I was simply being friendly. They were two different things, and it wasn't my fault if everyone took my friendliness the wrong way. Or hell, maybe it was my fault. Regardless, I refused to change my behavior, and I suffered the consequences for it. Nightly.

I glanced at the time and realized our youngest brother wasn't here yet. "Where's Nick?"

Frank shrugged. "He had a meeting with one of the social-media companies."

"Do you know which one?"

I asked with a grin because I knew that he had absolutely no idea. Frank didn't understand half the shit that most people used their phones for these days. He trusted Nick to make the marketing decisions for the bar, considering he was closest in age to the majority of our patrons and had his finger on the pulse of all things up and coming.

Frank grimaced. "Snap something. Snip something? I don't fucking know." He groaned out his frustration like a bitter old man, and I laughed.

"Why don't you go back in your cave and play with numbers," I teased, and he flipped me off. Frank handled all the finances for the bar, and he used to sit in the office and work all the time. But that was before Claudia came into the picture.

"But I like hanging out here with you. It's much more fun."

"Then be useful." I pointed at the almost-empty bottles of liquor lining the shelf.

He scowled, not wanting to take inventory since it was my job, and muttered something about our vendors before he disappeared behind the office door. I laughed and went to work restocking before the bar filled with customers.

When Nick eventually showed up, I inhaled a quick breath, grateful that my brothers and best friends were all together in one place. It hadn't been so long ago when Nick worked for our father and not here at the bar with Frank and me. All that changed one day, and it was the best thing to happen to us. And the bar.

"Ryan," Nick called out with a smile.

"Where've you been?" I scowled at him, pretending to be mad, but couldn't even fake it.

"Had a meeting with the VP of development," he said, then filled me in on all the potential plans they discussed.

There were special filters, collaborations, parties, and nationwide exposure ideas that included featured spots on the front page of the app. They'd even talked about global exposure, although I wasn't sure that realistically suited our needs. But I never ruled anything out, and I trusted Nick implicitly.

"That sounds amazing. Seriously." I nodded in appreciation. Nick was a fucking genius when it came to online marketing, and we all knew it.

"I'm excited about it." He was enthusiastic and fired up, and I loved when he was that way.

It was incredible to see someone in their element, the way their eyes lit up with passion as the wheels turned in their head. My brothers both said I got that way whenever I was crafting a new cocktail. But to me, it was about combining unexpected ingredients to create something magical. I loved making drinks, loved seeing people's reactions to tasting something that I designed. That first sip when they weren't quite sure what would be hitting their tongue, and then the look on their face when they realized just how damn good it was.

I was good at creating new drinks. And I knew it.

"I'm excited too, little brother." I smiled because his attitude was infectious.

"You okay? You seem distracted."

Apparently, I wasn't so great at hiding my emotions. I

filled him in on what had happened earlier with Grant, and Nick squeezed my shoulder in sympathy, saying almost the exact same thing as Frank had.

Even with their reassurance that Grant was a stubborn fighter, I still worried. And the damn hospital hadn't called yet. How long did it take a grumpy old man to wake up?

Finally, a little after five, I got the call I'd been waiting for. Grant was not only awake but was asking for me.

"You okay if I head to the hospital?" I asked Nick as he drew beer for a couple of our regulars.

He waved me off. "Of course. Just tell the old man to get out here before you go." He hooked a thumb over his shoulder at the office, referring to Frank.

"I'll be back."

"Take your time, and give him our best."

*

WINDING MY WAY through the hospital corridors, I slowed as I approached Grant's room. I peeked through the doorway, wanting to be sure he was alone and not surrounded by hospital staff monitoring his every move. I laughed at the thought, knowing how annoyed he would be at being poked and prodded.

"Get in here, asshole," his gruff voice called out, and I smirked as I sauntered in. Everything in his room was white and cold, except for the colorful plate of hospital food sitting on the tray in front of him. "Why were you hiding outside like some sissy girl?"

"I wanted to make sure I wasn't interrupting anything.

Excuse me for having manners," I fired back as I pulled the single chair in the room next to his side. He still looked pale, but at least he was breathing.

"Manners, my ass," he muttered, and I bristled.

"Hey, I have manners." When he waved me off with an annoyed expression, I changed the subject. "Scared the hell out of me this morning."

He took in a deep breath, his tired gaze on the doorway before finally meeting mine. "I can't even remember what happened." When I started to speak, to fill him in on everything I knew, he interrupted. "But I will tell you this. I think I saw an angel this morning, kid."

Grant tried to smile but the move was strained. Even still, I knew exactly who he was referring to.

"That you did." I grinned as her face flashed in my mind.

"She was real?" he asked, awkwardly spooning some green Jell-O into his mouth.

"Oh, she's real, all right."

Her image filled my thoughts, making me feel fifteen again, my body full of raging hormones I couldn't control.

"I have an angel." Grant sighed, a dreamy expression on his face, and I shifted in my seat.

Feeling ridiculously jealous for no good reason, I said, "She's *my* angel." I sat up straighter, puffing my chest out as I claimed her, making sure the old man knew she belonged to me, details be damned.

His eyes narrowed, and he dropped the spoon. "Pretty sure she's *my* angel," he snapped back.

I was going to have to fight him, this sick man old enough to be my grandpa. And I wasn't above it.

"Pretty sure she's too young for you, old man."

"Pretty sure she came to *my* rescue," he countered.

At that, I glared at him. "Pretty sure she didn't have a choice."

"We all have choices, and she chose me. Find your own angel, asshole."

At his last retort, I fought off a laugh. We were two grown men fighting over a woman that neither of us even knew. "Glad you're feeling better."

"I was until you showed up and pissed me off," he said between coughs. "Trying to steal my damn angel like you can't get one of your own. I've seen you at that bar."

I decided to let the comment go. For now. "How long do you have to stay in here?"

"Who knows? They said they need to monitor my heart and make sure I don't have any more episodes. Whatever the hell that means."

"It means they don't want you to die," I teased.

He snarled at me, threatening to throw to his little plastic spoon, holding it in striking position as if the damn thing would even hurt me.

"Do you need me to bring you anything?" I knew he'd grumble about it, but I'd do it anyway. "I can pick up whatever you need from your place, and stop by every day until they release you."

"I don't need a babysitter," he mumbled under his breath. He was such a pain in the ass.

"Good. Because I don't know how to babysit."

He pursed his lips, seeming to consider. "I could use a pair of pants and my fishing hat."

I suppressed a grin. "Pair of pants and your fishing hat. On it."

Grant snorted. "How can you be on it if you don't have a key? It's not like my door's magic and just gonna open on its own because you show it your pretty mug."

Frowning, he reached toward the bedside table and pulled open the drawer. For a moment, he fumbled, then fished out a set of keys and tossed them at me without warning. It was a good thing I'd kept my eye on him; the damn things nearly smacked me in the face.

After giving me his address, he frowned. "Aren't you going to write it down?"

"I don't need to write it down. Got it right here." I tapped my head.

Grant didn't know that I could remember things like that without trying. It's how I kept all the drink orders straight at the bar without a notepad. I just . . . remembered certain things.

Apparently, not all things. If I did, I would have remembered the angel's name, and meeting her.

Grant flicked a finger at me. "Write it down anyway. Put it in that stupid phone or something. Don't need you trying to walk into the wrong house and riling up my neighbors."

Rolling my eyes, I gave in and pulled out my phone, tapping in his address to make him happy. "I'll bring them to you first thing tomorrow morning, okay?"

"Fine."

As I tucked my phone back in my pocket, I said, "Wouldn't hurt you to be nice to me."

"Wouldn't hurt you to be nice to me," he repeated in a

falsetto, mocking me, and I suddenly felt like I was back at the bar, listening to Frank give me shit.

"All right, old man, I'm leaving. I'll see you tomorrow."

"Stay away from my angel," he said the moment I got up and headed for the door.

Turning around to face him, I said, "You mean, *my* angel?"

I stepped into the hallway before he could say anything else. As I left, I thought I heard the sound of something hitting the door frame, and when I glanced back, a single plastic spoon lay on the floor.

Grumpy ass.

GUYS LIKE RYAN
Sofia

NERVOUS ENERGY RAN through me as I waited for the world's slowest elevator to arrive on the proper floor. Surrounded by a handful of solemn strangers, I had no idea why I was so anxious, my stomach knotting tighter with each breath I inhaled. The doors finally opened and I moved to step out, my gaze on the floor as I watched my step.

"Hey."

A voice grabbed my attention just as a hand wrapped firmly around my arm, bringing me to a halt.

When I looked up into Ryan's panty-melting blue eyes, my stomach knotted even tighter. He was the reason for all that nervous, pent-up energy. Something inside me must have known that he would be here. I must have *sensed* his presence, regardless of how crazy that seemed.

"Oh, hey." I took a step back, pulling my arm from his grasp, but the spot where he'd touched me still tingled.

"You coming to see Grant?" he asked, blocking the elevator door, and I moved a few steps to the side to give the people exiting it more room.

Pretending not to be unnerved by Ryan's presence, I said, "Yeah, I just came to check on him. Have you seen him?"

Ryan's mouth twisted into a grin. "Oh yeah. He's a pistol, but he'll be happy to see you."

"He will?" How could an unconscious man I'd never met before this morning possibly be happy to see me?

"He will. I'm about to head back to the bar, unless you wanted to grab a coffee or dinner or something? I could wait until you're done visiting him first." Ryan frowned, seeming unsure of himself. "If you wanted, I mean."

I shifted my weight, unsure of how to answer. "That's probably not a good idea," I said, trying to convince him of what I'd already convinced myself.

A flirtatious gleam came to his eyes. "How could going out with me be anything but a good idea?"

The man was trying to bait me and I knew it, but I didn't have time for games. Looking into his beautiful eyes, I kept my gaze steady. "I don't want to give you the wrong impression."

"And what impression would that be, exactly?"

"That I'm interested in you."

I used my most convincing voice so Ryan would understand, but he didn't waver. No, his grin only widened and his gaze intensified. It didn't matter what I said . . . he obviously didn't believe me.

"So we'll get coffee as friends." He shrugged as if this was totally normal, the two of us being friends. "Friends get coffee."

"Friends?" A small laugh escaped me.

"Yep. How else will I get to know your name?"

I laughed again, annoyed at myself for giving in, even the slightest bit. "I forgot about that."

"It's okay. I've given you a nickname until you tell me."

He folded his arms across his chest as if he was the cleverest man on the planet.

"You've given me a nickname?" I wasn't sure I wanted to hear it. Some guys were immature and crude, so the last thing I needed was to hear Ryan call me something degrading or idiotic.

"Yeah. I had to call you something," he said, his tone still flirty.

"Let me guess." I paused before looking around at the hospital walls. "Peaches?"

He bent over, laughing. "Peaches? No. But I love it. Please tell me I can call you that."

"Not if you expect to live," I all but growled.

Ryan stood back up, his tall frame towering over mine as his expression turned serious. "Angel. I call you my angel."

My jaw dropped before I sucked in a shaky breath, pissed that his nickname for me had drawn out such a noticeable reaction. I knew I wasn't hiding it well. Hell, I couldn't hide it at all.

Angel? And not only angel, but *his* angel. No wonder half the bar patrons were in love with this man.

"I should probably hurry. You know, before visiting hours are over." I focused on the stark white hallway and the black room numbers on the wall. Anything to avoid those eyes.

"I thought we were getting coffee?" Ryan sounded almost pleading now, no longer the confident man from a moment ago.

"I never said that."

"Please?"

Stop begging me, Ryan, because I'm about two seconds from giving in. "I don't think so."

He swallowed hard, his throat moving as his jaw clenched. "Give me one reason why you won't."

A multitude of valid reasons flashed through my mind.

Because I'm a single mom.

Because you work at a bar.

Because you've dated half the women in town.

Because you probably drink more than most people.

Because your livelihood is based around alcohol, late nights, and loose women.

There were a million reasons, and those were just a few.

"You're just not the kind of guy I'm looking for, Ryan."

When the words left my mouth, his entire body tensed as though I'd just punched him in the gut.

"Look, I'm not trying to offend you, you're just not my type." I added the last part to lessen the blow, but it only seemed to make things worse.

His eyes narrowed. "How would you even know that?"

Unable to look at him, I dropped my gaze, and couldn't help but notice how his hands clenched by his sides. Apparently, I'd struck a nerve.

"Trust me, your reputation precedes you."

It was a bit of a low blow, but it was all I had to really drive the point home. If Ryan wouldn't take my word, then I had to use his own against him.

"What if my reputation is all off base?" He spat out the word *reputation* like it tasted bitter on his tongue.

I paused for a moment, pondering his question. Could his reputation be wrong, based on exaggerations and falsehoods, wishful fantasies, or maybe outright lies? I knew better than most people how the truth could be twisted and exaggerated, turned into a story that no longer resembled anything close to reality.

Was that the case here?

No, I'd seen Ryan in action. I'd watched the way he treated women, the way he flirted, and I'd heard what women said about his performance in the bedroom. Those things meant Ryan wasn't selective when it came to sex and having it. I needed a man who could keep it in his pants, who wanted to only be with me and would be satisfied with that.

"Angel, would you believe me if I told you not to believe everything you hear?"

Ryan's voice cut through my thoughts, and I looked up to see those gorgeous blue eyes looking down at me.

"You forget that I've seen you in action," I said, my tone far less harsh than it had been a few minutes earlier.

"Things aren't always how they seem. That's my job, and I'm really good at it."

I nodded and gave him a slight smile. "I'm aware."

"Still not going to give me a chance, are you?"

Ryan sounded so defeated, I almost crumpled on the spot. Instead, I shook my head, afraid I might not be able to form the actual words to resist him again.

"I'm not giving up," he said.

"You should."

"I'm not a quitter."

"And I'm not a pushover."

He leaned in close, so close that I could breathe in his natural scent. "I never thought you were. You have one hell of a backbone, angel, and one day, you're going to tell me exactly where it came from."

I fought back a gasp as Ryan moved to press the button on the elevator, and the doors immediately slid open. He stepped inside, and the doors closed.

It was only then that I released a long breath and looked around, remembering that we weren't alone. I glanced up and down the empty corridors, thankful that no one had heard our exchange.

Ryan Freaking Fisher drove me crazy and jumbled my emotions into a convoluted, confused mess. He refused to listen, just pushed and pushed and pushed, knowing full well that a woman had only so much strength before she caved. It was like he could smell my weakness like a shark scenting blood.

He seemed to be intrigued by me, but I wasn't stupid enough to think that it was based in reality, no matter how hot it was. No, Ryan was attracted to me because I kept pushing him away. Guys like him were always drawn to the chase.

But I wasn't playing a game. I didn't want him to chase me. I wanted him to leave me alone.

He thought he was interested now, but I could imagine the look on his face the second I told him that I was a single mom. That charming smile would falter ever so slightly, and the sparkle in his gorgeous eyes would dull as the reality of my situation set in. I'd seen it all before, and I couldn't bear to watch the disappointment transform Ryan's face.

There was no way in hell a guy like him would be interested in dating a woman with a kid. I had what most men called "baggage," but I'd never consider my son that. Matson and I were more like a package deal. You wanted me . . . you got a spunky eight-year-old too. You were lucky, not burdened.

It took a special kind of guy to see my situation in that way. And that guy was definitely not Ryan Fisher.

Forcing thoughts of Ryan from my head, I found Grant's room and stepped inside.

"My angel! You are real. I thought that asshole was lying to me."

Grant's unexpected welcome made me laugh out loud as I stepped closer to the side of the bed.

"Hi, Grant. I'm so happy you're okay." I smiled, unsure whether I should sit or stand. "You are okay, right?"

"I'm fine. Because of you. You saved my life," he said, reaching for my hand and planting a kiss on top of it.

"I was just in the right place at the right time. And I'm glad I was. Ryan helped too, you know," I said, not sure why I brought him up.

Grant's face twisted into a snarl and he tossed a hand into the air. "I don't care about that knucklehead. I only care about you. About us," he cooed, and I laughed again.

"Are you trying to woo me?"

"Is it working?"

"It might be."

"Good. I'm a much better catch than Ryan. You should definitely choose me."

"Oh, I already have," I said, trying to push Ryan's image from my mind.

Grant gave me a toothy grin. "I knew it. I can't wait to throw that in his stupid face."

The old man's indomitable spirit was amazing. He'd nearly died this morning, and now here he was flirting with me. The outrageousness of it made me smile.

"Sit." He pointed at the empty chair, and I did as I was told. "Now, tell me your real name, sweetheart. I should know it since we're dating."

"It's Sofia."

He grinned. "Sofia. A beautiful name for a beautiful woman. Does Ryan know it?"

My smile fell away. "No."

"Good." Grant laughed and then began to cough.

I jumped to my feet. "Are you okay?"

"I'm fine. Sorry. I'm just old, Sofia. But don't worry, we've still got plenty of time." He patted my hand, and I moved back to my chair.

"That's good, considering I just found you. I can't lose you already," I said in my sweetest voice.

"I plan on staying around and torturing Ryan for as long as I can."

"What is it with the two of you? You're not related, are you?"

His relationship with a man young enough to be his grandson made them an odd pair. I couldn't help but wonder how they knew each other and what their story was. It would make sense if they were related somehow, but otherwise, I had no idea how they would have become friends, considering their age difference.

"Related? I'd end it all right now if I was related to that pretty boy."

"Stop it." I playfully swatted at his arm. "How'd you two meet, anyway?"

The old man huffed out a long, annoyed breath. "He invaded my personal space one morning, and I haven't been able to get rid of him since. Ryan's like a stray dog that won't go away, no matter how many times you shoo him away. He always comes back for more."

"You probably feed him, don't you?" I said, hiding my smile. "Strays never leave if you give them food."

"Dammit. You're right."

Making fun of Ryan behind his back should have felt wrong, but it didn't. I sensed that we would have said these things in front of Ryan if he were standing here, so that made it okay in my mind. Plus, it was sort of fun to pick on him.

"Do you know how long you have to stay in here?" I asked, wondering how serious Grant's condition was.

"Eh, they don't tell me anything. Maybe they'll tell you since you're my wife and all." He waggled his bushy eyebrows at me.

"We're married now? I swear we were just dating a second ago."

"Oh yeah, did you forget? No prenup or anything. I get half of all you got, sweetheart."

"Half of not much isn't much."

"I find that hard to believe," he said. "I don't think you have not much, and I think there's far more to you than meets the eye."

I shifted in my chair, feeling slightly uncomfortable. I had no interest in sharing my personal business with a perfect stranger. Matson was the one thing I kept protected, private, and was none of anyone's business unless I deemed it so. Telling someone you had a child opened yourself up to a hundred questions, each more personal than the last.

My fierce hesitation came from all the rumors and lies that were spread during and after my pregnancy. Looking back at it now, I knew it was based in immaturity and high-school kids being kids, but it still hurt at the time. The things people said about me and accused me of were hard to deal with, especially since I was just a teen myself.

People I considered close friends claimed I got pregnant on purpose, to trap Derek, as if either of those things were even remotely in my character. Rumors spread that I was trying to get Derek's family to give me hundreds of thousands of dollars, when the truth was that I hadn't asked them for a dime. People acted like I was some sort of manipulative genius who had been planning this all along, that my entire two-year relationship with Derek had been some sort of setup and sham.

"Angel? Sofia Angel?" Grant's voice was soft as he snapped his fingers to get my attention.

"Sorry." I gave him a weak smile.

"You drifted."

"I did."

"Anything you want to talk about?"

"Not really," I said, hoping he wouldn't pry further.

"Okay." He shrugged and carried on like nothing had happened.

I glanced up at the clock on the wall and rose to my feet. It was getting late, and I needed to get home to my son.

"I'm sorry, Grant, but I have to go," I said, and the disappointment on his face reminded me of the way Matson looked when he didn't get his way.

"Did I say something wrong?"

"No. It's nothing like that," I said to reassure him. "I just need to get home."

"Okay. Will you come back tomorrow?"

"Of course." Maybe my mom would watch Matson again

for me. If she couldn't, I'd swing by here on my lunch break. Either way, I'd be true to my word.

"Promise?" Grant held out his pinky in my direction, and I linked mine around his and squeezed.

"Promise."

"We can go ring shopping then," he said with a wink, and I shook my head.

"Were you always this charming?" I asked as I moved toward the door.

Grant gave me a serious nod. "Always."

I grinned again before leaving for the night, making a mental note to ask my mom about tomorrow when I saw her.

Ryan briefly slipped into my thoughts before I pushed him right back out. I was likely to run into him again if I continued to spend time with Grant, and I convinced myself that that was the only reason he was invading my mind. It wasn't because he was persistent, or more charming than the old man in the hospital bed, or so damn easy to look at.

Nope. Ryan wasn't in my thoughts for any reason other than the fact that we now shared a mutual friend. One I was engaged to, apparently.

Ryan would understand. He'd probably even be happy for us.

I laughed at the thought as I left the hospital and headed for my car, ready to pick up the only male in the world who truly mattered to me.

FLOWERS FOR AN ANGEL
Ryan

MY ANGEL WAS keeping something from me, and I knew it. What it was exactly, I had absolutely no idea, but I was determined to figure it out.

As I made my way back to work, I found myself actually wanting to talk to my brothers to get their advice. I also hoped that both of their girlfriends would be there too so I could get a woman's perspective as well.

I was screwed. This was what I'd turned into. Within the span of a twelve-hour period, I'd become completely infatuated with someone I knew nothing about. Was that why she drove me so crazy, because of the mystery and intrigue?

Shaking my head, I searched my thoughts and feelings to be sure that this wasn't some kind of sick game I convinced myself I needed to play. I wasn't the kind of man who toyed with women's emotions, no matter what they might say about me. And the last time I had been so bent out of shape over a woman was . . . hell, never? I couldn't remember ever feeling quite this way before.

Pulling the heavy bar door open, I stepped into my second home. Thankfully, the evening crowd was somewhat thin, and I spotted Claudia and Jess sitting together at a back table.

I thought about heading straight for them before I realized that I should see what damage Frank and Nick had done to my bar in my absence. We were all equal partners, but behind the bar was my domain. Nick ruled the social media and marketing. Frank ran the finances and the books. The bar, the drinks, the concocting of new and amazing cocktails, that was all me. All mine.

"How's the old man?" Nick asked as he wiped down a glass.

"Ornery as ever."

Frank glanced over at me. "So he's okay?"

"I think so. He didn't tell me much, except that I'd better see him again tomorrow and bring him some pants." I made a face, and Nick howled.

"He cracks me up," Nick said through his laughter.

"I don't know what the hell is so funny about me bringing the guy pants."

Frank grinned at me. "You do realize that everyone bosses you around, right?"

My eyes narrowed in response. "Whatever. What the hell have you two done to my bar?"

I scanned the liquor bottles displayed behind the bar, noting how some of them were out of place, in the wrong order and facing the wrong direction. I groaned, muttering *amateurs* as I went behind the bar to fix it all.

"He's still grouchy," Nick said, talking about me but not to me.

Frank nodded. "I told you. It's the girl."

They were obviously trying to goad me, which was one of their favorite things to do. As much as I didn't want to give them the satisfaction, I needed their help, so I had to suck it up.

I stopped rearranging the bottles and turned to face them. "Can you guys be serious for two seconds and actually help me, or are you gonna be assholes all night?"

Frank opened his mouth to respond, but Nick put his hand below his jaw and closed it before he could speak.

"We'll be nice," Nick said, and Frank glared at him. I wondered for a second if he was going to lose it, but he stayed calm.

"Probably need the girls for this one." I tilted my head in the direction of their girlfriends.

"Love of my life," Nick shouted across the bar, and Jess's blond head popped up in response, a big smile on her face. "We need you."

Instead of chastising Nick like I expected, Frank yelled to his girlfriend, Claudia.

"You too, gorgeous."

I just stood there, dumbfounded at the turn of events. A year ago, Frank would have been yelling at both of us, calling us names because he was so damned miserable himself. But now, instead of reacting the way I'd grown accustomed to, he was acting . . . like a man in love. It was as sickening as it was fucking adorable. I couldn't even hate him for it, no matter how badly I wanted to.

Both women hopped up from the table and hurried toward us. Drinks in hand, they climbed onto stools at the bar, their gazes pinging between the three of us in anticipation. I couldn't help but laugh at how serious they looked.

Claudia's brown eyes widened. "What is it?"

"Are we in trouble?" Jess asked. "Ooh, I sort of hope we're in trouble," she teased before waggling her eyebrows at Nick and nudging Claudia with her elbow.

Claudia elbowed her back, then turned serious. "Wait. Is everything okay?" Her gaze swung to Frank before she looked at me, concern filling her features.

Frank shrugged. "Don't ask me. He's the one who wanted a family powwow."

He nodded toward me, and both women softened at the word *family*. But that's what they were. Claudia and Jess were the women my brothers were going to marry and spend the rest of their lives with. They'd eventually be my sisters-in-law someday, and that made us family. The realization made me smile, but I fought it off because this was serious.

"Okay, listen, I need your help. Or just your opinion." I held up one finger, asking for a moment of patience, then took care of the last two remaining customers before asking my brothers if we could close the doors a little early. The bar was dead, and I knew they wouldn't oppose the idea.

Once the customers had cleared out and the doors were locked, I resumed my position behind the bar and faced the girls. "So I met this girl," I said, and when both Jess and Claudia squealed, I rolled my eyes. "Before you get too excited, you need to know that she hates me."

"Impossible. No way," the girls said immediately, talking over each other.

"My best friend's in love with you," Jess said, meaning her friend Rachel.

"Mine too," Claudia added, talking about her best friend, Britney.

"See? Everyone loves you, Ryan. No way this chick hates you," Nick said before walking toward Jess. He picked her up and sat on her bar stool before placing her on his lap. It was downright adorable, but everything the two of them did was like that. She slipped one arm around his neck nuzzled into him, her blond hair spilling over his shoulder as she pressed her cheek to his.

"She hates me," I told them. "She said that she met me before, which is why she won't tell me her name or go out with me."

"Why won't she tell you her name?" Claudia asked, her face crinkled in confusion.

"She said she's already told me."

Claudia nodded in understanding. "So, she's been in here?"

"Yeah. She said she's been here once before."

"Only once?" Jess asked.

"That's the impression I got."

The girls glanced at each other in some secret unspoken communication that only females understood, then Claudia said, "You don't hear the way women at the bar talk about you."

"Yeah, they say some crazy shit, Ryan," Jess added.

"Like what?" I asked. Not because I didn't have a general idea of what they said, but I didn't know exactly what women talked about while I was working. I couldn't hear most of the things they said when the bar was hopping.

Jess rolled her eyes. "They talk about dating you, sleeping with you, how you're a tiger in the sack. They formulate plans on how to get you. Typical crazy-girl shit."

"They say that about me too, don't they?" Nick asked, and Jess smacked his shoulder.

"They'd better not," she said seriously, and Nick smirked at me. *Idiot.*

Claudia shot Frank a look. "Don't even think about asking me that."

He laughed, his hands in the air. "Wouldn't dream of it, baby."

"I don't see how any of that has to do with this girl hating me," I said, trying to bring the conversation back on topic. I wanted to understand what it was that I could have possibly done to this girl, and how I didn't even remotely remember it.

"Pretend for a second that you're a twenty-something-year-old woman," Claudia said before stopping abruptly. "Is she twenty-something? I just assumed." She cocked her head, her dark hair falling over her eyes before she tucked it behind her ear.

"I think so. She looks early twenties, I guess," I said with a shrug.

"Okay, so pretend you're a woman in your twenties and you're actually not looking for a one-night stand—" She stopped as my brothers both faked gasps. "It's been known to happen. We're not all looking to hook up and break up in the same night. Some of us want to find good guys."

"I am a good guy," I mumbled under my breath before she waved at me to be quiet.

"So you're in this bar and you see this guy," she said, "you know, you. You're the guy she's seeing, Ryan."

"Right, 'cause I'm the girl in this scenario," I said, following along.

"Sounds about right," Frank added, and I took a step toward him to punch his chest, but he jumped back out of reach.

"Anyway," she drawled out, glaring at Frank. "You see this guy and you think he's cute and he's flirting with you, making you feel special, and you think that maybe there might be something more there. But then you hear him talk to all the women in the bar that way. And you hear what all the women in the bar are saying about him."

Jess held up a hand. "Yeah. You hear them talk about sex, and whether it's true or not, you just assume that it is, because why else would so many women be saying the same things if they weren't? And then you realize he's just like every other guy in LA, so you feel dejected and disappointed. And no matter what he does from that point forward, there's no unhearing all the things you've heard."

"Yeah. He's kind of ruined to a girl who's looking for something serious," Claudia said, wrapping up her theory. "I mean, if that's what she's looking for. Or if that's the kind of person she is. I'm only guessing here and projecting how I would feel if it were me."

I bristled, rising to my own defense. "But what if the things they're saying aren't true? How is that fair to me?"

Nick gave me a knowing look. "You take your shirt off every night. Not the best defense there, brother."

I scowled, still thinking about what Claudia and Jess said, torn between being pissed off and feeling a little sorry for myself.

"So, how do I change her mind?" I asked, and smiles crept across both the girls' faces.

*

"You brought me flowers? You shouldn't have," Grant said when I walked into his room carrying an armful of colorful tulips. It looked like a box of crayons had exploded in my fist.

"These aren't for you." I narrowed my eyes and gave him a fake dirty look before tossing him the items he'd requested from his house.

"Then why'd you bring them into my room? Just to tease me?" He reached for the pants and the hat before smiling. "You're just a regular heartbreaker, aren't you, boy? Showing up here with flowers that aren't even for me."

I shook my head. "Has she been here already?"

"Has who been here?"

Grant knew exactly who I was referring to, but he refused to give me a straight answer as a sly smile spread across his lips. If he wanted to play games with me, then I'd play.

"You know who."

"Oh, you mean my angel?"

Not this again. "No, I meant *my* angel. Has she been here today?"

He laughed, knowing how much this conversation was riling me up. "She's *my* angel, *my* fiancée, and *my* future wife."

As he continued to torment me, my body filled with jealous heat. Hearing those words, no matter how untrue they were, still caused a physical reaction inside me that I couldn't control. The old man was claiming her, and I was about to explode into a thousand shards of glass. I didn't understand it, any of it, but I didn't question it either. Whatever it was that I was feeling, whatever insane and irrational thoughts and feelings filtered through my mind and body, I allowed.

I glared at Grant, whose sly smile had now turned into a full shit-eating grin. "Just tell me if she's been here or not, old man. Spit it out, already." I held my breath for only a second. "Or maybe you don't remember. Is that it? Your mind fading already?"

I must have pushed him a smidge too far, because he looked around for something to throw at my head. Again. Between him and Frank, I was always ducking the crap being tossed at me. Maybe I was the problem? Nah, that couldn't be right. It was their tempers and short fuses that made them want to pummel me with things every chance they got.

"She hasn't been here yet today, asshole. But I'll tell you this, she doesn't like you much."

I relaxed a little at his admission and the fact that there wasn't anything within his reach to throw at me. "Tell me something I don't know."

"She likes me a lot. A hell of a lot more than she likes you." He let out a gruff laugh, enjoying bringing me pain. "You think you can steal my angel from me with a few flowers? You've got a lot to learn, boy."

Glancing down at the flowers that I held on to like a lifeline, I shook my head, unwilling to let Grant deter me. He was only teasing me, but every word was like a razor blade slicing through my flesh. Little nicks here and there, and before you knew it, I'd be bleeding out all over the stark white floor.

"What do you suggest then?"

He cleared his throat and faked a cough like he hadn't heard me right. "Did you, dyin' for Ryan, just ask for my advice?"

Now it was my turn to choke out a cough. #DyinForRyan was one of the hashtags women posted when they talked about the bar. "How do you know about that?"

"I don't live in a cave. I've seen them all. #DyinForRyan. #FishWish, whatever the hell that means. #SpankMeFrank. #LickedByNick. I can't believe the gumption of the women these days." He sounded part disgusted and part impressed.

"Do you have a Twitter account?" I shook my head, unable to picture it.

"Instagram."

Grant's response was so deadpan, I had no idea if he was serious or not. I cocked my head, raising one eyebrow, letting him know so before he laughed.

"I don't really know how to use it," he admitted, "but I downloaded it after being in your bar. Wanted to see what all the fuss was about. Turns out I wasn't missing much."

"I'll make sure to pass that along to Nick."

"I'll tell him you were lying," he shot back.

"You gonna stop fighting with me over every single thing?"

"Probably not." He faked a yawn, pretending like my company bored him. "You ever going to put those flowers down?"

"Probably not."

"She won't want your damn flowers, you know."

"She might not think she wants them, but she does."

Glaring at me, he said, "She'd want them if they were from me."

Grant started to cough, slapping at his chest to get it to stop. I wasn't sure that sort of thing was even effective, yet we all did it.

"Then you should have gotten off your ass and bought her some," I told him.

This time he did find something to throw at me. A Sharpie flew through the air and hit me in the stomach before bouncing off and pinging to the floor. I didn't even attempt to grab it, even though I could have easily caught it with one hand.

I let Grant have his moment of satisfaction, striking me with flying objects, before I bent down to pick it up.

Where the hell did he get a Sharpie from, anyway?

SAY YES
Sofia

I STOOD OUTSIDE the doorway for a minute longer, wondering what else Ryan and Grant would say before I made my entrance.

Ryan had flowers for me—I gathered that much from what I'd accidentally overheard. It hadn't been my intention to eavesdrop, but when I arrived at Grant's door, I couldn't help but hear their banter. Neither had said my name, but my gut told me the *she* they kept referring to was me.

Part of me wanted to turn around and bolt until the coast was clear, meaning until Ryan was long gone, but my mom could only watch Matson for so long. She had a meeting tonight she couldn't get out of, so my time to visit Grant was limited.

I sucked in a breath and reminded myself that I wasn't there for Ryan Manwhore Fisher. Grant was the reason for my visit, and I wanted to make sure he was okay. Ryan being here was an unfortunate side effect that I had no control over.

As much as I wanted to pretend that I hated Ryan for being here now, all my girlie parts screamed the opposite. They definitely liked that he was here. I'd denied myself male attention for so long that I'd almost forgotten what it was like.

Ryan made it hard to keep my resolve. But in those moments of weakness, my son's face flashed in my mind and I steeled myself, instantly remembering that my life wasn't just about me anymore.

Matson was the reason for my standoffish behavior. I had to not only protect my heart, but my innocent son's as well. Ryan wasn't good for either for us, no matter how hard he tried to convince me otherwise. Agreeing to date him would be like begging for my heart to be shattered. I might be a strong woman, but even I could only take so much.

Drawing in a calming breath, I took a step into the room before I could talk myself out of it. The conversation stopped midsentence as both men turned their attention to me. Grant propped himself up higher in the bed, finger-combing his hair, while Ryan moved toward me like a wild animal stalking his prey.

I was definitely that prey.

"You look beautiful," he said, his blue eyes raking my body from head to toe.

An unwanted shiver raced down my spine, and I fought off the goose bumps that wanted to pepper my arms.

"These are for you." He held out the most colorful bouquet of fresh flowers I'd ever seen in my life. They were stunning in their simplicity, tied together with a piece of twine.

I snapped my jaw shut as I took them from his hands, the weight of them catching me by surprise. "Thank you," I said slowly, more than a little confused. Why would he bring me flowers, anyway?

"I'm not sure why he didn't bring me flowers," Grant

muttered, and I directed my focus to him, putting some space between Ryan and me.

"I'm not sure either. Ryan, care to answer that?" I asked.

It was adorable the way he shifted his weight from one foot to the other when I put him on the spot, clearly a little uncomfortable before he fought back with a dimpled smile.

"What the hell would he do with flowers?" He jerked his thumb toward Grant. "He'd probably throw them in the trash the second I walked out. Or give them to some nurse and pretend he bought them for her. I knew you'd at least appreciate them," he said with a wink.

A wink? Ryan probably meant it to be charming, but all it did was send me crash-landing back to reality where he was a womanizer, and I was, for whatever reason, his latest conquest attempt.

"They're very pretty," I said halfheartedly.

His shoulders slumped with his exhale. "Pretty enough that you'll consider going out with me?"

As I tried to form an answer, I moved to the side of the bed, placing the flowers on the nightstand to give myself a moment to think.

Grant burst out laughing. "You don't even have to answer, angel. Your face says it all. This is too good."

"But I want an answer," Ryan said over Grant's chortling, taking a step closer to me.

I turned to face him, almost forgetting that anyone else was in the room. "I can't go out with you."

"Can't or won't?" Ryan pinned me with his intense gaze as he took another step closer.

My breath caught, and I stumbled over my response.

"Does it matter?"

One more step. "It does to me. Can't or won't?"

Ryan was close now, so close I caught his scent with every breath.

His head cocked to the side, his eyes never leaving mine. "Can't or won't, angel?" he whispered.

How the heck was I supposed to answer that? I couldn't go out with Ryan because there was no point. He wasn't a good role model for Matson, and the bar life wasn't something I was interested in being a part of.

Ryan and his brothers had been on reality TV shows more than once, and were regularly featured in online and local magazines. He wasn't a celebrity, per se, but he was treated like one. That wasn't the type of atmosphere I wanted to raise my son in.

So no, I couldn't go out with Ryan. And I wouldn't for the same reasons.

"If you're done harassing my girlfriend here, don't you have a bar to run?" Grant said gruffly, and I could have kissed him, so grateful for the interruption.

Ryan's gorgeous blue eyes narrowed at Grant but softened when he looked back at me. Thank God he stepped away, because now I felt like I could breathe again.

"I do have to get back to work. Promise me you'll at least think about giving me a chance, angel. Just one chance. It's all I'll need."

Offering him a tight-lipped smile, I shrugged. "I'll think about it." It was a lie, and Ryan knew it.

He headed toward the door but stopped and turned to look right through me. "Here's the thing. You think you know me, but you don't. I know what the women at my bar say about me, but that doesn't make it true. I'd like to take you out and see if there's something more here than just what I feel every time I see you. I know you feel it too, but for some reason, you're pretending you don't."

An uncomfortable laugh bubbled up from his throat.

"Hell, maybe you really do hate me? But I'm betting that's not true either. Maybe you're scared of what this could be? I don't know. But I'll tell you this. I'm not giving up. One chance. One date. That's all I'm asking."

And with that, he walked out, taking all the air in the room with him.

Ryan was as infuriating as he was sexy, refusing to listen or take no for an answer. I was torn between wanting to be annoyed with him and wanting to jump his bones. Why was that alpha-male behavior so damn sexy? Or maybe it was only sexy because it was coming from him? I had no idea, but Grant clearing his throat reminded me that I wasn't alone.

"That was . . . interesting."

"That was something, all right." I struggled to catch the breath Ryan had stolen with his speech.

Grant studied me, searching my eyes for answers. When he found none, he pursed his lips. "I'm going to get serious with you for a moment."

Curious, I pulled up the lone chair in the room and sat down. "Okay."

"It's obvious that boy likes you. I can see it in his eyes, and it's more than just seeing you for how pretty you are. He's genuinely interested, and he's right . . . you keep pretending like you're not. Why is that?"

Did I want to confess all my insecurities and fears to this man I barely knew? Someone who would probably repeat everything I told him to the one person I was trying to keep all of this from?

"I can't tell you. You're on his side."

Grant let out a hearty laugh. "His side? Hell, I'm on *my* side. I want you all to myself, but that knucklehead is stubborn. He won't quit. So, tell me why you dislike him so much."

I sucked in a breath, wondering how much I was comfortable sharing. As a young single mom, I learned early on to keep the fact that I had a child to myself. The silent judgment that came after that confession was something that chipped away at me a little more each time it happened.

Guys didn't want to date girls like me; they wanted to party and be obligation-free. Dating someone with a kid was the exact opposite of that. The second most men found out that I had a son, they usually bolted, or made up some lame excuse to stop talking to me as quickly as they had started. It was almost as if I'd grown two heads the moment they learned the truth.

The worst part was that I'd started to believe there was something wrong with me . . . that my having a kid was a bad thing.

So I'd stopped telling people I had one.

I convinced myself that it was to keep my private life private, but the truth was that it was to keep me from feeling small and insignificant. It shouldn't have bothered me what people thought about me, but it did. All the glances at my left ring finger, which was clearly ringless, weighed on me. The wary look in people's eyes when they learned I was a single mom. There was never a positive response from anyone. No, they were always feeling sorry for me, judging me, or wanting to commiserate in some way.

So I kept my guard up.

The truth was that my son made me a better person. Matson was the best damn thing to ever happen in my life, and any guy who couldn't see that didn't deserve to be in it.

And this was exactly why I hesitated to tell Grant. He'd tell Ryan, and there was no way that Ryan would want to be a part of my life when he learned about Matson. I couldn't imagine him thinking that my son was anything other than a hindrance, and I refused to put myself in that situation again, no matter how charming the guy was. I'd rather be alone forever than with someone who couldn't see our worth.

"Was my question that difficult?" Grant said, breaking through my self-imposed trance.

"No," I said with a smile. "It's not that I dislike him, necessarily . . . I don't even know him, but I've heard things. I've seen things. Ryan's just not my type."

"I thought Ryan was everyone's type."

"He thinks so too." I rolled my eyes.

"Did something happen between you two before? Was he rude to you? Do you want me to fight for your honor?"

Giggling at the mental image of Ryan and Grant going at it, I reached for his hand and squeezed it. "He wasn't rude to me. But if you want to fight him just for fun, I'm not sure I'd stop you."

"Would you cheer me on?"

"Hell yes, I would," I said far too enthusiastically.

He gave my hand a quick squeeze. "I know you're keeping things to yourself, Sofia, and that's okay. You don't owe me anything. And I'll deny saying this if you ever repeat it, but you might be wrong about that boy."

Swallowing nothing but the air that seemed to thicken around us, I nodded, refusing to believe that could possibly be true. I supposed I could be wrong about Ryan, but I'd bet money that I was right about him not wanting to date a single mom.

"I don't think I'm wrong."

Grant nodded toward the flowers on the table. "He doesn't walk around giving girls flowers all the time, if that's what you think."

"I don't think that. But he doesn't even know me. And if he did, he probably would have saved his money."

I hated the way I sounded, but no one knew what it was like to be me. No one knew what I'd been through. It would have all been fine if I'd had a ring on my finger. People would have thought I was married, and being a young mother would have been more acceptable. Some days I was tempted to do it, to buy a fake wedding ring and wear it to avoid the judgment and pity on strangers' faces.

Grant gave me a sympathetic look. "Nothing about you could be that bad, Sofia. I can't even imagine what it is you're not telling me."

Guys from his era seemed more chivalrous and family-oriented. I imagined if Grant had learned something like this about the love of his life, he would have stepped in to be the man of the house, no questions asked. But guys today were more self-absorbed and cared about all the wrong things—like money, fame, and screwing as many women as possible.

"It's not bad. It's just different. I'm pretty sure Ryan wouldn't be interested, so I'm saving us both the trouble. That's all."

Grant pursed his lips again as he thought. "So he doesn't get a say in the matter? You've already made the decision for both of you? That's not fair. What if you're wrong?"

I knew what Grant was doing, pointing out the fact that I wasn't even giving Ryan a chance, but he was wrong. I was doing the right thing for all involved.

Shaking my head slowly, I said, "I'm not."

"How about this? When I get out of here, you and I will have our first date at Ryan's bar. Then you can decide during our date if you want to give him a chance or not."

It sounded absolutely insane. "I just told you I'm not interested in Ryan."

"You are, though. You know it. Ryan knows it. And that's why you have to say yes to my offer."

I huffed out an annoyed breath, but I wasn't annoyed at all. I stalled, all the while knowing I would agree to this ridiculous idea. "Fine."

"Is that a yes?"

When I said yes, Grant grinned like he'd never been more proud of himself and clapped his hands.

"I should probably get going." I reached for the arm-breaking bouquet of flowers and hefted them into my arms. "I'll see you tomorrow." Then I bent down and gave Grant a quick peck on the cheek before turning to leave.

"Angel, wait!" he said quickly, and I paused. "I need your number. You know, just in case."

A slow grin spread across my face. "Just in case, what?"

"In case you try to disappear on me."

My jaw dropped open in mock shock. "How dare you. I would never."

"You might," he teased, and I laughed out loud.

"You're right," I said as he held out his cell phone. Putting down the flowers again, I took his cell phone and typed my name and number into it before handing it back. "I wasn't sure which name to put it under, but it's in there under Sofia."

Grant stared at his phone before pressing a button for the nurse.

"Are you feeling okay?" I asked, suddenly concerned, but he waved me off.

"I just need to find out when I'm getting the hell out of here. I have a date to go on."

WHERE IS HE
Sofia

I LOOKED INTO my son's sweet eyes as I tucked him into bed. As much as I loved the fact that his eyes were a gorgeous shade of blue, I hated that they looked exactly like his father's. I could never forget where Matson came from, not when I looked into the almost identical eyes.

"Did you have fun with Nana tonight?"

Matson nodded his head vigorously, a smile plumping up his cheeks. They used to be chubbier but were slimming now as he grew taller, losing his baby fat.

"I'm glad." I pressed a quick kiss to cheek before kissing the other. I could never resist planting kisses on his sweet face, especially knowing that one day he'd make me stop.

He yawned, covering his mouth with his fist before asking, "Is the man from the hospital okay?"

"I think so," I said, realizing that I hadn't even asked Grant how he was feeling or what the doctors had said about his condition. Even if I had asked him, he probably would have lied or exaggerated the truth, not wanting me to be concerned or worried.

"Do you have to see him anymore," Matson asked, his forehead creased with as much concern as an eight-year-old could muster.

"I'll go see him tomorrow during my lunch."

He blinked, and I stared at his long, dark lashes, loving the way they accented his kind eyes. "You'll pick me up before dinner this time?"

My heart ached with the knowledge that any change to our normal routine tended to make Matson uneasy. I'd never pinpointed the reason for his fear, it seemed unnatural to me, but I didn't want to add to it. The last thing I wanted to bring to my child was unease. It was my job to protect him, to make him feel safe and comforted. It was a job I took extremely seriously.

"I'll pick you up before dinner. Sorry I've been late the last couple of nights."

"It's okay, Mama. That man needed you and I let him borrow you for a little while, but now I need you back," he said, his tone so matter-of-fact that I had to stop myself from giggling.

"Things will go back to normal tomorrow. Promise." I stuck out my pinky finger, and Matson wrapped his smaller pinky around mine and squeezed before shaking our hands up and down twice.

"Good night, Mama," he said through another yawn.

I kissed him again, on the forehead this time. "Good night, baby. I love you."

"Love you too."

*

KNOWING THAT I had a promise to keep to my son, I hustled

during my lunch break toward the hospital. It wasn't far in terms of miles, but there was no quick route that avoided the everyday traffic and numerous red lights. I threw my car into park in a visitor's spot and practically jogged into the hospital.

Opting for the stairs instead of the slow elevator, I was anxious as I made my way up, two stairs at a time, toward Grant's floor. I had no idea why I was feeling so apprehensive for no reason until I rounded the corner and stepped into his room.

His *empty* room.

Grant wasn't there. A vase of flowers sat undisturbed on the windowsill. The handful of get-well-soon cards he'd received were still propped up, marching in a neat row on the nightstand next to the bed.

I spun on my heel to exit the room at the same moment a nurse I didn't recognize from my previous visits walked in.

"Where is he?" I demanded, waving toward the empty bed.

"He's gone," she said matter-of-factly as she gathered the cards.

I almost fell apart right then.

Swallowing hard, I sucked in a breath and barreled back down the stairs. As I ran for my car, I noted the time, knowing I'd be cutting it close, but I had to hear it from Ryan directly. I had to know what happened.

Grant had seemed fine yesterday. What had gone so wrong since then?

When I arrived at Sam's, I tugged open the heavy bar door and walked in, pushing my sunglasses on top of my head. As I waited for my eyes to adjust to the dim lighting, I searched for Ryan behind the bar, but he wasn't there.

"Angel?"

I turned around to see him bent over a notebook at a table, his head cocked to one side as he eyed me.

"Ryan, what happened? How'd he die?" My voice cracked on my questions as I hurried toward him. "I thought he was fine."

He pushed out of the chair and stood up, meeting me halfway. "Who died? What are you talking about?"

"Who died?" I practically shouted. "Grant! What happened to him?"

Ryan's face fell, and his brow furrowed in confusion. "Grant, what?"

I couldn't believe Ryan didn't already know and I was going to have to tell him. I was sure he would have known before I did. The hospital would have called him, wouldn't they?

"He's not at the hospital, Ryan. They didn't tell you?"

"Wait." He raised one hand to stop me before placing both of them on my shoulders and squaring me to face him. "You were at the hospital?"

Staring into his ocean-blue eyes, I pretended to ignore how good his hands felt on my body, or how warm. "Yes, I was at the hospital. His room was empty, but all his gifts were still there, and the nurse said he was gone."

Ryan started laughing. The asshole actually laughed in my face.

I jerked out of his grasp and took a step back, appalled at his behavior and attitude. "Why are you laughing?"

"I took him home this morning. Trust me, the old man's fine."

My breath whooshed out of me, taking my anxiety with it. "He's not dead?"

Ryan shook his head, but the smile refused to leave his lips. "No."

"I just assumed . . . I mean, his cards and flowers were there, so it looked like—" I stopped short, unable to finish that sentence.

"He made me leave those things. Told me if I even thought about boxing them up and taking them to his house, he'd shoot me once we got there."

A laugh bubbled up from deep in my throat. "He's unbelievable."

"You're unbelievable." Ryan smirked.

A throat cleared and I turned to see one of Ryan's brothers behind the bar. Maybe the youngest brother, but I couldn't be sure. I definitely needed to brush up on my Fisher trivia.

No, I most certainly do not. Why did that thought even enter my head?

"Hi. I'm Nick." He offered me a friendly little wave.

Ryan groaned without even giving him a glance. "No one cares who you are. Go away."

"I bet she cares. Don't you?" Nick asked, then launched rapid-fire questions at me. "Are you the girl from the beach? The one who saved Grant? The one my brother won't shut the hell up about?"

All my words escaped me, so I could only nod. Nick knew who I was? Ryan talked about me? This was surreal.

Glancing down at my watch, I noted the time. "Shit," I mumbled under my breath as I backed away. "I have to go. I'm on my lunch break."

Ryan moved too, falling into step with me. "I'll walk you

out."

"You really don't have to do that." Trying to ignore him, I headed for the door. "It was nice to meet you, Nick," I said as I passed by him. His eyes were identical to Ryan's, but their hair color couldn't have been more different. Nick's was jet black, a stark contrast to Ryan's lighter brown.

"Nice to meet you too, uh . . ." Nick paused, looking sheepish. "I have no idea what your name is. Sorry."

"Sofia," I said before I could stop myself.

Dammit. I hadn't wanted Ryan to know my name, and now I'd given it up without thinking. These Fisher brothers made a girl lose all sense of reason.

"Nice to meet you, Sofia," Nick called out. "Come back again."

I tossed him a wave before I pushed the door open and walked out into the blaring sunshine. Dropping my sunglasses over my eyes, I sensed Ryan at my back before I turned to see him there.

"Sofia," he said, my name a breathy sigh as he closed the space between us. The way he said it sent chills down my spine. "It suits you."

"What does," I asked, but I knew exactly what he meant.

"Your name. It's beautiful."

"Flattery will get you nowhere." I tried to sound strong, but being so close to Ryan's body heat was like asking yourself not to burn when you were already on fire.

Ryan shifted on his feet and ran a hand through his hair. "I'm not trying to flatter you, angel. I'm really not."

God, he was so good-looking, it should have been a crime. My attraction to him had to be written all over my face, let alone my body. Every part of myself betrayed me, weakening my resolve.

"Then what are you trying to do?" I asked, trying to keep my voice steady.

"Get to know you."

I shook my head. "I've already told you. You're not my type."

"Do you have a boyfriend?"

I had to stop the sarcastic laugh that threatened to burst from my lips. "No."

Maybe I should have lied. If Ryan thought I had a boyfriend, I was fairly certain he would back off.

"You don't have a boyfriend." He held up a hand as he started counting. One finger.

"You pretend you hate my guts." Second finger.

"You also keep pretending you're not interested in me." Third finger.

"But I know you feel this energy between us, because there's no way I'm the only one who feels this." Fourth finger.

"All I can think is that there's something you're not telling me." Fifth finger.

Ryan held up his whole hand in front of me, one eyebrow raised as he waited for a response.

My head swam with his accusations as light-headedness consumed me. "I really have to go. I can't be late." I needed to get away from Ryan and all of his stupid finger-counting and pressure and gorgeous eyes.

A solid hand wrapped around my upper arm, and I looked at it as he spoke. "Just say you'll come back. One time. Please, Sofia."

Reaching for his fingers, I peeled them off my arm before I stepped into the parking lot. "I was already planning on it," I said casually before getting inside my car and driving off.

Ryan would probably assume I was coming back to see him, but I was only fulfilling my end of the bargain that I'd made with Grant. And now that he wasn't dead like I'd thought he was twenty minutes ago, I'd have to uphold it.

OFF MY GAME
Ryan

REFUSING TO MOVE an inch, I watched Sofia drive off until she made a right turn and disappeared from sight. If I could have run to a rooftop to watch the rest of her drive, I would have. This woman was turning me into a desperate man. But then again, she'd said she was already planning on coming back to the bar. Which meant that before I'd begged her like a starved man, she had planned to come and see me again.

The thought alone filled me with a mixture of feelings, some I didn't recognize and couldn't quite name. But one distinct emotion stood out above all the others—excitement.

One time, that was all I'd need, and I knew it. One visit from her and I'd break down her walls, or at least start scaling them like a fucking boss. I would make Sofia see that I wasn't who she thought I was. All her preconceived notions about me were wrong, and I planned to prove exactly that to her.

When I walked back inside the bar, I was met by Nick smirking at me. I'd forgotten all about him while I was lost in thoughts of winning my angel over.

"She's pretty," he said as he wiped the top of the bar, even though I'd already cleaned it earlier.

"I know she's pretty," I said as if that was the stupidest statement I'd heard all day.

The office door swung open and Frank stepped out. "Who's pretty?"

"The chick Ryan won't shut up about. You missed her, man," Nick teased.

"I miss everything," Frank grumbled.

"Maybe if you left the office every once in a while, you would've seen the pretty little thing our brother has the hots for."

Nick sure was mouthy for being the youngest, but since there was an eight-year age difference between him and me, and Frank was two years older than me, we weren't around much as he was growing up. Hence the reason Nick wasn't scared we'd beat the shit out of him for being so lippy.

When Nick added, "She looks familiar too," my jaw tightened in an emotion as foreign as it was intriguing.

Could I actually feel possessive over this woman I knew nothing about?

"What do you mean, she looks familiar? Familiar how? Like you've seen her on the street, or you slept with her, or what?" I knew I was ranting, knew I sounded like a fucking madman, but I didn't care.

Nick raised his hands, patting the air. "Calm down, psycho. I have no idea. She just looks familiar. I'm not sure from where, but it's definitely not from sleeping with her."

He might have been cool about it, but I felt anything but calm as visions of Sofia and my baby brother going at it filled my mind.

"Dude, I said I didn't sleep with her. Are you even listening?" He snapped his fingers in front of my face.

I snapped out of it, wondering how he knew exactly what I'd been seeing in my head.

Frank smirked at me. "I've never seen you like this."

I knew all too well how much he was enjoying my current state of crazy. I'd enjoyed his idiotic behavior over his girlfriend Claudia in much the same way before they started dating, and I hadn't hesitated to let him know. So I supposed I deserved all of this.

"I feel a little out of control and I don't know why," I admitted, feeling a little self-conscious. "But she said she'd come back, so that's a good thing." I tried to sound chipper, like my normal self, but I was off. My brothers knew it, and I knew it. There was no sense trying to hide it.

Nick's eyes widened. "She did?"

"When's she coming?" Frank cocked a brow and leaned against the bar top.

Shit. When was she coming? She didn't say.

I shrugged. "Honestly, I have no idea."

Nick and Frank's widened and they both howled with laughter, and I never realized just how annoying the two of them were until this moment.

"Did you get her number?" Frank managed to ask through his snickering.

"No."

Nick bent over laughing, holding his stomach. "You're so far off your game, it's comical."

I wanted to be pissed off, but he was right. Normally I was calm, completely cool when it came to women and how I handled them. I never got nervous or intimidated, but with

Sofia, I was flailing, a desperate man begging for whatever scraps she tossed my way.

Under my breath, I muttered, "I'm aware."

"What'd you say?" Frank leaned toward me, cupping his hand to his ear.

Narrowing my eyes, I glared at my older brother. "You heard me just fine the first time."

"So, what are you going to do about it then?" He lowered his hand and shoved it in his pocket.

"I don't know."

"You don't know?" both my brothers said in unison, sounding like an off-key boy band.

"Leave me alone," I growled.

"Remember when you harassed me about a plan for Claudia?" Frank asked, and Nick nodded, egging him on. "Well, now it's my turn. Payback's a bitch. So, what's your plan?"

I had an inkling of a plan, but not much else. It was more of an idea, really.

"You'll laugh," I said, not wanting to talk about it anymore.

It was all fine and dandy when I was making fun of Frank or harassing Nick for his stupid decisions, but being on this side of it wasn't anywhere nearly as entertaining. At least, it wasn't for me. They, on the other hand, were enjoying the hell out of it.

Nick rolled his hand in an encouraging motion. "Just tell us. You know I'm going to bug you until you spit it out anyway. Might as well just tell us now."

A groan escaped me. I'd never hear the end of this, no matter how hard I tried to avoid it, so I might as well spill it.

"I'm going to woo her."

"Woo her?" They both mocked me, imitating my voice before breaking out into hysterical laughter. Again.

The two of them might have been laughing at me, but the truth was that they didn't know shit about women. Both of them were idiots and made huge mistakes before they finally got the girl.

Me, I didn't intend to make mistakes when it came to Sofia. I planned on being the exception to the Fisher brother playbook they both seemed to follow. One that was apparently handed down from our father.

"Yeah, I'm going to woo her. Something you two clearly know nothing about."

"Excuse me." Frank's laughter died and his jaw clenched. "I get that you're trying to bash us here, but you're inadvertently bashing our women in the process. Choose your next words carefully."

"What he said." Nick pointed his thumb toward Frank, but he was nowhere near as threatening as Frank could be.

There wasn't a doubt in my mind that my brothers loved their girlfriends. And the personal hell that each of them had gone through in order to get their girl and stay together was nothing short of crazy. But I didn't want to do things the way either of them did. If there was going to be some big dramatic implosion before my happily-ever-after happened, it sure as hell wasn't going to be my doing.

I waved my hand in surrender, not wanting to genuinely piss my brothers off any further. I loved their girlfriends and knew that both Claudia and Jess would be my sisters-in-law one day. "I only meant to offend you two. Not the girls."

"Hard to separate," Frank bit out.

"Can we move on? Or back, actually?" Nick asked, leaning forward on the bar. "I want to hear all about this wooing you're planning to do."

"I just meant that I was going to romance her, okay? I want to be a gentleman when she comes in. Drive her home if she'll let me, ask her on a proper date, bring her flowers. You know, all the things guys do when they actually like a girl." I knew I sounded like a Hallmark Channel movie, but I couldn't have cared less. They already knew I was an over-the-top romantic, so this was simply confirming it.

Nick caught my eye. "Can I say something?"

I glanced at Frank, who was already staring at Nick as I braced myself for whatever was about to spill from his lips. "Go ahead."

"Can I just point out that you don't even really know her? You can't possibly *like her* like her already." Nick looked to Frank for backup. "Am I right or wrong here?"

Frank offered a slight shrug but not much else as I allowed Nick's words to sink in. He wasn't wrong.

"You're right," I admitted. "I don't know her, so I can't really like her already. I guess *liking her* is the wrong word choice. Let's just say I'm interested. I'm interested in getting to know her better so that I can like her. Better?"

I wasn't sure why I was explaining myself, but I felt the need to. As much as I wanted to run away and hide in a corner where they'd leave me alone, I couldn't avoid my brothers forever. And in their own way, they were only trying to help.

"What do you think you like about her? Why is she so different? Is it because she's avoiding you?" Frank's words were thoughtful, carefully chosen, it was obvious he'd been thinking on this longer than a second or two.

"That's a good point," Nick said. "Is it just the chase?"

Frank and Nick turned to each other and got lost in conversation about the thrill of the chase. They talked about not really liking a girl, but being intrigued for all the wrong reasons. I wasn't included in the conversation, and neither of them looked at me until I cleared my throat loudly, reminding them that I was still here and this conversation was supposed to be about me.

The chase part had been something I'd considered already. Hell, maybe part of my pull toward her had initially been based on the fact that she kept pushing me away. We always want what we can't have, right? But I wasn't that kind of guy, never had been. And they both knew it.

"It's not the chase. It's not some game," I said, then looked at Frank. "Was it the chase for you with Claudia?" I asked, knowing the question would strike a nerve.

"You know damn well it wasn't," he ground out through clenched teeth.

"Then what was it about her?" I asked. Frank wouldn't like being put on the spot, but I did it to prove my point. "Can you put into words what made her so different from any other woman you'd met before?"

"You know it was something I felt. It wasn't about words."

I blew out an exasperated breath. "That's how I feel. There's just something there. I don't know what it is. I don't know if it's real or some bullshit fantasy I've made up in my head, but I want to find out. I have to know for sure."

Nick nodded, clearly wanting to contribute. "That's how it

was with Jess. I could've had any girl I wanted at State, but none of them made me feel the way Jess did."

I glanced between them. "So you both understand that I have to do this. I just need to see."

My brothers nodded in unison as the doors flew open and a rowdy group of guys sauntered in. I was tempted to give them a round on the house for their perfect timing, but decided against it as I took their orders and got to work instead.

PHONE DATES
Sofia

WHEN I GOT back to the office, I weaved through the cubicles as I made my way toward my desk. My boss wouldn't care that I was ten minutes late coming back from lunch, but I did. If there was one thing I never wanted to be, it was irresponsible. Giving someone a reason to fire me was not on my to-do list. I had too much to lose and a son to support.

"You're late," Sarin said, chuckling as she approached my desk.

I glared at her. "Shhh, don't be so loud."

"Martin's not back from his lunch meeting. You're fine." She waved at me like I had nothing to be concerned about, when the truth was that I needed to check all the voice mails and emails that had come in while I was gone.

I tossed my purse into my desk drawer and slammed it shut a little too hard, making the framed picture of Matson and me fall over. I moved it back upright and grinned when I looked at his cake-stained face. My dad took the picture on Matson's third birthday, and it was still one of my favorites. I missed my son's chubby cherub cheeks.

"How was the old guy?" Sarin asked as she stirred her cup of coffee.

"He wasn't there," I said without looking up, scrolling through emails.

Sarin snapped her fingers at me, drawing my attention, and I looked up from my computer at her.

"He wasn't there? Where was he?" She blew at her drink before taking a sip.

"I thought he was dead," I said and she choked, spitting her sip back into the cup.

"You made me do that." She wiped at her chin with the back of her hand. "Hurry up and tell me what happened. I have to get back."

"He checked out. But I thought he was dead, so I ran to Ryan's stupid bar to ask him about it, and he asked me out."

"What'd you say?"

I huffed, making sure Sarin knew I was annoyed. "I can't go out with him, Sarin. I can't date a guy like Ryan Fisher."

"Fine, tell him to ask me out instead. He's hot as hell," she said with a wink.

"Not helping."

"Not trying. But for the record, you're being an idiot."

Folding my arms over my chest, I glared at her. "Excuse me?"

"You heard me."

"Explain," I said. This was something I definitely wanted to hear.

"He likes you. He's made that abundantly clear, and you won't even give him two seconds of your time. For no good reason either."

"No good reason? Matson is the best reason I have. He's the only reason I need," I said, trying to make my closest friend see my situation through my eyes. She knew about my past, about Matson's father, and I couldn't believe she was questioning my not wanting to go out with Ryan.

Sarin rolled her eyes. "But what does Matson have to do with Ryan? Seriously. I'm not a mom, so I don't always understand your reasoning, but please try to explain it to me. And make it quick." She tapped a finger on her wrist.

Is she for real? "In what universe is dating one of the hottest guys on the planet, who also happens to be a bartender, is featured on reality TV shows and online articles all the time, a good idea for someone like me?"

"I think in this universe. This one." She pointed at the floor. "Hell, he might be just what you and Matson need."

I sat back hard in my chair, staring at her in disbelief. "How does Matson need a bartender in his life? And how do I need a guy in my life who's pursued by every single woman in the city?"

"So that's what this is about? The fact that he's a bartender and girls hit on him?" Sarin scoffed at me. "It's just a job, Sofia."

I shook my head and swallowed. "It's not, though. He owns the bar, and he chooses to work there. That's a lifestyle. It's a single guy's dream, and I'm a single *mom*." I bugged out my eyes at her. "Pretty sure those two things don't go together."

"Well, I think you're wrong." She frowned, glancing at her watch. "Shit, I have to go. Put a pin in this conversation because we're not done with it."

Exhaling, I watched my best friend hurry away from my desk and toward her own.

Was I wrong? Glancing at the picture of Matson again, I smiled, knowing that I wasn't. He was my first priority, and it was my job to provide a good role model for him, both as a boy and as a future man.

And I honestly couldn't picture that role model being Ryan.

*

AFTER PULLING UP into my parents' driveway, I shut off the engine and started toward their house to get my son. Mom appeared in the doorway, her expression one I wasn't sure that I'd seen before.

"What happened? Are you okay? Is Matson okay? Is Dad okay?" My stomach churned as scenarios raced through my head.

She gripped my shoulder and shushed me, then told me everyone was fine. "Derek came by the house earlier." Her voice was calm and controlled, unlike my legs, and I reached out to steady myself.

"D-Derek?" I stuttered, unable to get his name out. "What did he want? What did he say?"

Regaining my composure, I looked around for my son and let out a relieved breath when I saw him sitting in the living room. Adrenaline surged, filling me with a feral protectiveness, like a mama bear who would attack anyone who threatened her cub.

"Oh my God, does he want custody of Matson?" My throat tightened, and I thought I might throw up all over my mom's pink hydrangeas.

"I'm honestly not sure what he wanted, *mija*."

"How can you not be sure? You talked to him, didn't you? What did he say?"

"He said he stopped by to see how we were. He wanted to know how you and Matson were, and if you still lived at home."

My head ached with the news. It had been over eight years since I'd heard from Derek. Eight years since he'd left for college after telling me to get an abortion. Why would he suddenly show up and start asking questions?

"Please tell me you didn't tell him where I live."

She clucked her tongue at me, her eyes narrowed. "Never. But I did tell him that you were happy, safe, and better off without him."

A small smile twitched my lips. "I bet he loved that." Derek had always been overly cocky and confident as a teenager, but I had no idea what kind of man he'd grown into. I assumed it was more of the same.

When Mom patted her hand above her heart, her tell for when she was uncomfortable, I asked, "What else happened?"

"I told him to leave and never come back."

"And?"

"He said I'd better watch my mouth. That Matson was his son too, and I could count on him coming back. He got really angry."

The color must have drained from my face, because my cheeks turned to ice with her words. "Matson is his son too?" I whispered, not believing that this could be happening. Why would he claim paternity now?

"Your father walked over and threatened to blow a hole in

his head if he ever showed his face here again, and you know what Derek did?"

My stomach twisted and my head pounded because I didn't know. I had no idea at all what could have happened after that. "What?"

"He laughed. He actually laughed. I think he respected being threatened."

"Is Dad okay?"

"Other than wanting to follow through on the threat, yes. He's fine. Just worried."

"What do we do? He can't just come into Matson's life out of nowhere and expect to be his dad. It doesn't work like that. Matson doesn't even know who he is."

"I know. We'll figure it out, *mija*."

"How?"

Suddenly, I was terrified. Would I lose Matson? Would I have to share him with the one person who'd disappointed me more than anyone else ever had?

Logically, I knew Derek had every right to know his son and be a part of his life, but emotionally, I wanted to be sure Matson was safe and protected. Was letting Derek in Matson's life the best thing for my son? I had no way of knowing. The truth was that I didn't know Derek anymore.

"It will be okay, Sofia." My mom gripped my shoulder. "Now, go get your boy and take him home."

I nodded, feeling numb, my movements robotic.

Derek coming back wasn't something I'd ever considered. After his family disappeared from my life, I'd stopped thinking about them at all and moved on. Derek rarely crossed my mind, except on those rare occasions when Matson would look up at me with his familiar blue eyes, drawing back into some high-school time warp. Sadness rarely consumed me, and I never spent time reminiscing.

The only good thing Derek had ever given me was my son, and now he wanted to be in his life? After eight years? I wanted to throw up.

"Mama!"

Matson's voice rang out as he jumped up from the carpet and ran toward me. He wrapped his arms around my waist and squeezed before I leaned over and hugged him, then peppered his face with kisses until he told me to stop, wiping them off with his hand.

"Don't you wipe off my kisses," I teased before kissing him again.

"I made you something," he said, his eyes lighting up with pride, and I beamed back.

"You did? I can't wait to see it."

Matson turned from me and ran toward the kitchen, blowing past my dad who had walked up to join us.

I stood up and smiled at him. "Hi, Dad."

"Your mother tell you about the visit?" he asked, his tone wary.

I nodded. "I'm sorry I wasn't here to greet him myself." I bit back a laugh as I tried to imagine my easygoing dad threatening Derek.

"Here, Mama." Matson was back and thrust a paper toward my hands.

I reached for it and turned it around to check out the drawing he'd made. It was of me pushing him on the swings at the park in Venice. He'd written in blue crayon I LOVE YOU

MOM, and my eyes instantly welled up.

"You don't like it?" His head tilted to one side.

I bent over again so we could be eye to eye. "I love it. It's the most perfect picture I've ever seen. I love when you draw us together."

"Thanks. Papa helped me draw the swings and get the waves just right."

"That was nice of him." I looked up at my dad and smiled.

"Can we go now? I'm hungry."

"Hungry?" Mom asked. "I just filled this belly a half hour ago." She poked at his stomach and tickled him as he tried to wriggle out of her grasp.

"What did he eat?"

"Half a grilled cheese and some carrot sticks."

"Yeah, and I'm still hungry, Mama. I'm a growing boy. Papa said the more I eat, the more I'll grow. And I want to be as tall as a building."

"As tall as a building? How will you fit in anything?"

"I won't have to fit. I'll be a building, duh." He rolled his eyes before slinging his little backpack over his shoulder and heading toward the door.

"Well then." I glanced at my parents, who were chuckling at Matson as they held each other. "I guess we're leaving."

"I guess so." Mom patted her heart again, that simple action telling me she was still worried about the Derek situation.

I gave my parents a reassuring smile. "Everything will be fine. Let me know if he comes back here."

Now I was the one who was reassuring people, when I still needed a little reassurance of my own.

As we drove home, Matson filled the silence with stories about his day, and how he beat the fastest kid in his class in a race during recess. He told me that some boys were mean to his friend Hayley, pushing her, and Matson stepped between them and told them *if you want to get to her, you have to go through me.*

Pride filled me at my little man's big heart. He was everything I'd ever hoped he would be.

"You like that, Mama? I did a good thing?"

I glanced at him in the backseat. "You did a great thing. That was very noble, and what a gentleman would do."

"What's a gentleman? What does noble mean? You aren't mad that I told that kid I'd fight him?"

"No, honey, I'm not mad at all. I think it was a nice thing to stand up for Hayley. We shouldn't let anyone pick on other people." I paused, wondering how to describe nobility and gentlemanly behavior to an eight-year-old.

"And boys trying to fight with girls. We don't do that," he said, and I agreed.

"You're right. Boys don't fight girls. And a gentleman always make sure that girls are treated with kindness. A noble person would never stand by and watch someone be mean for no reason. A noble person stands up and does the right thing."

"You think that's what I did, Mama? I did the right thing?"

"Absolutely, you did. I'm so proud of you."

I glanced at his face in my rearview mirror, and when I saw the size of his smile, my heart warmed. In that moment, I forgot all about Derek, and my thoughts filled with how sensitive and kind my son was.

Following the narrow driveway to the back of the bungalow, I shut off the engine and turned back toward Matson before getting out. Just a single look, and his face lit up again like I'd brought home ten puppies.

"I made you happy, huh?" he asked.

"You sure did."

We hopped out of the car and headed into our house through the back door like usual. Derek immediately popped into my head and I stopped short, glancing all around me, checking out my neighbor's backyard to be sure no one was watching. When the coast was clear, I released a quick breath and nudged Matson inside, then closed and locked the door behind us.

Was this how my life was going to be until Derek finally found out where I lived? Would I constantly be on the lookout, waiting for him to show up? I was suddenly thankful that the house wasn't in my name and that I was only renting.

"Mama?" Matson's voice made me realize that I'd been standing at the door, unmoving.

Shaking my head, I turned around. "Sorry about that," I said, and he giggled.

Matson and I went through our weekday routine of eating dinner, and then sitting together at the table and working on his homework immediately after. Heaven help me if my son had any trouble understanding his homework, because I wouldn't be any help. The way he was taught wasn't how I had learned things as a kid. As I watched him make his way through math problems, I felt confused and helpless.

"Is it unwind time now, Mama?"

That was what we called it when we sat in front of the TV and watched shows together. Some people probably considered me a bad parent for letting him watch so much television, but in my opinion, it helped us bond. I spent all day long without him, and if we wanted to watch mindless animated cartoons together, I figured there were worse things we could be doing.

"As soon as I finish up the dishes." I walked into the kitchen and turned on the faucet to fill the sink with hot water, squirting in a measure of soap. "Did you brush your teeth like I asked?"

Matson groaned, and then I heard his feet padding across the floor. I turned my head to watch him pass by, but he stopped.

"I'm going. See?"

I couldn't help but smile. "Yes. Thank you."

"Welcome," he muttered before disappearing.

After an hour of unwind time, I tucked Matson into his bed and read him his favorite book about dinosaurs.

Twice.

"One more time, Mama. Please."

He batted his baby blues at me, knowing damn well they were my kryptonite. I could have flipped it and asked him to read to me, but I secretly enjoyed these moments when he still wanted me there, still asked for me to read to him. One day it would all change, and there would be no going back.

As I pretended to ponder his question, he tilted his head, blinking his eyes even faster than before, and I laughed.

"Last time," I said, preparing him. If I didn't tell him that, he would ask me to read to him over and over until the sun came up.

Even after I finally stopped reading and walked out the door, guilt consumed me for not reading it just *one more time*. What harm would it have done?

I pushed the thought aside and filed it in my brain under the category I liked to call Mama Guilt. Nothing was ever enough. I could always do more, be more, spend more time, have more, give more—more, more, more. But I also knew that if I didn't take the time to give myself some self-care, I wouldn't be the best mom I could be.

I considered that balance as I made my way to the couch and flipped the channels for a show to watch that was way more grown-up and far less Disney.

No sooner had I found a trashy reality show when my phone pinged with a text message. I glanced at it, seeing only a phone number instead of a name, and it wasn't a number I recognized.

Wary, I opened the message.

UNKNOWN NUMBER: *Still on for our date, angel?*

Nerves shot through me as I wondered how the heck Ryan had gotten hold of my phone number. He was a resourceful guy, so I figured he had his ways, but I was slightly unnerved.

Another text pinged.

UNKNOWN NUMBER: *Don't even think about hanging this old man out to dry. And if you tell Ryan I called myself old, I'll be forced to call you a liar in public. Don't make me do that, Sofia.*

I laughed out loud, both with relief and at Grant's words. Tucking my feet underneath me, I leaned into my couch and added him to my contacts, then typed out a quick response. I decided to tease Grant a little before agreeing to our date.

SOFIA: *I'm impressed that you text. I pegged you as more of a caller.*

The bubbles danced as I waited for his response.

GRANT: *I thought texting was less rude at this hour. Were you sleeping?*

Giggling again, I glanced at the time, even though I didn't need to check it. Matson started getting ready for bed at eight thirty on the dot each night, and I made sure that I was done reading and out of his room by nine. It was barely five after.

GRANT: *You're stalling.*

Patience, Grant, I thought. *You need to work on your game.*

GRANT: *Sofia!*

I couldn't stop laughing, and before I could even respond to his text, my phone blared out its ringtone, the music way too loud. I quickly silenced it before answering, hoping it didn't disturb Matson.

"You have zero patience," I said instead of saying hello.

"You took too long," Grant grumbled. "And you're right. I like talking better than typing on this stupid thing. My thumbs are too big, anyway. I always press the wrong buttons, and it has to correct it for me. Half the time it sends something that makes no sense at all. Like why would I ever tell someone to water the zoo?"

I laughed again, still not getting a single word out before he continued.

"I was thinking we could go to the bar on Thursday or Friday, your choice."

I pondered for a second as I considered my options. Thursday would be less crowded, but Matson needed me to stick to our weekday routine. I didn't want to mess it up any more than I have been lately.

"Friday works," I said before I could talk myself out of it. I needed to ask my mom to watch Matson, and she'd want to know what I was up to, but it wouldn't be a problem. Part of me hated leaving my son any more than was necessary, but I had promised Grant I'd do this, and the sooner I agreed, the sooner it would all be over. This ridiculousness could stop, and we could all move on with our lives like we'd never even met.

"Friday, it is," he said. "I'll pick you up at eight. That way it won't be too crazy in that godforsaken place."

"Oh, you don't have to do that," I said, but Grant cut me off.

"This is a date, Sofia. How can I make Ryan jealous if we arrive in separate cars? I'll pick you up. Text me your address."

He was so bossy. "Okay. I will."

"Good night, angel. Sleep tight."

"Good night, Grant. Don't forget to water the zoo."

I pressed END on the phone and convinced myself that none of this meant a damn thing. I'd go, have fun with Grant, and never think about Ryan or his ridiculously charming self again.

SAM'S BAR
Sofia

THE REST OF the week went by in typical fashion. There had been no more unannounced visits from Derek, and that only slightly calmed my nerves. I knew he hadn't shown up out of nowhere for no reason, so I waited anxiously for him reappear. Thinking about what he could possibly want made me sick to my stomach every single time, so I tried to push it out of my mind.

That proved to be easier said than done, especially where my son was concerned. I'd woken up twice this week from nightmares involving him taking Matson from me in a public place. I never remembered the exact details, except Derek was there, screaming at me with Matson in his arms, and I couldn't reach them in time.

Work was busy, as usual, and Sarin entertained herself by harassing me about my upcoming date with Grant. She called it *Spyin' on Ryan*. Even though I told her I wanted nothing to do with him, she never believed me. I wouldn't have believed me either. There must have been some subconscious reason that made me agree to go.

Friday night, I convinced my mom to watch Matson at my house so I wouldn't have to wake him up to bring him home after being out. I figured it would be easier on him to be in his home and in his own bed. It gave me comfort too, knowing my son wouldn't be disrupted by my unusual Friday night outing.

Most single moms needed time away from their kids. They tended to be desperate for an escape, a night out, a day away. I wasn't sure why, but I didn't feel that way. Maybe it was because I was away from Matson for most of the day while I worked, getting home past six and sometimes later, depending on what was going on at the office. All I knew was that I enjoyed being around Matson, and I hated being away from him. If I worked from home, however, I'd probably feel differently.

"You know if you get tired, you can always stay here. I can sleep on the foldout," I said to my mom as she watched me getting ready in my bathroom. Matson was in the living room, eating my her famous homemade enchiladas and watching his favorite animated movie for the hundredth time.

"I'll be fine." She stroked my long hair, her fingers sifting through the soft curls I'd added to the length. "Your hair looks beautiful, *mija*."

I grinned. "Thank you, Mom. It looks just like yours." Staring at our reflections in my mirror, I noticed the way we resembled each other in more ways than just our highlighted hair. There was no doubt that I was Mira Richards's daughter.

"So, tell me more about this Ryan." Mom waggled her eyebrows at me, and I scowled.

"I told you I'm going out with Grant."

She clucked her tongue. "Yes, but not really. It's not a real date."

"I know."

"You told me he wants you to see Ryan, right?"

Why did my mom remember everything I mentioned to her in passing? Couldn't she forget some of the details? Or why couldn't I lie to her like a normal daughter?

"Yeah. He wants me to give Ryan a chance. See him in action or something. Even though I've already seen him in action before."

"I'm confused by all of this. Ryan is a bartender? Or he owns the bar?"

"Both. He owns the bar, and he bartends," I said, basically summing up all I knew about Ryan in just a few words.

"And he's cute?" She gave me a knowing look.

"Does it matter?"

"It always matters."

"He's very good-looking," I said, trying to sound unaffected as I thought about how gorgeous Ryan Fisher actually was.

Mom gave me a cryptic look. "It's the good-looking ones that get us into the most trouble."

"Not if you don't let 'em," I said confidently, certain that there was nothing Ryan could do to change my mind.

She laughed. "True. And you're good at not letting them."

"I just want to make the right decision for Matson and me. It's not enough if the guy is good enough for me, but not for him, you know?"

Mom wrapped her arms around me and pulled me close. "Of course I know. You're a great mom, Sofia. I'm proud of you. But at some point, Matson will need to know what love looks like between a man and a woman." Her voice was so romantic and nostalgic.

"That's why he has you and Dad," I said as if that solved everything.

"Your heart can't always stay locked behind a door no one has the key to. Sometimes you need to let it come out and breathe. That's how it grows."

Smiling at her, I said, "Well, it's not coming out to breathe tonight. It's not even getting involved in this."

I believed what I told her, honestly thought my heart wasn't involved when it came to Ryan. Hell, I believed it wasn't interested in him at all.

I should have heard my heart laughing all the way to the bar, but I didn't.

*

WHEN GRANT RANG my doorbell, I had to stop both my mom and Matson from rushing to the door. I still wasn't ready to go there with Grant, so I answered the door before I hurried out of it. My jaw dropped when I stepped outside and saw the classic brown Cadillac waiting at the curb, whitewall tires and all.

Feeling like I'd stepped back into a time I'd only ever seen in movies and pictures, I told him, "This is a beauty, Grant," as he opened the door for me. Seated on the cool white leather, I glanced around, impressed at how everything was in pristine condition, almost like new.

Once Grant was situated in the driver's seat, he turned to me. "Aside from my beautiful wife, this Caddy was my baby. Never had any real babies, you know," he said, his tone almost wistful as he pulled away from the curb.

I'd assumed they didn't have children, since no one was at the hospital except for Ryan and me, but I hadn't been sure until now.

"Does she have a name?"

"My wife or my car?" He glanced at me as he navigated through the busy streets.

"I meant the car, but both, I guess."

"The car's Miranda. My wife's name was Carol. Lost her a little over a year ago. Life's not the same without her here. It downright sucks, if you want to know the truth. That woman lit up my damn life. She made every day brighter. I hate being here without her."

"I'm sorry. She sounds lovely."

"She had to be to put up with me, right? An absolute saint, she was. But full of piss and vinegar too." He laughed. "You couldn't tell Carol to do nothing she didn't want to do. She was a rebel before her time."

"I'm sorry I didn't get the chance to know her," I said, and I meant it. She sounded like a strong woman.

"She would have liked you."

We stayed silent for the rest of the quick drive, fifties music drifting softly from the speakers. Grant pulled Miranda into an almost vacant lot behind Sam's that I hadn't even known existed. Only two cars and a motorcycle were there, so I assumed it must be employee parking.

"Will we get in trouble for parking back here?"

Grant guffawed. "That little shit even thinks about towing my baby, I'll hang him up by the balls."

Shaking my head, I stopped myself from rolling my eyes as he reached for my hand and placed it on his arm. We walked around to the front entrance and Grant pulled the door open for me, not even stopping to give the bouncer a glance. I gave the tall, beefy guy an apologetic look, but didn't stop either as I followed Grant inside.

Sam's was hopping, which I'd expected. I zeroed in on the bar and wasn't surprised to see Ryan behind it, a huge grin on his face as he leaned toward three girls wearing party hats. They had their hands all over him, pawing at his chest and shoulders, and my stomach flipped. I wanted to turn around and walk right back out the front door, but Grant must have sensed it.

Tugging me toward him, he shouted in my ear, "It's not his fault they grab at him like that," then pulled me away from the bar and toward the tables in the back. A couple got up to leave right as we reached them, and Grant pulled out one of the chairs for me before taking a seat across from me.

A deal was a deal, so I was determined to stick it out for at least one drink, but I had no idea how much longer than that I could last. To be honest, I wasn't even sure what I was doing here in the first place. Yes, I'd agreed to the date for Grant's sake, but now that we were here, all I wanted was to leave. The girls pawing Ryan, the look on his face revealing how much he loved the attention—these were the exact reasons why I hadn't wanted to get involved with him.

The truth was that I wasn't equipped to handle that level of competition on a daily basis. How could one woman ever date Ryan and feel secure?

"Angel."

Ryan's voice met my ears, and I thought I must be hearing things. Glancing to my right, I saw him standing there, his arms crossed.

"You came," he said, then looked at Grant. "With the old guy."

Grant's eyes narrowed. "I can hear you, you know."

"Are you sure?" Ryan teased.

"Why don't you take your pretty-boy mug back behind the bar and make us something drinkable," Grant said before giving Ryan a little shove.

I pressed my lips together to suppress a laugh. The two of them always behaved like children when they got together. Why would tonight be any different?

"Do you have an alcohol preference, Sofia?"

The sound of my name coming from Ryan's lips prompted all my girlie parts spring to life, making me aware of just how long it had been since I'd had a man inside me. Once I'd opened that door, I found myself desperately curious what it would feel like to be with Ryan. I imagined he'd be gifted in size, and I almost moaned at the thought of him entering me.

No, no, no, no, no, I chided myself.

But out loud, I said, "I don't care. Rum. Vodka. Tequila."

"You like tequila?"

"Are there people who don't?"

"What about you, old man?"

"Whiskey," Grant said gruffly. "Now, go away." Once Ryan was out of earshot, Grant laughed. "Isn't it fun picking on him?"

"I don't pick on him."

"You should," he said, and I turned my head to watch Ryan.

Nick, the brother I'd met the other day, was behind the

bar too. Together, he and Ryan worked quickly, making drinks and serving them before heading to the next person. I realized how stressful a job like this had to be as I watched them move nonstop, each with a constant smile on their face.

Ryan glanced up, and our eyes met across the bar. Even with the distance between us, I could tell that he was looking right at me as I watched him. A crooked grin brightened his face, and I couldn't help but smile in response.

"Stop flirting with the enemy." Grant slapped a hand on top of the table, jerking my attention to him.

"I wasn't," I lied, but my dreamy smile gave me away.

"See, you do like him," Grant said, calling me out.

I turned my smile into a frown. "I don't even really know him."

"That's why we're here," he said as if I was the most naive person in the room, then pointed with his chin.

I looked in the direction he'd pointed and watched as Ryan maneuvered his way through the crowd, a drink in each hand. Women tried to stop him, but he continued right toward us without so much as a glance. They grabbed at his shirt, pulled at his pants, but he kept moving like nothing was going on around him. I almost felt sorry for him before I decided that he probably liked being manhandled by women every night.

His bright blue eyes met mine as he smiled. "Adios Pantalones for the angel, and a Guy Hater for the grumpy old man. Seemed fitting," he said as he placed the drinks in front of us.

"Guy Hater? Stupidest shit I've ever heard," Grant grumped as he took a cautious sip.

"Good?" Ryan asked, clearly wanting approval.

Grant took another swig. "Damn good. But next time I'll take a plain whiskey on the rocks. I don't need anything froufouing it up for me. I can drink whiskey like a man."

"Sir, yes, sir," Ryan said with a mock salute before turning to me. "What about yours?"

"You really made me a drink that means *good-bye pants*?" I asked, curious about his beverage choice and wondering if I should be offended or not.

"It's the best tequila drink in the house. Ladies love it," he said with a shrug. "If you want something different, I can make it." He reached for my drink, but I pulled it toward me.

I sniffed at it before taking a cautious sip, allowing the liquid to caress my tongue before it traveled down my throat with a slight burn.

"This is amazing," I said, impressed.

Ryan puffed out his chest a little. "Thanks. Are you having a good time?"

"Yes. The company is wonderful." I sent a glance Grant's way before asking Ryan, "Are you?"

"I'd be having more fun if you ditched this zero and got with the hero." He pointed at himself. "But, of course I'm having fun. I love my job."

Ryan's pride and genuine joy was as infectious as it was attractive. Seeing him in his element was sexy as hell, the way his confidence radiated from him.

"Is it always like this?" I asked.

"Always," he deadpanned.

"And you want to do this forever? Tend bar, I mean?" I wasn't sure why I felt the urge to ask him personal questions about his future plans, but I decided to blame the alcohol.

Instead of the tequila making my pants come off, it had clearly shut off all logic and reasoning, and destroyed my filter.

"I don't know. I guess that all depends. I mean, I enjoy it, but I'm sure one day it won't fit in with my plans."

"What do you mean? What plans?" I finished the rest of my drink as I waited for his answer. I'd downed the entire thing in less than a minute, I realized. That couldn't be good.

Ryan picked up the empty glass and twirled it between his fingers. "I want a family someday. I don't think I can bartend every night while my wife and kids are at home without me. I won't want to be here then. I'll want to be with them."

My heart shot into my throat, and I tried to swallow around it as he looked at me and then back at his brother tending bar.

"I gotta get back over there." He thumbed over his shoulder. "I'm sorry. Talk to you later?"

I nodded, unable to speak as his words played in my mind over and over in a loop. He wanted a family someday. He wanted to get married. He wouldn't bartend while his family sat at home without him.

Oh my God. Ryan Fisher was one hell of a romantic.

"See? He's different than you thought he was, isn't he?" Grant asked with a grin like he'd just won the lottery.

"I think he may be," I said slowly, turning it all over in my head.

Grant might have been right. Maybe I'd been all wrong about the kind of man Ryan was. Maybe everything I thought about him was completely wrong. Had I judged him unfairly before I had all the information?

"There's a lot more to the boy than meets the eye, Sofia. I

wouldn't say that if it wasn't true."

My entire body warmed with more than just the alcohol swimming in my veins. "How well do you know him? I mean, really?"

He took another gulp of his drink before sloshing the liquid around in the glass. "I've spent a fair amount of time here harassing him, the same way his brothers do. We've had some deep conversations over breakfast in the past. I'd say I know him pretty damn well."

Waving my hand toward the bar, which still crawled with females vying for both Ryan and Nick's attention, I said, "This lifestyle . . . it's just not really me."

Grant gave me a serious look. "To be fair, I'm not sure it's really him either. Don't get me wrong, Ryan's good at his job. He's the most talented craftsman I've ever met. He's truly gifted." He let out a gruff laugh. "I didn't even know there *was* such a thing as a cocktail craftsman before I met Ryan. Back in my day, the bartender either poured you a beer or threw a few things together for a cocktail. Simple, yet effective. Nowadays, it's a damn art form, and Ryan's one hell of an artist. But while making these drinks might be right up his alley, I don't think this scene is."

I swallowed hard, sitting silent for more than a few minutes, thinking about how wrong I'd possibly been on every level when it came to Ryan and his character. I couldn't help but wonder how I hadn't sensed it before now. Had my intuition become so off-kilter that it couldn't be trusted? When had my gut instincts about people been so wrong?

No sooner had my self-doubt started than it was abruptly cut short. My jaw dropped as I watched the next few moments play out like a scene from a movie in sickly slow motion.

An eye-catching brunette walked behind the bar like she owned the place, not a care in the world as she wrapped her arms around Ryan's waist. He turned toward her, and his whole face lit up like she was the greatest thing he'd seen all day. When he placed a kiss on her forehead and she grinned up at him, the bile in my stomach pushed up to a threatening level.

They laughed and teased each other, neither one caring who watched. But I stopped watching.

I had to.

Jumping up from my chair, I stumbled to find my words—and my footing. "I need to get out of here. I'm ready to go."

"Sofia, why? What happened?" Grant peered up at me, confused, but I couldn't stay in the same room as Ryan for one second longer.

"You can stay. I'll call a car." I tried to wave Grant off, but his words stopped me.

"No, no." He pushed himself out of his chair slower than I would have liked, his car keys jingling. "I'll take you home."

I bolted from the bar, feeling like an absolute idiot. I hadn't been wrong about Ryan at all.

I'd been exactly right.

DISAPPEARING ANGELS
Ryan

AT SOME POINT during the chaos, I'd lost track of Sofia and Grant. I swore it had only been a minute, but the next time I looked up, desperately searching for her, both she and Grant were gone.

Hustling out from behind the bar, I practically jogged toward their table, hoping to find some remnants still there. I convinced myself that they wouldn't have left without saying good-bye as I weaved through the crowd. But as I reached their table, nothing but empty glasses and two one-dollar bills stuck under Grant's Guy Hater remained. There were no car keys, no sunglasses, no sign at all of them having only stepped away momentarily.

They had definitely left, and apparently weren't coming back.

Snatching up the money, I shoved it in my pocket before reaching for the discarded glasses and giving the table a quick wipe.

This wasn't how I wanted the night to go. Granted, I had no idea that Sofia was even coming to the bar tonight in the first place, but once I saw her here, I didn't want her to leave. In fact, I had the whole night planned out in my head the moment I spotted her.

I was going to ask her to stay until we closed, to which she would have agreed, of course, after a little hesitation. That would have forced the old man to go home at some point, because there was no way he could have stayed up that late. Not anymore. Plus, I was pretty sure that Grant turned into a pumpkin or a fat mouse once the clock struck midnight.

With cock-blocking Grant out of the picture, I would have given Sofia all my attention, getting to know her better with each hour that passed. Even with all the other females in the bar, I would have been determined to make her feel special, like she was the only girl in the room. And after the bar closed, she would have met my brothers and their girlfriends. The three ladies would have chatted, the conversation easy and natural, while us guys cleaned up and counted out.

I would have made her laugh. She would have seen me in my element, surrounded by my family, and when I asked to drive her home, she would have agreed right away. On the way to her place, I would have taken a slight detour, stopping at my favorite late-night eatery and buying her anything she wanted. Taking my time, because I wouldn't have wanted the night to end, I would have kept ordering food until she called me out on it, her eyes barely able to stay open.

It would have been the first of many dates, and I would have asked for another as I paid for our bill. She would have smiled and nodded, excited at the thought of seeing me again, and that's why I wouldn't have kissed her when I finally dropped her off at home, even though every single part of me would have been dying for a taste of her. No, our first kiss would have happened on our second date. The minute she opened the door, I would have started date two with a kiss, instead of ending it with one.

"Ryan!"

Frank's deep voice cut through my thoughts like a pesky gnat, and I blinked before meeting his eyes.

"Stop yelling," I said with a groan.

"What the hell planet are you on?"

"Same as yours, unfortunately."

Yeah, I was snippy, irritated because the night I'd envisioned had evaporated before my eyes. Sofia had left, and she didn't even say good-bye.

"What's the matter with you? You were fine ten minutes ago." Frank leaned toward one of our customers, listening to his order as he waiting for my response.

"Ten minutes ago, Sofia was still here," I muttered.

Frank's head shot up. "Sofia? The girl? She was here?"

"Sofia's here?" Nick sauntered over carrying two beers. "Here you go, man." He handed the glasses off to a guy and took his credit card.

"She was. But she's gone now."

"Where'd she go?" Nick asked.

"I don't know." I knew I sounded irritated, but they were asking me questions I didn't have the answer to.

Frank gripped my shoulder before he hit it twice. "She'll be back," he said with an encouraging smile, and I wanted to believe him.

"Out of the way, ladies and gentlemen." Nick glanced toward the door and his voice rose above the din of the crowd. "The most beautiful woman in the world has entered the bar."

He excused himself as he made his way through the crowd

to his blond-haired girlfriend who stood in the center of the room, her cheeks a bright red. It happened every time Jess came into the bar. Nick made a spectacle out of her arrival, and she blushed to her hairline as the crowd parted around her to watch the show.

Even in my sour mood, I couldn't help but smile as he grabbed her and kissed her like he hadn't seen her in months. My little brother loved his girl like she made the moon and stars shine in the night sky. He had been an idiot when it came to her initially, but he'd made damn certain that his days of making stupid mistakes in their relationship were over. They had some huge hurdles to get over, but once they did, they never looked back. Since then, they'd been solid, respectful and kind to each other. They had the kind of relationship that people in their early twenties aspired to, but had no idea how to make happen. Yet there they were, showing the rest of us up and making it look easy.

Once Nick stepped away from Jess, he kissed her on the cheek and then smacked her ass. She jumped, looking around the room until her eyes met mine. She gave me a wave and a big smile before I pointed at a table near the social-media wall. Jess craned her neck to see where I was pointing, and when she caught sight of Claudia, Frank's girlfriend, at the table with her best friend, Britney, she slipped through the crowd to join them.

"You want me to make her drink, or you got it?" I asked Nick when he made his way back behind the bar.

He shrugged. "Go for it. You make them better."

As I mixed Jess's favorite, a No Bad Days, I asked, "Frank, are Claudia and Britney good, or do they need another?"

He shrugged and headed for the girls' table to find out. Claudia beamed at her man as he neared, and that familiar pang of envy hit me all over again. My brothers both had standout women, and I couldn't even get the one I wanted to talk to me.

Finishing up Jess's vodka cocktail, I swirled an orange peel around the rim of the glass and looked up at Frank as he slipped back behind the bar.

"Britney and Claudia both want an Adios Pantalones," he said.

"I bet they do," I teased, biting back a laugh as Frank's jaw ticked.

My joking that his girlfriend wanted me always sent Frank over the edge. He had a bit of a jealous side that I'd never seen before he started dating her. I couldn't help but wonder if Claudia's Colombian temper had rubbed off on him, or if there was something about being with the right girl that triggered us men. Whatever it was, it made me laugh.

"Just make the drinks," he growled, and I moved Jess's drink near the back register so it wouldn't spill or be handed off to someone else.

"I'll take another one of those stupid guy drinks," Grant's rough voice bit out, and I immediately perked up, looking past him for Sofia. "She's not here," he said, answering my question before I could ask it.

"Where is she?" I asked, curious why he had come back without her.

"I took her home."

Although I was still confused, I nodded, then hurried through making Claudia and Britney's drinks. Once I'd handed all three to Frank so he could deliver them, I turned my attention to Grant while I made the drink he swore he'd never drink again.

As I measured, I glanced up at him. "Thought you didn't want one of these next time."

He mimicked me, repeating my words like a middle-schooler. When I didn't react, he growled, "You want me to tell you about the angel or not?"

My back stiffened. Grant knew damn well that I wanted to know everything, but dividing my time between him and our customers proved to be harder than I'd hoped. It was a Friday night, after all, and the bar was packed.

"Hold that thought, old man. I'll be right back." I moved away before abruptly stopping and facing him again. "Don't disappear on me."

His hands up in the air, he gave me a nod, a silent promise before tapping his wrist. Apparently, he was on limited time.

After making cocktails for a group of giggling women, I headed back to Grant with a Guy Hater in hand and slid it toward him.

"This place is a damn madhouse," he grumbled before taking a sip. "At least the drinks are decent."

"Gee, thanks." I pretended to sound bored at his weak compliment.

Grant glared at me. "Stop whining and give me your ear for more than five seconds."

Leaning down, my elbows on the bar between us, I looked him dead in the eye and gave him an expectant look.

"So, what happened earlier?" he asked.

"What do you mean?" I had no fucking idea what he was

talking about.

Grant frowned and took another sip of his drink. "Well, you must have done something to piss her off."

Blinking at him in confusion, I scratched my head. "I didn't do anything. I just looked up and you guys were gone."

"Yeah, well, one second she was fine, and the next she couldn't get out of here fast enough."

"You said you drove her home," I said, and he nodded. "She didn't tell you why she was upset?"

"She only mentioned something about you being exactly the kind of guy she thought you were. I tried to get her to tell me more, but she wouldn't. She's hiding something, and I thought that when I picked her up, I'd figure out what it was, But I still have no idea. She's a tough nut to crack, that one." Grant finished off his drink and shoved his empty glass toward me.

"Want another?" I asked, and he shook his head. "Look, I have no idea what upset her."

Honestly, I hadn't done anything out of the ordinary while Sofia was here. As a matter of fact, I was so aware of her presence, I'd consciously made sure I didn't do anything that could make her think I was interested in any other woman in the room.

Grant grunted. "I don't know either, but I wouldn't bet on her coming back here. I tried to put in a good word for you."

"You tried?"

"Yeah, of course I tried. I talked you up, and I swore she was thinking that you were a good guy there for a minute."

"Wow, a whole minute?" I winced at how pathetic that

was.

He leaned closer over the bar, lowering his voice. "It's longer than she ever thought you were a decent guy before."

"Gee, thanks."

"I'm on your side, you know." He tried to smack me upside the head, but I ducked out of the way.

"Sure sounds like it." I pulled the towel from my back pocket and wiped down the bar top out of habit.

"Look, Ryan, I don't know what she saw, or what she thinks she saw. But something upset her. She barely talked at all on the ride home. It seemed like she was berating herself. Like she should have known better or something. Hell, I don't know." He shrugged. "She's a woman, so who knows what the hell they're thinking half the time."

"What do you think I should do?" My rag slowed and then stopped as I gave him my full attention.

"I want to tell you to give her space, but I think if you do that, you'll never see her again."

"Then give me her number," I demanded without a second thought. It was either that, or I'd force him to show me where she lived. Then I'd start not-so-secretly stalking her.

"Took you long enough to ask."

Grant reached for his phone and pulled her contact information up on the screen. I entered it quickly into my own phone before he changed his mind.

"Thanks," I said sincerely, all joking aside.

"I think she's good for you." He met my gaze and gave me a serious nod. "And I think you might be good for her too."

I didn't know if Grant was right, but I knew I wanted to find out. If Sofia and I decided we weren't right for each other,

I'd move on and put her behind me. But she hadn't even let me try yet.

And as far as this woman was concerned, quitting wasn't an option.

IT FINALLY MAKES SENSE
Ryan

As I stared at Sofia's phone number in my phone from the comfort of my California king bed, I considered sending her a text but decided against it. It was well after three in the morning, and I had no intention of starting a conversation with her at that hour.

I was tempted to delete her number completely since she hadn't been the one to give it to me in the first place, but my practical side wouldn't allow it. Sofia was difficult, and I needed every advantage I could get when it came to her. So the number stayed.

Thoughts of her tanned face, hazel eyes, and brown hair blurred my vision, and before I knew it, my hand was down my sweatpants and sliding up and down my hardening cock.

My fantasy played out as I imagined gripping the back of her head with my free hand, my fingers tangling in her hair so she couldn't pull away from me. I held her face still, my dick hardening even more as I continued stroking it to visions of her.

I pulled her lips toward mine, my movements not at all gentle or sweet as I thrust my tongue into her mouth, showing her exactly who was in control. She moaned, liking the fact that I was going all alpha male on her as I deepened the kiss before moving to suck and bite at her neck.

Tugging at my sweats, I pushed them past my balls and kept working my dick, my hand moving at a rapid pace that felt so damn good.

Sofia's body was at my whim, mine for the taking. She gave up control and I took it, my hands roaming every inch of her as I discarded her clothes. She arched her back, pushing her tits closer, her nipples erect as I took them in my mouth one at a time. I sucked her perfect nipple between my lips, my tongue flicking at the sensitive bud before biting down a little too hard. The sound that escaped her only made me do it more. She liked it, that little bit of pain that brought on even more pleasure.

My dick could barely take another moment, and I'd just gotten started. I pulled my cock harder, moving my hand faster as my breathing grew erratic.

I worked my way down Sofia's stomach to her gorgeous core. Burying my face in her pussy, I devoured it like it was my last meal, licking and pressing my tongue inside her as she squirmed beneath me.

Fuck, yes.

Seeing her this turned on only pushed me closer to the edge. I neared my release as I plunged my cock inside her. She was hot and wet, her walls gripping me so tight that I immediately came after a few more strokes.

My hand slowed its pace, but didn't quite stop, as I attempted to catch my breath and slow my erratic heartbeat.

If fucking Sofia in real life was half as good as my fantasy, I was in for some serious trouble.

*

AFTER GOING THROUGH a series of stretches the next morning, I took off down my regular jogging path. I had stopped running listening to music with my earbuds a while back when I realized I was missing everything around me.

Music helped me block out life as I ran, but running along the beach, I wanted to hear what was going on around me. I found that I enjoyed the noise.

The crash of the ocean's waves against the shore, the creaking of swings as kids swung back and forth, the chatter and laughter of tourists and locals, the songs of talented street musicians. The sounds all swirled together, making me feel more connected.

My feet pounded the pavement, following the familiar path with ease. The beach was crowded today, due in part to the recent warm temperatures. Santa Monica was almost always hopping, but the activity turned up a notch when it got hot out. Birds squawked, diving and hopping around on the sand in search of discarded food to steal.

Children laughed and shouted as I neared the playground. The sound of a couple arguing drew my attention for a second before I tuned them out and continued on my way.

One of the voices sounded vaguely familiar, however, even though it was strained. I slowed down, scanning for the couple in question. Glancing in every direction, I almost gave up before spotting them, a man and a woman arguing a short distance from the kids, but not far enough away. The woman was pleading, begging the man to leave, her hands waving wildly back and forth.

"Sofia?" I said out loud, my eyes narrowing as I stared, and she turned.

"Oh, thank God, Ryan."

Thank God?

She ran toward me but kept glancing back at the playground, as if she was scared to get too far away. The guy followed her, his hands balled into fists.

Oh, hell no. If he thought for one second that he was going to hit her, he'd better think again.

"Who the hell is this? He's not Matson's father," the guy said, clearly agitated as he pointed at me.

I had no idea what he was talking about, but he looked like a grade-A douchebag, an unhinged one at that, and I wanted to punch him for it.

Sofia looked more agitated than I'd ever seen her, and my entire body came alive with a possessive need to protect her. I moved to shield her body with mine.

"Is there a problem here? Sofia, is this guy bothering you?" I asked, straightening to my full height so I could tower over the short little prick.

"Yes," she said, just as he said, "No."

I'd give this guy a fucking problem if he didn't leave her alone. Taking an aggressive step toward him, I felt a perverse satisfaction as he stepped back. *Yep.* Douche-face was afraid of me. *Good.* He should be.

"Who the hell is this asshole?" he yelled at Sofia while pointing a well-manicured finger at me.

"I'm about to be your worst nightmare if you don't get that finger out of my damn face," I growled, my eyes narrowing to take in his perfectly styled hair and pressed clothes. He couldn't have looked less suited for a day at the beach.

"Touch me and I'll have your ass thrown in jail," he shouted.

I couldn't have been less concerned about his threat. I'd go to jail right now. Hell, I'd lock myself in there. It's not as if my brothers would leave me stranded. Not to mention the fact that we had the best lawyer in town on standby for any issues regarding our business or personal lives. This wasn't the first time I'd threatened by some entitled asshole.

"Touch Sofia and they'll have to put me in jail to keep me from killing you," I growled at him.

The guy pulled his cell phone from his pocket, hovering his finger over the screen. "Care to repeat that?"

"Are you serious?" I glanced at Sofia before glaring back at this tool, who was doing a shitty job of getting me to threaten him on video.

"Derek, just go. You shouldn't be here." Sofia tried to sound strong, but I noticed the tremble in her voice.

"I have every right to be here, and you know it," he said, clearly trying to bait her. Shoving his phone back in his pocket, he took a step toward Sofia, but I blocked his path and he stepped back.

"I think you should leave," I demanded.

"Or what?" he spat out as he took another step back from me.

"Or else we're going to have a big fucking problem. Right here. Right now. And I'll call the cops myself. You want that?" I moved toward him again and watched as he stepped even further back.

He glared at her, and all I could think was that if looks could throw punches, Sofia would have been knocked out cold. "This isn't over, Sofia. Not by a long shot. You know the kind of power my family has and what I'm capable of. He's my son too."

"Leave," I said again, my tone threatening, and he turned to stomp away.

Refusing to take my eyes off of him, I watched until he disappeared from view. He only turned around once to look back, his phone aimed high, probably taking a picture. But I'd worry about that later.

Turning toward Sofia, I took her into my arms. Her entire body relaxed as I pulled her against my chest, resting my chin on her head as I ran my fingers through her hair, calming her. She went nearly limp against me with relief, her breathing deep and ragged, but my curiosity forced me to end this magical moment before I was ready.

"Want to tell me what that was all about?" I asked, even though I already had a fairly good idea.

"Not really," she mumbled against my chest.

"Was he talking about your son?" I asked, unable to hide the lilt in my voice. When she nodded against me, I said, "So you have a son."

"I do." She pulled away and pointed at a kid with hair and skin the same color as hers who was playing on the monkey bars. "That's him in the dark blue shirt."

He happened to be looking at us at the exact same time, and waved to Sofia.

As she waved back, I asked, "What's his name?"

"Matson."

I repeated the name in my head a few times, thinking how unique it was, and wondered where it came from. "That's a cool name."

A slight smile played at her lips. "Thanks."

"How old is he?" I wasn't experienced with kids, so I had no idea how old he was. She could have told me he was five or ten, and I would have believed her.

"He's eight."

Eight seemed like a good age. For what exactly, I had no idea.

"So that dickhead was his father?"

Her entire body tensed at my question. I'd never been a violent guy before, but I found myself filled with an overwhelming urge to break every bone in his fucking body if he ever scared her or her son again. And there was no doubt that Sofia was scared.

"Unfortunately."

A million more thoughts swam in my head as I watched her son run around the swings, kicking up sand behind him.

Whatever attraction I'd had to Sofia grew tenfold in those moments after learning she was a mom. That knowledge transformed her in my mind to someone unlike any other woman who came into my bar, and in the best possible way. Learning this changed everything for me . . . the way I saw her, the way I felt about her. A life with her and her son played so clearly in my mind, I had to remind myself that none of it was real.

"Why didn't you tell me?" The question came out in almost a whisper as my confusion mixed with a sudden clarity. Her attitude had been so standoffish because she had a kid. It wasn't that she really hated me; she was only trying to protect herself and her heart because she assumed I'd break it.

"Why does it matter?"

"What do you mean, why does it matter?"

"I saw you with that girl last night, Ryan. You take your shirt off every night because women ask you to. Why do you care what I do?"

My grasp on the conversation faltered. "Wait, what? What girl?" I had absolutely no idea what Sofia was talking about. "There was no girl."

"So I made up seeing that gorgeous woman wrap her arms around you behind the bar?"

I stared at the sandy concrete, desperately searching my memory to conjure up the moment she was so certain happened. "I honestly don't know," I said, then stopped. "Oh. Long brown hair? Tanned skin?"

"Nice of you to actually remember her," Sofia said with a bit too much snark for my liking.

"That's my brother's girlfriend, Claudia." Satisfaction shot through me as Sofia swallowed and her face reddened slightly. "And for the record, I hate taking my shirt off."

Sofia rolled her eyes. "Then why do you keep doing it?"

"Because I've never had a reason to stop," I said, although that wasn't quite true. The fact that I hated it should have been enough reason for me to stop, but so far it hadn't been.

"Then you must not hate it that much," she said, holding her ground.

"Trust me, I do. I'll stop tonight. I'll never take my shirt off at the bar again. Will that make you happy?"

"Don't do anything for me, Ryan. Do it for yourself," she said, and I hated how her words made me feel small inside.

"You're changing the subject." Getting this conversation

back on track, I asked, "Why didn't you tell me you had a son?"

Her demeanor quickly changed, and I felt the power shift back into my court. "I don't know," she said with a shrug, but I refused to accept that bullshit non-answer.

I deserved the truth and I wanted to hear her say it, so I continued to push. "Yes, you do. You could have told me. Why didn't you?"

"I didn't think it mattered or would have made a difference."

She looked everywhere but at me, and that's how I knew. Sofia was lying. She knew damn well it would have made a difference, but not in the negative way she probably assumed it would have.

"Nope. Try again."

She shifted her weight and kicked her flip-flop against the concrete. "I just didn't think you'd be interested in dating a single mom." She gave me a quick glance before looking away again.

Now we're finally getting somewhere. And even though the judgment stung, I brushed it off.

"You just assumed that? Based on what, exactly?" I crossed my arms and swallowed hard. A defensive move on my part, but I was starting to feel exactly that.

"Your occupation, for starters." Her eyes held mine a little longer this time before she looked away. More truths.

"You didn't think I'd be interested in dating you because I own a bar?" Shaking my head, I tried to make sense of what exactly she was saying. How had my owning a bar correlated with my wanting to date her or not? One had absolutely nothing to do with the other.

"Something like that," she said dismissively.

My insides reignited, my adrenaline still pumping from earlier. Instead of calming me down, this conversation was riling me back up. Uncrossing my arms, I reached for her chin and waited for her eyes to meet mine.

"Tell me the truth, Sofia. For once since we met, just tell me the damn truth."

As I waited, she stayed silent. Her face pinched with an emotion I couldn't quite place—either confusion as she sorted through her thoughts, or hope that if she stayed quiet long enough, I'd eventually go away and leave her alone.

Finally, she said, "I didn't think you'd want to date me, okay? That's the truth."

Those damn eyes continued to look over my shoulder and then back toward her son. They looked everywhere except at me. And while I stood there, excited at the possibility that this woman was an even more perfect match for me, it suddenly became clear that Sofia didn't see me the same way.

"Except it's not. Is it?" The realization hit me like a fucking sledgehammer to the rib cage. Sofia didn't think I was good enough. She hadn't pushed me away to protect herself or her heart; she pushed me away because she didn't want me.

Past conversations replayed in my head like a bad soundtrack I couldn't make stop. Sofia had told me over and over how I wasn't her type, and said I wasn't the kind of man she was looking for. She might be lying about it now, but she hadn't been lying then. When she pictured the perfect guy for her, she didn't see me. Hell, she never even considered it. She'd blown me off the second she met me. I was never an option. In her opinion, I wasn't good enough.

"What are you thinking about?" Her voice was so wary, I wondered how my expression must look for her to sound that way.

"Just how ironic all of this is," I managed to say, although I wasn't sure how. My throat felt like I'd swallowed a handful of sand.

Her head tilted to one side as if she wasn't following my meaning at all. "Ironic? How is any of this ironic?"

I fought through my emotions to find the words . . . and trust me, I was damn well getting emotional. "I just found out you're a mom, and no matter what you think, I'm even more attracted to you because of it."

I paused, giving my words time to sink in. I wanted her to hear to hear me—*really* hear me—before I continued.

"But you're not," I said sadly. "I mean, I'm even more interested in dating you because you have a kid, and you aren't interested in me at all for the exact same reason. It's ironic."

"It—it's not," she stammered. "I just mean—"

I put up a hand to stop her. "It doesn't matter. You made yourself clear to me many times. You told me I wasn't right for you. I guess I should have listened."

"Ryan . . ."

I tried not to wince at how soft and sympathetic her voice now sounded. Pity was the last thing I wanted. I didn't need Sofia feeling sorry for me because of the way she felt. If she didn't think I was good enough for her, so be it. She was wrong, but that was on her, not me. And it would be her loss.

"Mama?"

Both Sofia and I looked down at the same time to see her

son standing nearby, looking between us. Neither of us had seen him coming.

"Who are you?" he asked me, shielding the sun from his blue eyes with his hand.

"Hi. I'm Ryan. I'm a friend of your mom's." I gave her a quick glance before I dropped to a crouch so I could be eye level with him. "And you are?"

"I'm Matson Richards." He shoved his hand toward me and waited for me to shake it.

We shook hands, and I pretended to wince like his grip was too strong. "It's nice to meet you, Matson Richards. I was actually just leaving."

"Oh. Do you have to go?" His head cocked to the side, making his brown hair flop over his eyes. He looked up at his mom. "Does he have to go?"

"Sorry, buddy, I have to get to work."

His face scrunched in confusion. "But it's Saturday. Grown-ups don't work on Saturdays."

A small laugh escaped me. "Some grown-ups do. Otherwise, every place would be closed. Does that make sense?"

He shook his head. "No."

Shit. How do I explain this?

"Okay, Matson. I'm sure you don't just sit at home every Saturday, right? What else do you and your mom do on the weekends?"

His face lit up. "Sometimes we go to the movies. I love popcorn. Do you like popcorn?" When I nodded, he said, "Mama likes to go grocery shopping. I don't like it when she makes me go with her, but she usually buys me a treat, so then it's okay." He sucked in a big breath before launching into more. "And she loves Target, so we go there a lot. But I don't see why she likes it so much. It's not even fun. Sometimes we go out to eat at my nana's favorite restaurant. I like it because I get to eat a lot of chips and salsa, and no one tells me to stop."

I couldn't help but laugh. This damn kid was adorable. "See? All those things that you do and those places you go to, like the movies, the restaurant and the grocery store." I made a face that made him giggle. "There are people working there, right?"

"Like the lady that brings us the chips and salsa?"

"Exactly. Is she a grown-up?"

His lips bunched into a pucker as he stared at the sky. "Kind of. She's not like a grown-up like you and Mama. But she's not like me either."

This kid was too smart for his own good.

Before I could finish making my point, he gave me a wise nod. "I get it now, Ryan. Some grown-ups have to work on Saturdays so I can see movies, or Mama can go to Target and buy things we don't need."

Sofia let out a laugh. "Hey, I can hear you, you know."

"It's true, Mama," Matson said with a shrug. "You say it all the time."

"You're right. I do." She hugged him, the love she had for her son radiating from her like sunshine.

The boy gave me a hopeful look. "Sorry you have to work. Maybe you can come with me and Mama to get chips sometime."

Ten minutes ago, I would have jumped at the idea. But I hadn't forgotten how easily Sofia had dismissed me. How wrong she'd been about me, and how she hadn't even given me a chance.

"Maybe." I stood up.

Matson asked his mom if he could keep playing, and ran off once he had her approval.

Watching him go, I said, "He seems like a great kid," and I meant it.

"He is. The best. You were really great with him."

Sofia seemed a little choked up, and I wasn't sure if it was because of my interaction with Matson, or if it was about the dickhead from earlier. Or maybe it was from something else entirely.

I crossed my arms over my chest and stared at her. "You sound surprised."

She fidgeted nervously, all her usual bravado gone. "I guess I am."

"That's really fucked up, you know." I hadn't planned on saying it exactly like that, but I couldn't stop the harsh words from coming out. "You saw me in my bar once, maybe twice, and somehow that gave you the right to judge me? You think you know me, but you don't. And I clearly don't know you. Hope you have a nice life, Sofia. I mean it."

Too pissed off to care about her feelings while I was caught up in my own, I walked away. And when she called my name, instead of stopping or turning around, I picked up the pace and jogged toward home.

SELF-DOUBT
Ryan

I FUMED THE rest of the way back to my place, my feelings growing and twisting in perfect time with each pound of my feet against the pavement.

Thump. She's wrong about me.
Thump. Maybe she has a point.
Thump. Am I good enough to be in a kid's life?
Thump. Of course I am.
Thump. Right?

It was only once I got home that I realized how hard I'd been running. Sweat dripped down my face, burning my eyes. My T-shirt was soaked, clinging to my chest and arms like a second skin. I tried to slow down my heart rate by sucking in long breaths and walking up and down the street in front of my place at a moderate pace.

I stretched for a moment to cool down my body before heading inside and upstairs to shower. Too bad none of it had had any effect on my emotions, which were still running on overdrive.

My anger mingled with the steam, heating the bathroom as I scrubbed myself clean. Disappointment rained like water down my back. Confusion made my emotions swing back and forth. But when my hard-on betrayed me, wanting her when it was supposed to hate her the same way I did, I got pissed off all over again, refusing to even touch it if it was going to betray me like that.

Annoyed with myself, I dried off and got ready for work. It was earlier than I needed to be at the bar, but I didn't have anywhere else to be, and I was too pissed off to sit still. I closed my eyes and groaned as I imagined Frank giving me crap, calling me a princess for being so emotional, but I refused to let that stop me.

I wanted to talk to my brothers, needed to know that I wasn't wrong for being this upset. Despite the shit they both loved to give me, there was no one I trusted more.

Okay, except for my mom. But I'd call her later if I needed to, once I sorted this all out my head and had a little clarity.

*

"YOU'RE EARLY."

Frank's voice boomed out the second I walked through the back door of our bar. It was like he sensed my arrival before he could even see it was me. Then again, only employees used that entrance, so I guessed it made sense.

"I was bored," I lied, and he narrowed his green eyes at me. I tried to avoid his scrutiny by looking past him at the handful of customers.

"You're never bored," he shot back.

Ignoring him, I slipped behind the bar, hoping to work on some new cocktails before we got too busy. After gathering a lemon, a bitters liquor, apple brandy, and maple syrup, I measured ingredients and added them one by one into the glass, taking a small sip after each addition.

"What's the matter?" Frank asked from behind me as I focused on the cocktail.

"Why do you think something's wrong?"

"Because I know you. And you have that look."

I stopped stirring and turned to face him. "What look?"

"That one." He waved his finger at my face. "It's the one that tells me when something's bothering you. Plus, you get two little lines right here," he tapped me between my eyes and I jerked back, "whenever you're upset."

I smoothed my expression, trying to make any possible lines go away, but all Frank did was laugh. No one had ever told me that before, but then again, maybe no one knew me well enough to know that about me.

"Where's Nick?" I sipped the concoction I'd just made before pushing it toward Frank, who still hadn't moved. "Try this."

"He'll be here later. Wanna wait until we're both here so you don't tell the same story twice?" Not waiting for my answer, he took a sip. "Shit, this is good."

I nodded, because it was. "I'm going to add it to the board tonight. We'll see how it sells."

"What are you calling it?"

"Bad Apple," I said without thinking.

"Bad Apple? You're usually more creative than that," he teased, even though he hated most of my drink names.

"It fits the drink and my mood."

Frank's eyes widened. "Forget waiting for Nick. Talk to me." He dropped his notepad and pen on the counter and leaned back against the bar. "Is it the girl?"

Squeezing my eyes closed, I pinched the bridge of my nose while I thought about how exactly to say it. "It's the girl," I said, but then stopped.

"What about her? What happened?" When I didn't answer right away, he said, "Look, I know I give you a bunch of shit all the time about being sensitive and girlie, but I don't mean it. Well, you are sensitive and girlie, but I just like to tease you about it. If I thought it really bothered you, I'd stop, you know?"

I nodded because I knew it was the truth, and Frank went on.

"You and Nick helped me a lot with my situation when I didn't think I wanted any help. But I needed it. I don't know how I would have gotten through everything without you two."

"But that's what brothers do," I said.

"Exactly." Frank gave my shoulder a light punch. "That's what brothers do. So, talk to me. Tell me what's going on."

"Sofia has a kid," I blurted, then waited for Frank to wince or look horrified, have some sort of reaction, but he seemed unmoved.

"So?"

"So, she didn't tell me."

"Okay . . ." He dragged out the word, still not catching on as to why I was so upset.

"She didn't tell me she had a kid because she doesn't think I'm good enough to be around him." There. I'd spelled it out for him plainly.

Frank's face pinched into a pissed-off expression. "She said that?"

Now we were getting somewhere. I wanted someone else to be pissed off like I was. I needed my brother to get mad with me. Or at least tell me I had a right to be mad.

"She told me that I'm not the kind of guy she wants in her life. Said I'm not the type of man she's looking for. Can you believe that?" I asked, resisting the urge clutch my stomach. Repeating her words out loud was like a knife to the guts.

Frank stayed quiet, processing what I'd just said. Being the most levelheaded and rational of the three of us, he rarely spoke without thinking first.

But his silence gave my self-doubt enough time to rear its destructive head again. What if Sofia had been right?

"I'm sorry, little brother. It's clear that she doesn't know you," Frank said with a slight shake of his head. "Because anyone who would say something like that about you can't know you. Out of the three of us, you'd absolutely be the one who would date someone with a kid. Hands down. I can even picture it in my head."

"Then why couldn't she?"

Frank lowered his voice, his words slow. "Because she doesn't know you, Ryan."

"She didn't even try."

He folded his arms across his chest. "Is that why you're upset? Because she didn't give you a chance, or because she misjudged you?"

Scratching the back of my head, I pulled at it, cracking my neck. "I'm pissed that she made the decision for me without even asking. I had no say at all. I kept pursuing her, begging her to go out with me, and it was stupid. She was never going to say yes. And she was never going to tell me why, either."

"It's a little messed up, to be honest."

"Which part?"

Frank sighed. "All of it, I guess. I have no idea what it's like to be a parent, so I can't know what she was thinking, but it's her loss, man. It's totally her loss."

I knew that. Somewhere deep down in me, I knew that was true. But why didn't it feel like it? Why did it feel like I was the one losing somehow?

"I'm just so fucking mad," I admitted.

Frank stepped close and clapped a hand on my shoulder. "I would be too. I'd be pissed. Especially if I knew she was dead wrong. That's the worst part, how absolutely off base she is."

"The worst part for me is how much more I wanted her after learning she has a son, you know?" I swallowed, my throat feeling thick. "It was like a switch flipped on inside me, and everything made sense."

"What made sense?"

"How she pushed me away all the time and didn't want me to get close. At first, I thought it was a defense mechanism. Then I realized it was because she didn't think I'd be good enough for her son."

"Did you tell her that?"

"I told her a lot of things." I winced slightly as I thought back on what I'd said.

"How'd she take it? What'd she have to say about it?"

"I might have run off," I said, bracing for Frank's reaction.

He laughed. "You ran away from her?"

"It was either leave or end up fighting someone. I was

kinda riled up." Then I remembered the encounter that brought me to Sofia in the first place. "Oh, I almost forgot."

"Hold that thought," Frank said before greeting a couple who had walked in.

While I waited, I whipped up a few Bad Apples and poured them into sample glasses. Walking around the bar, I handed them out to our customers to try—on the house, of course—before I made my way back to Frank, who was free again.

"Go on." He circled a hand in the air, encouraging me to get it all out. We were running out of time to have a serious discussion before the bar got busy.

"The whole reason I even saw her today was because she was fighting with some guy. He was threatening her. She seemed really upset."

"Who was it?"

"Her kid's father, apparently."

Frank shrugged. "Maybe you dodged a bullet with that one. Sounds like there's a lot of drama there, and that's the last thing any of us need."

I couldn't help but agree with that assessment, but something still didn't sit right with me. Their interaction hadn't seemed cordial at all. It had been strained, uncomfortable, and confrontational.

"What's with the face, sourpuss?"

Grant's gruff voice snagged my attention, and I smiled for what felt like the first time all day. Turning to face him, I put on a straight face so I could give him shit.

"Who let you in, old man?"

"Who's gonna try and stop me?"

I drew him a beer like he usually ordered, but when I slid it to him, Grant grimaced.

"Maybe I wanted whiskey."

I pushed it closer. "Drink this first."

"Gonna tell me what's eating you?" he asked, but Nick arrived before I could respond.

"The best-looking Fisher brother has finally arrived," Nick called out, but his smug expression quickly faded when he saw my face. "What's wrong?"

"I've been asking him the same thing since I sat down," Grant said with a harrumph, and Nick gave me a quick once-over.

"You've been here for two seconds." I narrowed my eyes at him.

"Tell us," Nick insisted, and Grant huffed out an agreeing sound.

"Not now. Later." I wanted to put Nick at ease, but he wouldn't give up that easily. My little brother was nothing if not persistent. He reminded me of someone else I knew.

Nick raised an eyebrow at me. "Don't make me wait until we close. I'll die of curiosity before then, and I'll create a hundred crazy scenarios in my head. At least give me the CliffsNotes version."

I couldn't help but smirk as I led him out of the customers' earshot. "I found out Sofia has a son, and that's why she wanted nothing to do with me. Because she thought I wasn't good for her or him. The end."

"No way. She has a son? How old is he?"

Odd first question. "Eight."

"And she thought you'd be, what, a bad influence on him

or something?" Nick sounded sincerely perplexed as he dropped his keys in the drawer and then adjusted the baseball hat on his head.

My jaw worked back and forth. "I guess."

"That's fucked up."

"Thank you," I said, feeling marginally better for the support.

"No, really. I mean it. She wasn't obligated to tell you she has a kid, but for her to honestly think that you'd be a bad influence on him is ridiculous."

A thought hit me, and I walked back toward Grant's seat at the bar. "Did you know, old man?"

"Did I know what?" He sipped his beer, his attitude surly.

"That she had a kid."

"Who has a—" He paused midsentence as the dots must have connected in his head. "Sofia has a kid?"

"You didn't know?"

"I had no idea."

"I guess the whole bartender thing isn't what she's looking for in a baby daddy," Frank said, and I stopped myself from chuckling at the words *baby daddy* coming out of his mouth.

"Or maybe it is." Nick jerked his chin toward the front entrance, and the three of us turned in time to see Sofia walk in, scanning the bar.

For me.

TOTAL HYPOCRITE
Sofia

After Ryan turned his back and walked away like I had just torn apart his world, I felt a little lost. It was absolutely absurd of me to feel that way, yet there it was, a hollowed-out pain in the upper left side of my chest. I tried to stop him, calling out after him, but he pretended he didn't hear me when I knew he had. Instead, he broke into a jog as I watched him with my jaw hanging open.

I supposed I deserved that.

With my feelings jumbled up into a chaotic mess about Ryan, I'd almost forgotten about Derek. He had shown up at the park, clearly knowing where Matson and I would be, so I assumed he'd had me followed. I wouldn't put anything past Derek or his family, but I didn't understand what he wanted now, after all these years of silence.

"Matson!" I called out my son's name, and he immediately stopped running and turned toward me. I waved him over. "Let's go."

Matson was such a good boy. He did what I asked without argument and rarely complained. Every once in a while, he would question why he couldn't do or watch something, and when I'd tell him, "It's not appropriate for you right now," it usually satisfied him.

"All set?" I asked after snapping his helmet into place.

"Yep. Don't forget your helmet, Mama."

After fastening mine, we took off on our bikes back to our bungalow. Matson rode in front of me so I could keep an eye on him. When he was younger, he had to follow behind me because he didn't know how to get places. I spent half the time riding in circles because I was so paranoid about not being able to see him, that all I did was look backward to make sure he was still there. He would always light up with a smile, completely clueless as to how worried I was.

"You still there, Mama?" Matson shouted into the wind, and I couldn't help but smile. I used to ask him that too whenever he was behind me.

"Still here!" I shouted back as we turned down our street.

Matson navigated his bike onto the sidewalk and made the sharp turn into the small driveway, and we followed it to the back of the house. As I opened our one-car garage, he dropped his bike to the ground and skipped toward the back entrance.

"Uh, excuse me," I said and he stopped, slowly turning to face me with a concerned expression. "Is that where your bike goes?"

His chin dropped to his chest. "No. Sorry."

"Come back here and put it where it belongs, please," I told him, and watched while he picked his bike up and walked it inside the garage, then placed it gently against the far wall. "Thank you."

"You're welcome," he said automatically as he waited for me.

After I closed the garage door, Matson took my hand and

held it as we walked toward our back door. I loved that my eight-year-old son still held my hand, and I hated knowing that it wouldn't last forever. Someday soon, he'd be too embarrassed to hold my hand in public, and my heart would surely break a little when that day came.

"Can I open it?" He looked up at me with big blue eyes and I handed my keys over. The key refused to go in at first, and I resisted the urge to help as Matson turned it upside down and tried again. When it slid in easily, he turned it, opening the door for us with a proud smile.

Closing the door behind us, I clicked the lock into place. "Matson, remember to lock the doors behind you, okay?"

"Why? It's not dark out."

How could I explain to my son that bad guys didn't only exist in the dark? I didn't want to scare him, but I needed him to make safe, smart choices, especially if Derek was lingering in the area.

"Just for right now. Let's lock the doors all the time."

"Who was that man earlier, Mama?"

"Ryan?"

"No, I met Ryan." Matson's face pinched with childlike concern. "The other one. The mean one who was yelling."

"He's no one, baby." I wasn't ready, couldn't tell him that the scary man was his father. Not before I knew what it was Derek even wanted, or how long he planned on sticking around.

Matson narrowed his eyes, thinking, then gave me a nod. "I like Ryan," he said, and my heart skipped.

"You do?"

"Yeah. But I don't like the other man." When I nodded

but didn't say anything, Matson asked, "Is he why we're locking the doors all the time?"

That was a question I didn't want to answer but couldn't avoid. "Yes. He's the reason why."

Matson nodded again like everything suddenly made perfect sense, when it shouldn't have made sense at all. "Okay."

"Want to take a quick shower before we go to Nana's?"

"We're going to Nana's?" His face lit up, and I realized I hadn't even asked my mom if we could come over yet.

"Actually, I should ask her first, huh?" I laughed and Matson did too.

"I can ask her if you think it would make her say yes," he said, and I chased him around the kitchen, stopping only once I caught him. "I just meant I think she likes me better," he choked out through his laughter as I tickled his sides.

"Likes you better? We'll see about that."

I pulled out my cell phone and dialed my mom's number. Thankfully, she and my dad didn't have plans, so she said we could come by. I promised to bring dinner so she wouldn't have to cook, and although she tried to argue with me, I eventually won.

"Chips and salsa?" Matson asked as soon as I hung up, and I smiled at my sweet boy.

"Most definitely."

He kept staring at me. "So, what'd she say?"

"About?"

"Liking me better?" he asked with a sly grin, and I pretended I was going to chase and tickle him again. "Just kidding, Mama. She probably likes us both the same."

"She's not going to like you if you don't take a shower." I

pinched my nose as if he smelled.

"I don't smell!" he shouted before his smile fell. "Do I?"

"No, but you'll smell nice and clean for Nana and Papa if you shower."

"Fine," he said with a groan.

As he stomped down the hall, I checked all the windows and doors, making sure that the blinds were closed and everything was locked. I'd always been concerned about my general safety since I lived alone and was a single mom, but I'd never truly felt unsafe until now.

Derek's presence made me wish I'd gotten Matson a dog when he asked for one a few years ago.

*

I PARKED IN my parents' driveway before turning around and looking at Matson in the backseat. He wanted nothing more than to sit up front with me, but it wasn't safe with the airbags. The manufacturer recommended that no one under twelve years old sit up front, and I followed their suggestion, much to Matson's chagrin.

"Will you grab my purse and I'll carry the food?"

"Sure," he said, then unbuckled his seat belt and reached for my bag.

Mom opened the front door before we could ring the bell, and she hugged Matson like she hadn't seen him in years, instead of only yesterday. My body warmed with a rush of gratitude. I was incredibly lucky to have my parents so involved in my life.

"We got your favorite, Nana," Matson said.

"I can tell. It smells amazing." Mom ushered us inside and quickly closed the door. "Go wake up Papa."

Matson laughed. "Captain's chair or bedroom?"

"Captain's chair, of course," she answered, and I rolled my eyes at the special names the two of them had created for certain things. "Hello, *mija*. Are you going to tell me what's going on?"

She gave me a hug, and I nodded against her shoulder as my son ran off down the hallway.

"I need to talk to you in private, though. Not with Matson around."

We walked through the entryway and into the living room where my dad was being woken up by his rambunctious grandson. I continued into the kitchen, placing the paper bags filled with food onto the counter.

"Who let you in?" Dad teased Matson before grabbing him and pulling him onto the chair with him. "Now we both sleep."

"It's not time for bed, Papa. We brought chips!"

My dad shot out of the chair like it was on fire, leaving Matson sitting in it alone. "Chips? Feed me, my boy."

Matson grabbed his hand and dragged him into the kitchen, where Dad greeted me and placed a kiss on my cheek.

"Hi, Dad. Sorry to wake you."

"Men should always be woken up for food. Remember that."

I glanced at my mom with a smile. "I'll remember."

"And I'll remind her," Matson said, trying to help.

I had to stop myself from asking him whose team he was on, anyway. I figured I'd probably lose that contest, and I wanted to pretend I was my son's favorite person on earth for as long as I could.

As we seated ourselves at the round dinner table, I reveled in being surrounded by the people I loved, thankful that I had them in my life and my son's. I had no idea how I would have done any of it without my parents in my corner. They were my lifeline when I needed one, when I was certain I'd drown.

And here I was, about to ask them for more.

For a moment, I felt guilty for always asking, asking, asking instead of giving, but I needed them and their help. My parents needed to know that Derek apparently wasn't going away anytime soon. I hated bringing drama to their front door, and felt responsible for it like it was somehow my fault.

Pushing aside my depressing thoughts for now, I focused on the moment happening right in front of me. So much happiness surrounded that little round table. I wanted to bask in it, soak it all up, before it came crashing down in waves of concern.

After dinner, my mom suggested that Papa and Matson go watch a movie while we cleaned up the dishes and had girl talk. It was the perfect diversion, one my father couldn't agree to quick enough.

"Not wash dishes? I'm in. Come on, Matson, before they change their minds," he said before hurrying away, Matson running behind him.

When they were gone, I sighed. "Derek showed up at the beach where Matson and I were today."

"What?" The plate Mom was holding dropped into the sink with a splash, and she reached for it to wash it again. "Sorry. Did he talk to you? Did he talk to Matson?" She rinsed off the plate and handed it to me to dry.

"No. Yes. I mean . . ." I was fumbling, my emotions getting the best of me. Forcing myself to calm down, I toweled off another dish. "He didn't talk to Matson, but he did threaten me. He told me he had every right to see his son, and he wasn't giving up."

Mom cursed softly in Spanish under her breath. "What does that boy want?" she asked as she scrubbed.

"I keep asking myself the same thing."

She stopped her scrubbing and frowned. "After all this time, showing up here and demanding to be a part of Matson's life. Why? He can't have suddenly grown a conscience. He must want something."

As awful as the thought sounded coming out of my mom's mouth, I couldn't disagree with her. "I thought the same thing."

"That boy doesn't do things out of the kindness of his heart. He never has. He might have had me fooled for a while back when you two were in high school, but not anymore."

"I know, Mom. Me either."

After handing me the last dish, she pulled the drain plug. Reaching for a towel, she dried her hands before placing them on her hips. "I'm worried, *mija*. Do you think he's dangerous?"

I wanted to scoff at the suggestion of a former boyfriend wanting to hurt me or my son, but the truth was that I had no idea. I couldn't pretend to know Derek anymore, not that I truly ever had. As uncertain as I was about his intentions, I didn't want my mom to worry. She did enough for me every single day, and the last thing I wanted was to cause her stress, so I lied.

"I don't think so."

She shook her head. "He seemed a little loco when he stopped by the other day."

I filled an empty glass with ice water before hopping onto the countertop. "He seemed angry today too. Super agitated with Ryan."

"Ryan was there?"

I took a gulp of water. "He happened to be jogging by when Derek and I were arguing." My mom's face lit up, and I pretended not to notice. "He made Derek leave. I think he told him he'd kill him. It's all a little blurry."

"I might like this Ryan person. He's the one who owns the bar with his brothers, right?"

I'd told my mom all about Ryan after Grant's heart attack. "Yeah."

"He must like you if he threatened Derek's life." She leveled me with an inquisitive gaze, letting me know that I wasn't getting away without talking about this. But that was why I'd insisted on coming here in the first place. I needed her opinion.

"He's made that pretty clear. But I think I ruined any chance I might have had."

"What do you mean? What did you do?"

Swirling the ice inside my glass, I avoided my mom's question for as long as I could until she cleared her throat and tapped a foot on the floor. Giving her what she wanted, I said, "He didn't know about Matson."

"He was mad when he found out?" she asked, jumping to the wrong conclusion, although I didn't blame her. Most guys in the past hadn't reacted well when they learned I had a kid.

"No. He wasn't mad at all. He was happy, actually."

Mom's widening smile brightened her whole face. "He was happy. Then what's the problem?"

"It's just that. Well, I told him every time he asked me out that he wasn't the kind of guy I was looking for. That he wasn't my type. And today, when he put two and two together..." I paused, knowing she'd finish my thought for me.

"He was hurt?"

I nodded. "He was most definitely hurt. And angry."

"Anger is still hurt. They come from the same place."

"I know. But I'm not sure he'll forgive me."

Mom clucked her tongue. "What happened, exactly?"

I searched my mind for the memory. Considering all the adrenaline that had been pumping through me on the playground, I probably wasn't remembering everything clearly.

"He found out about Matson. He said he was more interested in me, and then he said that I was less. And that was why I'd pushed him away all this time. Then he got really mad and took off."

"He has every right to be upset," my mom said, her sympathy for Ryan making me feel even worse.

I looked down at the glass in my hand and closed my eyes for a second. "I know he does. I was wrong to judge him before I even knew him."

"So, why did you? You don't normally do that, so I'm surprised." She paused before adding, "And curious why you did with him."

I'd been asking myself those same questions since I'd run into Ryan at the hospital. Why had I been so adamant on shutting him out? Why had I refused to give him a chance with me? It was deeper than all the standard reasons I usually had in those situations, that much was certain.

"I think I was scared," I said softly.

A sympathetic smile spread across my mom's face, but she said nothing. The silence stretched out as she waited for me to continue, but I knew that she understood. She had been with me since the day I found out I was pregnant, and every moment in between.

She knew how hard it was for me to be a single mom, and how tricky it was for me to date. It eventually seemed easier to avoid the potential heartache altogether, and up until Ryan, no guy had tried hard enough to break down the walls I'd put up to protect myself. To me, that was just further proof that each guy wasn't the right one. I'd convinced myself that the right one would stay. That he would fight for me.

"I assumed Ryan wasn't the right kind of guy to have in our life."

"Because he owns a bar?" she asked, sounding surprised.

"In part, yes. Being a bartender is a certain kind of lifestyle, one that I didn't want to be a part of. Mom, you've never seen the way women throw themselves at him. It's like he's royalty or something, and he's so flirtatious back."

My mom put up a hand to stop me. "Sofia, it's not Ryan's fault if women throw themselves at him. I'm assuming he's a good-looking guy and he's single. So, of course they'd try. And just because he's flirtatious doesn't mean he means it. It could all be part of his job. The more flirtatious he is, the better the money he makes, I'd bet."

"But I don't want a guy who acts like that."

"Remember, *mija*, he's single. He's never had a reason not

to."

Crap. She had a point. A good one. I hated that sometimes.

Mom leveled a serious look on me. "I think you should head on over to that bar and apologize."

"Now?"

"Right now. Before too much time passes and he starts thinking that maybe you were right. That maybe he wasn't the kind of guy who would be good for you."

"He still may not be," I said, not entirely convinced. The truth was that I still didn't know Ryan any better than I did yesterday. I only knew that my having a son hadn't scared him off. Which was a huge plus.

"He may not be, but he deserves a shot. And you deserve to know the truth. At least if you rule him out, let there be a real reason for it. Not something you made up in your mind."

My adrenaline started pumping as nerves shot through me. What if he hated me and didn't want to talk? What if I'd ruined everything?

"Okay, but wait. Matson—"

"Will be fine. I'll watch him. Go. You owe that man an apology, and you need to give it to him while he'll still listen. Men are sensitive creatures, believe it or not. Sometimes underneath all that bravado and machismo is a boy who wants to be loved."

I jumped down from the counter and searched for Matson to tell him I wouldn't be long.

"Where are you going, Mama?"

"I need to go talk to Ryan. I won't be late, but you're going to stay here while I'm gone, okay?"

"Okay. Tell him I said hi, and I hope he'll still eat with

us." Matson leaned toward me, cupping his hands around his mouth as he whispered, "But don't tell him we got the chips and salsa without him tonight. He might be sad."

I suppressed a giggle. "I won't. Be good for Nana and Papa."

My mom walked me out, rubbing a hand down my back for support. At the front door, I stopped and turned to face her.

"What do I say when I see him?"

"Start with a little honesty. And then maybe make out with him or show him your boobs."

"Mom!"

She chuckled. "I'm joking, but just tell him the truth. And you need to be honest with yourself as well. You can't let fear rule your life. Sooner or later, you need to let someone in. Matson deserves a good man in his life to look up to. And you deserve a man who loves and respects you."

Tears pricked my eyes, but I blinked hard to keep them from falling. I wasn't tearing up about Ryan exactly, but my mom's words had struck a nerve.

I hadn't realized I'd been shoving down my own wants and needs for so long. I'd practically given up on the idea of ever being with someone, and I'd thought I was okay with that.

Apparently, I wasn't okay with it at all.

"Wish me luck," I called out as I walked toward my car.

Mom stood on the porch and waved. "You won't need it."

She was so convincing, I found myself wishing I had half the confidence she had in me right now.

APOLOGIES
Ryan

As Sofia approached where I worked the bar, her body language seemed confident but her eyes betrayed her uncertainty. She was a walking contradiction, and I assumed I must look the same.

"Angel," Grant said, interrupting the conversation our eyes were having.

She blinked twice, breaking the spell, and turned to him. "Hi, Grant." She gave him a hug and a genuine smile. "Didn't think I'd see you here."

"I like to slum it sometimes." He finished his beer before tapping his glass on the bar top, signaling he wanted another.

As I reached for his empty glass, my eyes met hers and she gave me an uneasy smile.

"Hi, Ryan."

Pursing my lips, I nodded, my eyes asking the questions my mouth refused to voice.

Why are you here? What do you want?

Once I'd slid Grant's newly filled glass toward him, Sofia looked around before asking, "Can we go somewhere private and talk?"

I scanned the crowded bar, thinking it wasn't the best time

to take a break, but Frank stepped over and spoke close to my ear.

"I'll cover you. Go talk in the office."

Thumbing toward the dark door behind me, I turned and made my way there without seeing if Sofia was following or not. When I got to the door, I looked back to see she was behind me, then pulled the door open and held it wide for her. I followed her inside, moving to sit in Frank's desk chair.

I motioned for her to sit across from me in the only other empty chair, and she hesitated for a few seconds before sitting down. It felt so formal, my staring at her with a desk between us like she was about to be interviewed. In a way, she sort of was, considering that I had a few questions.

"Ryan, I'm sorry." She clasped her hands together and stared down at them before meeting my eyes again. "I'm sorry for how I acted and how I treated you. I think I might have been wrong about you, and it wasn't fair or right of me to judge you."

She *thinks* she *might* have been wrong about me? What kind of lame apology was that?

I almost fucking laughed, but I stopped myself the second I looked into her eyes. She sat there, so open, so vulnerable, and the last thing I wanted was to make her defensive and regret walking in here tonight.

Still hurt, I said, "I know that it can't be easy for you being a single mom, but why did you think—"

"I know I judged you without knowing you, which is wrong. And I made assumptions based on your job and what I'd seen of you here. I did exactly to you what I hate being done to me."

Confused, I sat back in my chair, studying her. "What do you mean?"

Sofia sat up a little straighter, as if she was steeling herself. "I've always felt like strangers were making assumptions about me because of my situation. When I was pregnant, people checked my hand for a ring. They did the same thing when I had an infant in my arms. I was always being judged unfairly, or at least it seemed like it. And I did the same thing to you."

"What kind of guy do you think I am? Why do you think I'd be so bad for you?" I asked with a grimace. "For your son?"

"You seem like such a playboy. A lot of women give you attention, and it looked like you enjoyed it. I don't want a guy who needs attention from other women. I would hate having that kind of life. And I don't want a role model like that for Matson."

Before asking Claudia and Jess for their opinion on Sofia, I would have never guessed how my life might look to others from the outside looking in. I knew the kind of man I was, the kind of man I wanted to be, but it wasn't fair of me to assume that anyone else could see that just from looking. I always put on quite a show at work.

"I'm a one-woman kind of guy, Sofia. I'm not a playboy. I might have gone through a phase at one point, but it didn't last long. It wasn't me. I want to settle down. I want a family. I want to find the kind of love my brothers have."

Her mouth formed a crooked smile before it faded. "I would have never guessed any of that by looking at you. Or by watching you at work."

"Obviously." I realized that I sounded like a bit of a dick, so I took my tone down a notch. "Can I ask you something?"

"Sure." She unclasped her hands and started playing with a pen.

"What are you so afraid of?"

The cap of the pen flew onto the floor and she bent over to pick it up. "I feel like I'm afraid of everything right now. Of falling in love. Of never falling in love. I haven't had a relationship since I had Matson, really. At least, nothing that ever turned even remotely serious. I'm scared of giving you my heart and having you completely obliterate it. Because I think you could do that, Ryan. I think if anyone could destroy me, it would be you."

A harsh cough bubbled up from my throat, and I pounded my chest. I hadn't expected that answer. "It works both ways, you know. You could completely obliterate me."

"Could I?" She sounded unconvinced.

"Sofia, I'm sensitive. If I haven't made that clear by now, let me tell you again. I've got a soft heart. I'm a hopeless romantic. I want all that fairy-tale bullshit that they peddle to girls. I want it." I pointed at myself. "Me."

"I don't trust easily." An uncomfortable laugh escaped from her beautiful lips. "Obviously. It's always just been Matson and me for the last eight years. And my parents, of course. But I have a really hard time letting anyone in. I don't know how."

I nodded because that made complete sense. "It's easier to keep people out, and that's why you push so hard. Somewhere deep down, you want to see who will scale the walls you put up. I was willing to."

"Was?" Her eyebrows drew together.

"Still am."

Her face instantly relaxed. "You are?"

"Hell yes, Sofia." I pushed out of my chair and stalked around the desk.

"You're not at all what I thought you'd be, Ryan Fisher." She batted her eyelashes as she looked up at me.

"I know."

I smirked at her, then pulled her from the chair and pressed my lips to hers. I probably should have waited until our first date to kiss her, but I didn't want to wait another second.

Sofia kissed me back, her tongue meeting mine aggressively, momentarily catching me off guard. I thought she might be shy or reserved, yet Sofia was anything but. She matched my intensity, gripping the back of my shirt as I held her tight, afraid if I let go, she might disappear again. She felt natural in my arms, like she belonged there, like she was made for me, and kissing her felt like anything but the first time. Our mouths moved in sync, our tongues tasting and teasing, nipping at each other with lips and teeth.

When she finally pulled her head back, breaking the kiss, I leaned in. I wanted more, as much as I could get of her. Because, dear God, that was perfect.

Sofia pushed my chest slightly and looked up at me through her lashes. "I wanted to ask you before I forgot."

"Ask me what?"

"On a date."

My hands slid down her back and rested on her hips. "You're asking me out on a date?"

"Yes, Ryan. I came here to apologize and make it up to you. I want to."

I hesitated, not because I didn't want to go out with Sofia, but because it went against everything I believed in to have her take me out. I wanted to be a gentleman, to be chivalrous. "What did you have in mind?"

"I thought you could come over to my place, and I'd cook us dinner. If that sounds okay?" She bit lightly at her bottom lip, apparently nervous again.

A smile broke free. "Will Matson be there?"

"Would you like him to be?"

"I would, but it's up to you." I definitely wanted to spend more time with Matson. He seemed like a cool kid, but that decision wasn't mine to make.

Sofia stared at the floor, her head moving slightly with the silent debate she was having with herself before she looked back up. "I think it's probably best if we have a few dates first, just us, before we involve him. I don't want to confuse him, or have him get attached to you if—"

"If we don't last," I said, finishing her sentence for her.

"Yes. I don't say that to be mean. I just want to protect him."

She was a good mom, and I respected that. Plus, she said a "few dates," which meant she had more feelings for me than she was willing to admit.

"I understand."

A knock at the door stopped our conversation, and Nick peeked in. Taking in our embrace, he said with a smirk, "Hey, man, some crazy dude is out here asking for you."

"Who?"

"No idea." Nick shrugged and closed the door.

I narrowed my eyes in confusion, wondering who it could

be. "I'll be right back." I looked at Sofia, who was still flushed from our make-out session.

"No, it's okay, I need to get home. My mom is watching Matson for me so I could come talk to you."

I turned and gave her one last quick kiss on the lips before grabbing her hand. "Okay. I'll walk you out."

I led her out of the office and into the chaos of the bar. Derek's gaze instantly met mine from across the room, and I stopped short in surprise before Sofia slammed into my back. "Sorry, angel."

Derek's narrowed gaze trailed down to my hand, still linked with Sofia's, and his expression shifted from angry to downright murderous. My protective instincts kicked into overdrive as Sofia's grip on me tightened.

As Derek worked his way through the crowd toward us, I squared my shoulders, keeping my body as a buffer between his and hers. There was no way in hell I was letting him anywhere near her. When he got close enough to talk, I put out my hand to stop him.

"What are you doing here?" Sofia's voice blew past my ear, and Derek's mouth formed a devilish grin.

"I didn't know you would be here, Sofia." His gaze flicked between her face and mine, as if he wasn't sure which one of us to maintain eye contact with. "I came here to talk to Ryan. But if you're here fucking around with him, then who is watching our son? Where's Matson? Who has him, your mom? Hasn't she done enough to help you over the years? You can't even raise our kid properly. Can't you do anything right?"

"That's enough," I snapped, searching the room for my brothers. Frank's gaze met mine and he raised an eyebrow in question. I gave him a slight shrug in response, knowing that he'd keep an eye on the situation as it unfolded.

"Or what, Ryan? You going to threaten me again?"

He rolled his eyes and something seemed . . . not quite right, like he was on something. Not that I had a lot of experience with people on drugs, aside from the few who came into the bar sometimes, but he seemed off somehow.

"I might," I ground out, my jaw tight.

"Why did you come here?" Sofia asked again, peeking out from behind my shoulder.

"I told you. I came to talk to your boyfriend."

"What about?" I asked, clearly annoyed. "And as you can see, I'm a little busy." I waved my hand around the packed bar.

His laughter sounded demented. "So you're too busy for me, but you're not too busy for her. I see how it is. Not a wise move, Ryan Fisher. Not a wise move at all."

He knew my full name. I guessed it wouldn't have been that hard to figure out once he knew where I worked, but I was still a little weirded out by it. I was actually more concerned that he showed up here at the bar, though.

"I think you should leave." My voice dropped to a dangerous low rumble, and I sensed Sofia stiffen behind me.

"Do we have a problem here?" Frank appeared at my side, a towel and glass in hand.

"I was just asking Derek here to leave."

"Doesn't look like he was listening," Frank said to me, and I held back my grin as we continued to talk around Derek like he wasn't even there.

"Sure doesn't," I said, keeping my voice light.

"Did you ask nicely, Ryan?"

"I asked plenty nice."

"Maybe you hurt his feelings," Frank said playfully, not looking at Derek.

I shrugged. "He might be hard of hearing."

"Hate when that happens." Frank finally turned toward Derek. "Are you going to leave willingly, or would you like some help getting tossed on your ass out of my bar?" Frank took a step toward him, no longer playing around, and Derek threw his hands in the air.

"I'll go. For now." He pointed a finger at me. "This isn't over. And next time I tell you I want to talk to you, you better make time to listen." He turned to walk away.

"Don't fucking threaten me," I yelled at his back before adding, "And stay the hell away from Sofia."

He stopped, faced us, and mouthed the word *no* before turning away and walking out the door.

"Who the hell was that?" Frank asked.

"My son's father," Sofia answered before I could.

"I'm sorry for that. I'm Frank, by the way." My brother extended his hand, and Sofia took it in hers.

"Sofia."

"It's nice to finally meet you."

"You too." She smiled, but I could tell she was still tense.

"Next time you come back, we'll get you set up with the ladies." Frank pointed at the table in the far back of the bar where Claudia and Jess were sitting with some of their friends. "That gorgeous brunette is my girlfriend, and the blonde is Nick's."

"Thank you, Frank." Sofia smiled, but it didn't reach her eyes, and Frank walked back to tend bar.

Glancing around, I noticed a fair share of attention focused in our direction, Grant's included. He looked concerned but I shook my head, warning him to stay out of it.

"I'm going to follow you home in my car. I want to be sure you're safe, and I don't trust that guy." When she swallowed and opened her mouth, I sensed she was about to argue with me, so I stopped her. "Look, Sofia, I know you're used to being alone and handling things on your own. But that's not how it's going to be with me and you, okay? You're going to try to do things by yourself, and I'm going to fight you on it every time because you're not alone anymore. We're giving us a shot, right?"

She avoided my gaze, looking anywhere but my eyes, and I realized that was her tell. She was uncomfortable, maybe enough to attempt to lie.

"Sofia?"

Those gorgeous hazel eyes finally looked directly at me. "Yeah?"

"We're doing this, right? Me and you?" I asked again, my thumb caressing her hand as I pulled her closer, fully aware we had an audience. I didn't care who knew, who saw, or who thought what. All I wanted was this woman in this moment with me.

"Yes."

When she maintained eye contact, I relaxed, knowing I had some of her trust.

"Then you're going to have to let me in," I said as I pulled her into a tight hug. "And you're going to have to get used to me helping you."

I didn't know Sofia that well yet, but I knew people

enough to know that the ones hiding behind the tallest walls tended to have the largest hearts. They were simply scared of getting hurt. They didn't hide because they hated love; they hid because they had so much of it to give.

"I don't know how," she murmured against my chest. "But I want to try. With you."

"Then I'm either following you home, or I'm driving you. Your choice."

She nodded and let out a sigh. "You can follow me. Thank you, and I'm sorry for all of this."

"Don't apologize. It's not your fault."

Although I tried to reassure her, I could see the self-imposed guilt written all over her face. That was going to have to change.

After I gave Nick a quick rundown of what happened, he wanted to shut the bar down so all the Fisher brothers could escort Sofia home, but I convinced him that wasn't necessary. So, he and Frank practically shoved me outside, wanting to be sure that I didn't worry about the bar when I needed to be focused on Sofia's safety.

And I was.

And even though my brothers didn't know her well yet, I could tell they were worried too.

SO THIS IS DATING
Sofia

I HAD NO idea what Derek was up to, but showing up at Ryan's bar and demanding to talk to him was more than a little disconcerting. How had he even found out who Ryan was, or where he worked? I had no idea but didn't have to think too hard. Derek's family had power and money, two things that could get you any information you wanted.

But why? Why had he shown up here, and what did he want to talk to Ryan about?

Ryan walked me outside the bar, scanning for any signs of Derek before helping me into my car and hopping in the passenger seat.

"I thought you were following me," I said.

"I am, but you're driving me to my car first. I don't want you to be alone. He seemed off, right? Like he was on something, maybe?" Ryan glanced in the side mirror, keeping an eye out for anyone following us.

"I don't know," I said because I honestly didn't. "I haven't seen him since before Matson was born." As Ryan directed me, I drove around the bar, making my way to the back lot where he and his brothers parked.

"Why not?"

"His family wanted me to have an abortion. They thought I got pregnant on purpose, and accused me of wanting Derek's money. He broke up with me the day I told him, instead of waiting until after we graduated like he had planned. I was seventeen and terrified. And I was about to have a baby that no one but me wanted."

"And Derek said nothing?"

"He and his family fell off the face of the earth. At least, in my world they did. Not a single call, text, or email. I eventually blocked them on social media to avoid exactly this happening, but to be honest, I figured if they hadn't shown up by the time Matson was two, they never would."

"Sofia . . ." Ryan said my name so softly, it almost sounded like he pitied me.

"Don't feel sorry for me," I said sharply. "I don't want or need that."

"Hey, I wasn't feeling sorry for you, but I'm allowed to think that story sucks. Because it does." He was adamant, his tone honest and kind. Ryan cared about me, that much was apparent.

"You're right. It is a crap story. But it's only a part of mine. And I don't feel bad about it anymore. It's in the past, you know?"

He reached for my chin, gently turning my face toward his. "I'm not sure I've ever met anyone as strong as you."

Ryan's compliment made me uncomfortable. It wasn't the first time I'd heard those words, but they always sounded strange to me.

My life was what it was, hard times and all. But what were people supposed to do when faced with hard times? Quit? Give up? Those never seemed like real options to me, so I always did whatever I had to do to get by. It never seemed like being strong or brave to me; it had always just felt like life.

"Did I say something wrong?" Ryan asked, his hand on my thigh as I pulled into the gravel lot.

"No. This is all new to me, that's all."

"I know. It's new to me too. I haven't had a girlfriend in years," he admitted.

A strangled sound came flying out of my mouth. "That can't be true."

"I told you." He smiled. "I've been waiting."

"You are romantic."

"Told you that too." He moved to open his door before stopping. "I want you to park back here from now on. I mean, if you ever come to the bar again."

I let out a quick chuckle. "If I ever come back."

"Dammit, Sofia. When you come back, park here."

"Yes, sir." I gave him a mock salute.

He leaned back into the passenger seat and gave me a soft kiss. "I'll follow you. Don't ditch me."

I grinned. "I won't."

The lights to a sporty white Audi lit up and he slid inside. After the engine turned over, I pulled out of the lot, making sure there was enough room between cars for Ryan to turn at the same time I did. Leading him through the streets of Santa Monica, I eventually pulled into my parents' driveway with him right behind me.

When I exited my car, Ryan got out of his as well.

"What are you doing?" I asked.

"I want to talk to your dad," he said, like it was no big

deal.

"My dad?" I practically choked.

"Come on, Sofia." He reached for my hand and pulled me toward the front door like he'd been there a million times before.

"Ryan, stop." I dug in my heels and pulled back on his arm. "Stop."

"What's the matter?" He stopped and turned, giving me a questioning look.

"I don't need you to talk to my dad for me."

I wasn't ready for a discussion about Derek with my father. Not before I knew what he even wanted, or why he was suddenly here. My parents would be consumed with worry, and to be the cause of turmoil in their daily lives was the last thing I wanted. Until I was certain that I needed them involved, I wanted my parents as blissfully unaware of all the craziness as possible. Maybe Derek would leave as quickly as he'd shown up?

Ryan looked down at me, his blue eyes practically sparkling in the moonlight. "You're right," he said easily, and I felt silly for bracing myself for a debate that clearly wasn't coming. "I'm sorry. I don't know what I was thinking."

I reached up and cupped his cheek, the scruff prickling my palm. "I know what you were thinking. And it's sweet, the way you want to protect me. But I'm a grown woman."

"And your ex is clearly unstable."

"He might be. But *I'll* talk to my parents about it. Not you. Not yet." I stood my ground while still attempting to sound appreciative. I'd never had a man want to take care of me before. It was as shocking as it was endearing. I loved it as much as I feared it.

"Okay. But you will talk to them, right?"

I nodded, afraid that if I said the words out loud, he might catch on that I was lying. Ryan seemed to read me far too easily.

"I should get in there so I can take Matson home. I'll call you." I leaned up on tiptoe and planted a long kiss on his lips, my tongue searching for his.

Kissing Ryan was as good as I'd hoped it would be. He knew exactly how to handle me, his tongue eliciting moans from somewhere deep inside me. My body begged me to strip him naked on my parents' front lawn, but my brain pinged out a message that it might not be the best idea.

Brains were dumb sometimes. They ruined everything.

"Text me when you're home so I know you're safe." He brushed his thumb down my cheek and kissed me once more.

"I will."

"We have a date to set up too." He grinned, and I smiled back.

"We do," I said, and felt my stomach flip with anticipation and excitement.

"Talk to you later, angel." He pulled open the driver's door before adding, "And tell your parents, please. They deserve to know what's going on."

"I will," I promised halfheartedly, watching as Ryan pulled out of the driveway and drove away.

I didn't tell my parents like I'd told Ryan I would, and my mom was none the wiser. She was more excited about the fact that I'd smoothed things over with Ryan and was going to give him a chance. When I told her about the eventual dinner date, she tried to give me fifty different family recipes—all authentic, she said—before I convinced her to walk away from her recipe box. Actually, my dad got her to stop, claiming that I was turning an unusual shade of green, and she'd better stop before I puked all over their hardwood floors.

Matson cracked up at that, then grew serious, wanting to be sure I was okay. After reassuring him that I was fine and Papa was only joking, he started laughing again.

Our drive back home was uneventful, but I checked my rearview mirror more than normal and was more aware of our surroundings than I usually would be. I realized that I had little to defend myself with if something happened. The pepper spray in the glove compartment had to be expired.

After walking through the front door, I texted Ryan to let him know we were home safe and sound, and then got Matson ready for bed. Ryan texted back right away, and my heart flipped inside my chest. All these feelings were brand new, and they were as exciting as they were terrifying.

"You have a date, Mama?" Matson asked as I sat on my knees, tucking him into bed.

"Who told you that?"

"I heard Nana talking about the way to a man's heart was through his tummy. She said you were going to cook for him. Can I come?"

My heart cracked a little at his request. I never did things without Matson and hated excluding him from this, but it was in his best interest. How did you explain that to an eight-year-old?

"I think the first time Ryan comes over, it should be just me and him. I want to make sure that I like him and he likes me before he spends time with you."

"It's Ryan? But we already like each other. I should be there," Matson said through a yawn.

"I'll think about it," I said seriously, and he smiled.

"Thanks, Mama. I won't ruin your date." He snuggled deeper into his covers and turned his back to me.

"Oh, baby, you could never ruin anything. It's not about that." I kissed his cheek before standing up. "I love you."

"Love you too, Mama. 'Night."

"Good night."

*

THE NEXT DAY, Ryan and I fell into a routine of texting throughout the afternoon and ending each night together on the phone.

Grant had even called to make sure that everything was okay, and after reassuring him, the teasing texts began rolling in. He informed me that it wasn't *cool* of me to choose Ryan over him, and that he knew I only did it because I wasn't into older men. He let me know that once I grew bored with Ryan, he'd still give me another chance . . . *if* he was available. Grant warned me that a guy like him was a catch and wouldn't stay on the market long, but I knew he was full of it. Grant only had eyes for one woman, and that woman no longer walked this earth with him.

Each night once Matson was in bed, I found myself pressing my cell phone against my ear and being put on hold every few minutes while Ryan served a customer. Since he didn't have a normal work schedule, I was a little concerned about how the logistics of dating him could possibly work. Being a single mom meant I had priorities that other girls my age didn't have. I couldn't go out every night of the week, and Ryan couldn't come home to Matson and me after a rough day at the office for a sit-down dinner.

Trying to set up an actual date with him was harder than it should have been. He only had one night off during the week, and it was a school night. He suggested that we have lunch instead on the weekend, but for some reason that seemed less like a first date, in my opinion, and he confessed that he felt the same.

As much as I hated messing up Matson's school schedule, I opted for Thursday night for our first date, and planned to send Matson to my mom's. When Matson informed me that he was okay with it all "since it's Ryan," relief filled my body.

"How do your brothers do it?" I asked Ryan Wednesday night while lounging on my sofa, snuggled into a soft throw, my phone hot against my cheek.

"Do what?" His voice boomed through the phone as music played in the background.

"Keep their girlfriends happy when they're never home? It's not like you guys have normal business hours. Do they ever even see each other?"

He laughed. "The girls are here a lot."

My life revolved around Matson. I couldn't have it revolve around a bar scene. "I can't do that, though."

"I know."

"So if the girls aren't at the bar, then what?"

"We each have one night off during the week. But, Sofia, it's our choice how often and long we want to work, you know?"

"No, I don't know. What do you mean?" I kicked the throw off my feet and wrapped it around my legs instead.

"We're all here because we want to be right now, but we don't have to be. We could give our other bartenders more hours, and we've talked about it before. Scaling back. I know that once Frank and Claudia start a family, there's no way Frank will want to be here as much as he is now. And he won't have to be. I don't have to be here either. I've just never had a reason to cut back before."

I smiled to myself, biting on my bottom lip before releasing a small sigh of relief.

"Sofia?" Ryan's voice cut through the silence.

"I'm here."

"Did I scare you off?"

"The opposite, actually," I admitted, still grinning. I'd assumed, wrongfully again, that Ryan would never leave the bar. That he would always close it down on weekends, and be there as much as possible. The Fisher brothers were the face of Sam's bar, and I assumed they would never walk away from the publicity and marketing they brought to it.

"You want me even more now?" he asked with a laugh.

"Something like that."

"No, really. Tell me what you're thinking."

"I just never thought you'd leave the bar. Which was part of the reason I ruled out dating you in the first place. I couldn't see myself being serious with a guy who didn't come home until two in the morning every night."

"Three. Sometimes four," he said, and I gasped.

"Really?"

"Sometimes. Depends on the night and the crowd," he said, and my heart stopped for a second before beating again in its normal rhythm. "You still with me?"

I nodded, forgetting for a second that he couldn't see me. "Still with you. Just surprised." I honestly couldn't imagine the upside-down, backward schedule sort of life, and wondered how he'd done it for so long.

"It's a lot of late nights, I know. But it doesn't have to be. And it won't always be that way."

"What do you want, then? Like what's your ultimate goal?" If he had already thought about stepping away from the bar at some point, in what capacity would he do that?

"I think my ultimate goal is to still have a presence at the bar. It would probably be a mistake for all three of us to disappear completely and never be there."

I found myself nodding along. "I agree."

"Do you?" He sounded surprised.

"Of course I do. You guys are the face of Sam's, and half the reason why your customers come there in the first place. If you take that away, what would that potentially do to your bottom line?"

"Exactly," he said, his tone lightening. "So I know that I'd like to still be there. It's important to all three of us that we're always hands-on to some degree with the business. None of us want things going on there that we don't know about, or wouldn't be proud of. Frank always wants to be the one to handle the books. To keep things on the up and up, you know? And Nick would have a hard time putting the marketing in anyone else's hands, I know that for a fact, even if he doesn't. I love creating and crafting new drinks, so I want to continue being the one who does that."

"I think that's smart."

"Which part?"

"All of it," I said as hope and happiness weaved through me. "What about your hours?"

"That's the part we haven't nailed down yet. I think it's important for us to be there on the weekends . . ."

I grasped onto his words, deflating a little at the thought of Ryan working on the only two days I had off. My defeatist attitude didn't last long as he continued.

"Not both days," he said, "but we'd each be there on either Friday or Saturday until the bar closed. So I'd have only one really late night on the weekend. And then we'd all still work during the week, but more normal hours. Leave the bar around seven or sometimes eight, I'm not sure. We haven't worked out the details because none of us are quite ready to scale back just yet, but when the time comes, we will."

"Will you hire more staff?"

"Yeah, we'll have to hire a manager and a couple more bartenders. It's either that or sell the place, which we've talked about doing too."

"You'd sell Sam's?"

"None of us want to, so probably not. But it's always an option."

Stepping back was one thing, but selling was a whole other ball game. It shocked me that I was saddened by the thought. "What would you guys do if you didn't have the bar?"

He laughed. "I have no idea. Probably wish I had a bar to work at."

Yawning, I glanced at the time. Making sure I read the

numbers right, I swore under my breath at the late hour.

"Ryan, I need to go to bed."

"I know. I've kept you up late every night this week. Sorry."

"You're a bad influence," I teased.

"That's the rumor. Go to sleep, angel. I'll talk to you tomorrow."

I grinned, loving whenever he called me the nickname he and Grant had coined for me.

"And hey," he said right before I said good-bye and hung up. "Anything from Derek lately? You haven't said."

I thanked my lucky stars that Ryan asked this on the phone and not in person. He had an innate sense of when I wasn't being completely honest, and he would have called me on this the second the next words left my mouth.

"Nope. It's been quiet."

"He can't have just disappeared, right?"

"Probably not." I swallowed, my mouth dry from the lie.

Ryan cleared his throat. "You'd tell me, right? If he was bothering you, you'd tell me?"

"Of course I'd tell you. If there was anything to tell," I said, trying to sound convincing.

"All right. I'll see you tomorrow night for dinner. Can I bring anything?"

"Nope. Just you."

"Just me, it is. Sleep well, angel." And before I said another word, he ended the call.

I hated lying to Ryan, but I didn't want him worrying about my ex-boyfriend, the same way I didn't want my parents to worry. I couldn't stand the idea of being the cause of so much stress, and until there was actually something to be worried about, I planned to keep everything to myself.

The other night when I got off work, Derek was waiting by my car in the parking garage. Before I got close enough to ask him what he was doing there, he walked off, giving me the evil eye. Just as he reached the ramp, he stopped and turned in my direction to point a finger at me.

"What do you want, Derek?" I'd shouted at him. My voice echoed off the concrete walls, repeating his name back at me.

He broke out into an evil laugh before walking down the ramp and disappearing from sight.

I had no idea what it all meant, but I refused to be intimidated by him. He wanted me to know that he knew where I worked, but I wasn't surprised by that. He'd found out who Ryan was and where he worked, so of course he could find out where I worked as well.

Part of me wondered if he'd always known. Maybe he'd been keeping tabs on me the whole time.

FIRST DATE
Ryan

M Y PHONE PINGED with a text.

> SOFIA: *Thank you for the flowers. You didn't have to, but they're gorgeous.*

A picture message arrived right after the text. A giant bouquet of roses filled my screen, stark-white flowers overflowing a white vase, not a bit of color showing, not even the green stems.

I stared at the messages from Sofia for a solid five minutes before I even thought about responding.

Glancing over at the two dozen pink roses I'd bought earlier at the farmers' market, flowers I planned to take to her house tonight, I was more than a little confused. She had clearly gotten flowers at work. But if I hadn't sent them, who did, and why did she think they were from me?

> RYAN: *I'd send you flowers every week for a year, but I'd never send you anything so devoid of color when all you do is add so much of it to my life. Basically, angel, I didn't send those. So, who's the secret admirer?*

His name flashed in my mind the second I pressed SEND

on my response. *Derek*. It had to be. Unless there was some other guy trying to court my girl, but it seemed unlikely. Not that Sofia wasn't worthy of all the admiration in the world, but I'd spent the past few nights with her on the phone for hours on end, and there were no other men in her life.

Trust me, I'd asked.

SOFIA: *You didn't???*

I was about to type a response when my phone vibrated with another text.

SOFIA: *Are you messing with me? They're from you, right?*
RYAN: *Angel, I didn't send them. And if it wasn't me, then . . .*

I baited my message, hoping she'd bite and land on the same page as I was. Her response took less than a second.

SOFIA: *Derek.*

My vision blurred as the possessiveness I was growing far too familiar with coursed through my veins, heating my entire body.

He knew where she worked. He'd sent her flowers with no card. What did this asshole want? What was he up to? What game was he playing? And why?

Hating having so many fucking questions and none of the answers, I quickly typed out another response.

RYAN: *That's what I thought too. We can talk about this later. See you tonight, angel.*
SOFIA: *Okay. See you tonight.*

I spent the rest of the afternoon attempting to calm myself

down, realizing that a freaked-out Ryan was no good for anyone, least of all Sofia and Matson. I tried calling my mom to ask her advice, but when she didn't answer, I opted out of leaving a message. I'd been almost desperate enough to call Grant, but I didn't want to upset him, especially after his health scare at the beach. He never told me how fragile his heart was and I never dared ask, knowing that he'd damn well bite my head off.

Navigating the internet, I did some research on stalking, intimidation, and harassment. I got loads of information, but nothing made me feel like I had any real power over the situation.

I even called the police station and asked what people could do when they felt threatened by someone, but they had little advice to offer aside from suggesting Sofia file a temporary restraining order. She could even file an emergency protective order if she felt her life was in immediate danger. I planned to talk to her about it later to gauge where her head was at, but I didn't want to scare her if she wasn't already.

I hated not knowing how to handle this situation. If Derek wasn't Matson's biological father, I would have considered simply beating the shit out of him and making sure he knew to stay the hell away from Sofia, or he was going to have more problems than the broken nose I'd give him.

But he was Matson's dad, and that added variables to the situation I wasn't sure how to deal with. I was in uncharted territory.

*

DRIVING TO SOFIA'S house, I was torn between being excited at the prospect of being alone with her, and a little sad that Matson wasn't going to be with us. I completely understood her reasoning for sending him away, but I still wanted to hang out with the both of them. Sofia and Matson were a package deal, and the last thing I wanted was to make her feel like I preferred one without the other.

When I knocked on her door, I heard her yell before the door opened and she stood there wearing a big smile. Her cheeks looked flushed, like she'd been running around, and I leaned through the doorway and planted a kiss on one before handing her the bouquet of pink roses.

"These are from me," I said lightly, trying to joke, but she didn't laugh.

She brought the flowers to her nose and inhaled the scent, her eyes closing with the long breath. "They're beautiful and they smell amazing. Thank you." Then she dropped them to her side as she stood on tiptoe to give me a kiss.

God, I loved kissing this woman.

Reaching around her waist, I pulled her tight against me, and all my basic instincts kicked in. I wanted to feel her body, longed to feel her chest pressed against mine.

I touched my lips to hers and quickly deepened the kiss, exploring the inside of her mouth. My tongue teased... touching, tasting, and searching for hers. It was erotic on the most primal level. My senses heightened, I was aware of every single thing about her, like the way her body moved against me before she tried to pull away to gain control. When I wrapped my arms tighter to bring her closer, refusing to let her go, she fell into me, deepening everything—our kiss, our touch, our connection.

As we kissed, her hair fell between our merged faces, wisps of it clinging to my scruff and my wet lips. I loved all of it. Except that I needed to stop, or else I never would.

Finally, I pulled away, practically breathless. "If you don't stop kissing me like that, I'm going to take you to bed and have my way with you before dinner."

"Who says I'd stop you?" she asked, her eyes flashing with desire.

"Don't tempt me, angel," I warned. For a second, I wondered how long it had been since a man had been inside her, but then I pushed the thought away. The last thing I needed was to imagine someone else touching my girl. I'd go stark raving mad with the thought.

"Consider yourself tempted." She turned around, pressing her ass against my jeans before moving away.

"Not so fast," I growled as I reached for her free arm and yanked her back to me.

Her body spun around, facing mine, and I gave in to my instincts. My fingers tangled in her hair, my lips pressing kisses all over her face, her neck, and her shoulders at a fevered pace. She dropped the roses to the floor and reached for my neck, digging her fingernails into my flesh. Our bodies twisted together, our skin fusing as if we couldn't get enough. The fabric between us felt like too much, and I pulled at her top, wanting it gone. I wanted nothing between us.

The sound of someone's stomach growling made us both pull away and laugh.

"Yours or mine?" I asked, not knowing whose stomach it was.

"I have no idea, but let's blame you."

"Blame accepted." I wiped my mouth with the back of my hand.

Her breath continued to come out in short pants as her lips stayed parted. "Maybe we should eat first."

"It does smell amazing." I sniffed at the air as she bent down to retrieve the discarded roses.

"Sorry about dropping them," she said with a wince, and I wrapped my arm around her waist.

"I'm sure they'll survive."

She led me through the entryway and into the small kitchen. I glanced around, taking it in, loving the size and feel of her bungalow. It was perfect.

"Sit," she told me, pointing at one of the barstools at the built-in island. I did as I was told and watched as her dark blue jeans hugged the curves of her ass so spectacularly, a hundred songs should have been written about it.

"I hope you like Mexican. I never even thought to ask." She looked at me, her brow furrowed.

I shook my head, clucking my tongue. "You're always making assumptions about me."

"Crap. What Southern Californian doesn't like Mexican?"

A hearty laugh escaped. "I love it. I was just giving you a hard time."

"Oh, thank God," she said on a relieved breath.

Sofia plated my dish with huge servings of enchiladas, Spanish rice, and salad, then filled her plate with the same but in daintier portions.

"Does it look like I haven't eaten in a week or something?"

"You don't have to eat it all," she said, sounding embarrassed as she pulled up the seat next to mine.

"It looks amazing. Thank you." One bite, and I was in heaven. "This is delicious."

"It's a family recipe my mom forced me to make," she admitted.

I grinned at Sofia while I chewed. "Tell her it was a hit."

"She'll love hearing that." She laughed and rolled her eyes. "Do you know how to cook?"

I practically choked on my rice. "No. All I can make for us are cocktails. Don't get me wrong, they'll be delicious, but we'll still be hungry."

"So, then I'll cook and you'll bartend. Sounds like the perfect compromise to me."

"I accept."

I shoveled more food into my mouth. She'd plated me way too much food, but it was so good, I couldn't stop eating it.

Finally, I couldn't ignore the elephant in the room any longer. "Can we talk about the flowers?"

"From Derek?" she asked.

I nodded. "Did you actually like those?"

She looked away for a second. "I did when I thought they were from you."

Her words were so sincere, my heart softened. "What'd you do with them?"

"Threw them in the trash." She spooned some rice into her mouth.

"Should've brought 'em here so we could set them on fire," I muttered under my breath.

"Next time."

Sofia gave me a teasing glance, trying to make me smile,

but all it did was drive me half crazy. The thought of that douchebag sending her flowers again didn't go over well.

"There won't be a next time," I snapped back.

She reached across the table and touched my arm. "I was only joking."

I sucked in a calming breath. "I know. Sorry. What are your favorite flowers?"

Smiling at my attempt to change the subject, she said, "Why do girls have to have a favorite? Why can't we just love them all?"

"You can. Do you?"

"Kind of. I mean, look at them." She pointed at the pink roses near us with a smile. "They're so beautiful."

"So you love roses the most?"

"I love them, yes. The most? I don't know." Her nose crinkled as she stared at the ceiling, pondering my question seriously. "I've always loved sunflowers. They make me happy whenever I see them. And wildflowers in general." Her eyes practically sparkled as she spoke, and I took mental notes.

"What about them?"

"They're a little messy and wild, kind of all over the place. I like that about them. The fact that they're not perfect."

Her response was unexpected, and I loved it. Sofia seemed to have it all together, so it touched me that something messy and wild drew her, like something forbidden she couldn't risk being as a single mom.

"Back to Derek," I said, and her smile dropped at the mention of his name. "So I guess he knows where you work."

She shrugged, not seeming surprised at all. Not that she hadn't already come to that conclusion on her own, but I expected a more visceral reaction from her. Instead, all I got was a tight-lipped nod.

"Why aren't you surprised?"

"That he knows where I work?"

"Yeah. Weren't you shocked or caught off guard?" I put my fork down and wiped my mouth with a napkin.

"Not really. Derek's family has a lot of money. His dad owns a large law firm in downtown LA that his grandfather started. Every male in the Huntington family has a job with the company. It's expected for them to join it; they don't have a choice. For as long as I've known him, it was set in stone that he'd take over the firm one day for his father. Actually, it was one of the first things he ever said to me before we started dating."

"You guys met in high school, right?" I asked, even though I already knew the answer. It seemed insane to me that someone's life could be that planned out for them. But then I thought about my little brother, Nick, and I understood exactly how that kind of shit happened.

"Yeah. He told me that the firm was his future, and I had to be okay with being second to it. If I had a problem with that, then I needed to walk away and pretend we'd never met."

I gave her a searching look. "And you never thought that was weird?"

"I was fifteen, Ryan. I thought it was ambitious. I'd never met anyone who talked like that about their future, or even knew at that age what they wanted to be when they grew up. He was different, and I was intrigued."

Putting myself in her shoes for a second, I could see how she might have felt that way. It made sense.

There was more to their history, and I found myself wanting to know it all—the way her mind worked, the way she saw and thought about things. Even though the topic wasn't ideal for a first date, or comfortable at all for me, I loved getting to know her better.

"When did you stop seeing him that way?"

She swallowed her last bite of food before answering. "His family was very close, very tight-knit. I assumed it was out of love, the same way that my parents and I are with each other. But I realized toward the end of our relationship that it was out of necessity. The Huntington family had too much dirty laundry on one another to be anything but close. It wasn't that they loved each other at all, as much as it was that they needed everyone to keep their mouths closed. The best way to ensure that was by staying together. It was like the saying 'keep your friends close, but keep your enemies closer'?"

I nodded.

"Well, what do you do when your enemies are related to you? I don't think Derek ever stood a chance at being a decent human being, really, now that I look back at it. He was raised in chaos and controversy, controlled by manipulation. To him, all his crazy behavior is perfectly normal."

Her voice completely calm and unemotional, as if she were reading the menu at Taco Bell, she said, "They have cops on their payroll, Ryan. Judges' phone numbers on speed dial. And they use everything they have at their disposal to get whatever they want. That's why nothing Derek does surprises me. He has the means to find out whatever he's looking for."

"You know this sounds like something we'd read about," I said, "not something in real life, right?"

Actually, I couldn't believe the similarities between Derek's story and what my younger brother went through. I would have bet money that Nick's story was a once-in-a-lifetime type of thing. But hearing this, I realized just how naive I was about what went on in other people's homes.

Sofia huffed out a laugh. "I know. It's crazy, right? I wouldn't have believed it if I hadn't seen it with my own eyes. And when the family found out I was pregnant, that's when it all fell apart. Derek told me his plan was to dump me after graduation, but my pregnancy news sped up his timeline. I'd overheard his grandmother saying that I was too soft and would eventually destroy the company if Derek and I stayed together. She said I wouldn't be able to keep their secrets if my life depended on it. But his grandfather said that having a Mexican in the family might give them more street cred."

"What?" I stared at her, part of me horrified and the other part disbelieving. "You're joking, right?"

"I'm not. Please picture a seventy-year-old saying the words *street cred*."

"I can't laugh about this right now. I'm too pissed off that you had to go through that." I put my elbows on the table and fisted my hair, tempted to pull the strands out one by one in my frustration. "I didn't even know you back then, but hearing it all now really pisses me off. I don't like it."

"I'm not upset anymore about any of that, Ryan. Truly. The only thing I'm concerned about now is why Derek's back after all this time. I still don't know what he wants with Matson."

Leaning back into my barstool, I sat quiet for a moment, letting all this soak in. I hadn't considered before how Derek's family history might be affecting his behavior, but I should have. You would have thought with all the insane bullshit Nick had gone through that I might have considered the possibility of a manipulative family controlling Derek, but I never had.

Reaching for my glass of water, I finished it off.

"Are you okay?"

When I saw Sofia's concerned expression, I felt like an asshole. I should have been consoling her, not the other way around.

"Just processing. And still mad that you ever had to go through that."

"Ryan—"

I held up my hand to stop her. "Look, I know my feelings aren't logical or rational, okay? But I don't like the thought of anyone hurting you. I don't care if it happened twenty years ago or if it happened yesterday. My feelings about it are the same. Okay?"

"Okay," she said softly. "Thanks."

"For what? Being irrational and overreacting?" I smirked at her, totally feeling like the soft little girl my brothers always accused me of being.

"For giving a shit," she said, staring at her plate.

Ha. Some women do like nice guys.

"By the way . . ." I paused, waiting for her to look back up at me, and almost got sidetracked by how pouty and red her bottom lip was from her biting it through our whole conversation.

"Yes?"

"I loved this. The food, the conversation, all of it. Thank you for cooking for me, and for doing this. But I want to be very clear that I plan on courting you."

"Courting me?" She rolled her eyes. "Have you been talking to Grant again?"

"No, I haven't been talking to Grant." I scowled at her. "That old man wouldn't know what to do with you if he had the chance."

"But you do?"

"You know damn well I do. And you deserve to be romanced, okay? I want to court you properly. Like a gentleman. Be a good example for Matson."

I hoped that last bit would melt whatever hardness was left in her heart when it came to me, although I presumed there was little left. I meant every sappy word that came out of my mouth. I believed in treating a woman well, and I wanted to be more than just a good role model for Matson. I wanted to be a good man for Sofia.

Her soft gaze met mine. "Can't really argue with that, now can I?"

"No."

"Didn't think so." She let out a sigh as her cell phone rang. Glancing down, a frown replaced her smile. "It's my mom. Hold that thought."

She answered the call, her brows pinched together as her tone went from carefree to concerned. My gut reaction as I listened to her side of the conversation was that Derek had done something, and my stomach clenched as I waited for her to get off the phone and tell me what was up.

After telling her mom she'd be right there, she ended the call and looked at me. "Matson doesn't feel well."

I pushed out of my chair before gathering the dishes and placing them in the sink. "You'd better go get him."

"You're not upset?"

"Why would I be upset?"

A small line appeared between her brows. "Because we barely even got to have our date. And this is the kind of thing that happens in my life."

This woman was a paradox. She was so secure in some ways, but so insecure when it came to dating, worried about how I'd react to her life.

"What happens? Your son gets sick and you have to take care of him? That's what you're supposed to do, Sofia. And one day, we'll do that together. It won't matter if he's sick, or upset, or just wants to hang with us. One day if something like this comes up, we'll handle it together."

My certainty about us might have seemed fast, but not to me. I'd been dancing around Sofia for a while now, trying to get her to go out with me, so this didn't feel like a first date. My feelings for her had already been established before tonight. And once I found out about her son, it was like a switch flipped inside me, and my desire for her only grew.

She swallowed, drawing my attention to her throat, making me want to nip and suck at the delicate skin there. "You're so certain about everything."

I took a step toward her. "About you, yes."

Leaning down, I reached for her and tilted her head toward me before my lips met hers. Our mouths opened instantly, our tongues finding each other in a desperate dance that was anything but sweet.

We wanted each other, that much was clear. But it would have to wait.

Right now, she had a son who needed her way more than my dick did.

SMASHED
Sofia

KISSING RYAN WAS the equivalent of a sex dream, considering that's all I'd experienced the last few years. His kisses were explosive, erotic, all-consuming, and fulfilling. At least, until you opened your eyes and realized it was all a dream.

Thank God when I opened my eyes after kissing Ryan, he was still there, all six-foot-one of him, ready and willing to do it again if I asked. And I had a feeling I'd be asking often.

As we walked outside to our cars, Ryan dropped my hand. "What the hell?"

Confused, I focused on where he was staring, and my stomach bottomed out at the sight of his smashed front windshield. It looked like someone had taken a baseball bat to it, leaving a hole in the center with a hundred cracked circles spiderwebbing out from it.

I looked up, assuming that something had fallen from the sky or a nearby tree and landed on his car, but there was nothing above it. Glancing in the gutter and along the sidewalk for the culprit, I came up empty as well. "What in the world? How did this happen?"

Ryan gave me a knowing look. "Angel?" he said patiently, willing me to get on the same page as him.

"Oh my God. Do you think Derek did this?"

"It was hit right here." He pointed at the hole in the center of the glass where the crack originated. "With purpose. Unless a brick fell from the sky and landed on my car, I'd say this was absolutely intentional."

"Should we call the police?"

"There's nothing they can do."

"But he damaged your car. He can't just get away with damaging your personal property." I sounded like a lunatic, my words contradicting what my brain already knew. Of course Derek could get away with damaging personal property. I'd just told Ryan earlier that Derek could get away with virtually anything.

"We don't have any proof it was him." Ryan sighed, calmer than he should have been under the circumstances. "The police would need proof in order to do their job. We don't have any."

"I'm so sorry," I choked out, shame and embarrassment tightening my throat. I felt like this was all my fault, even though logically none of it was. I didn't control Derek, but if you took me out of the equation, there would be no Derek in Ryan's life. And if there were no Derek, Ryan's windshield would still be intact.

Ryan took my hand, squeezing it to reassure me. "It's not your fault. You didn't make this happen."

"But I'm still sorry. This never would have happened to your car if it wasn't for me."

"You didn't do this," he said again, this time more forcefully.

"But it's because of me—"

He placed two fingers on my mouth, immediately quieting me. "It's not your fault. And it's just a car. I'll get it fixed. It's not a big deal."

I flung myself into Ryan's chest, wrapping my arms around him, and he held me tight. He rubbed his hands up and down the length of my back, molding his body to mine.

God, he felt good, and I knew he felt the same way. My hips pressed against his hard-on, and I had to force myself to stop before we got too carried away. I needed to go get Matson, and Ryan was one hell of a distraction.

As I pulled away from his warm, hard body, a stark realization hit me. "I guess he knows where I live." I tried to sound not bothered by that truth, but I was concerned. The work information I'd easily accepted, but this was something else entirely, a violation of my privacy that took more effort than a couple of clicks on a keyboard.

The bungalow I rented wasn't in my name, and there was no way of associating me with it on any legal forms that could be found in the courts or online. The only way Derek could have gotten this information was to have me followed.

My stomach churned with the realization that my safe haven was no longer safe.

It was funny the things you became aware of once they were stripped away. Like how I'd never thought twice about my safety here, living here as a single mom—until now. The bungalow had been the perfect home for us, but now it felt exposed. As if its windows and doors had disappeared, and anyone could see in anytime they wanted.

"I think he always has," Ryan said, his voice calmer than I could stand in the moment.

My body trembled as my mind raced, all my thoughts converging on one overriding question. *Are Matson and I safe here, living alone?*

"You think he's always known?" I clutched my stomach, willing it not to empty its contents from dinner onto the sidewalk. "Why would you say that?" I shifted my weight from foot to foot, trying to distract my guts from betraying me.

"Just a hunch." Ryan stepped closer, placing his hand on my cheek to calm me. "But even you said he has the means to find out whatever he wants to, Sofia. He found out where you worked. Of course he'd want to know where you live."

"He went to my mom's first. He thought I still lived there," I said, remembering my mom telling me about that unsettling encounter. "Then he demanded to know where I was."

"I assume she didn't tell him?" His thumb drew patterns on my cheek, an attempt at calming me that clearly wasn't working.

"Of course not." Then the realization dawned on me. Derek would never accept simply not knowing.

"So he found out on his own. That seems to fit his personality. Any idea what he wants? He hasn't told you, right?"

I swallowed around the lump in my throat, speaking numbly without thinking. "Other than him saying that he wanted to see Matson that day at the beach. That was the most we've talked in eight years. He keeps showing up places, but he never says anything."

Ryan stiffened and dropped his hand from my face. In an instant, I realized the mistake I'd made.

"He keeps what? Showing up where?" Ryan took a step back before looking deep into my eyes, questioning me.

"Sofia." He blew out a harsh breath, his jaw ticking. "I knew you were keeping something from me whenever I asked you on the phone, but I thought I was just being paranoid. I thought I was being crazy."

I had no idea that Ryan had been beating himself up over the questions he asked me. The very questions I'd evaded and then lied about, knowing I could only lie to him on the phone because he knew exactly when I wasn't telling the truth in person.

"I'm sorry. He showed up in the parking garage at my office the other night. When I left work, he was just standing there by my car. It's a private garage, Ryan. I don't know how he even got in. He didn't say anything, though. He was just . . . just standing there, watching me."

Ryan reached for my chin and forced me to look up into his eyes, now the darkest blue I'd ever seen them. "You can't keep this stuff from me. Not anymore. I know what we have between us is new, but if you feel anything like I do, then you know that *this*," he waved a finger between us, "isn't going anywhere. *I'm* not going anywhere."

My eyes blurred and I blinked hard. I wanted to believe every single thing that Ryan said to me, but I was scared. Scared that he was too good to be true. Scared that he didn't really know what he was getting himself into. Scared to give him my heart, just for him to discard it when he realized I wasn't worth all the drama.

Ryan's face was stoic, his eyes unblinking. "Whatever I need to do to convince you, I plan on doing it. However long it takes, I'll wait until you believe me. I'm in it for the long haul, angel."

He obviously believed the things he was telling me, but for how long? What if a year from now this was all too much, too hard, too much of a hassle, and he wanted to quit?

"I've never done this before," I told him, needing him to understand. "I've never had someone like you in my life. I don't know how to handle someone wanting to take care of me and Matson. I don't know how to be a teammate. I've never had one before."

"I know," he said softly. "I get it, and I understand. I haven't either. But I need you to promise me something."

"What?"

"That you'll try. Hard. To let me in. And to let me be there for you."

I pulled in a deep breath before nodding slowly in agreement. Ryan seemed to know exactly what I needed, and I wondered how in the world I'd gotten so lucky to have this amazing man in my life . . . wanting *me*.

"I'm going to push at your walls, but I don't want to push you away in the process. I'm going to test you. You're not going to like it, angel. But remember, it goes both ways. I have walls too."

God, he was so sensitive. This tall, gorgeous man with the hard, sexy body was so damn soft underneath. It melted my heart to know him in this way. To know that I was getting the parts of Ryan that no one else saw, aside from his family. The women who came into the bar wanted the tough, flirty exterior he showed them there. They had no idea what was hidden underneath.

"Tell me you understand," Ryan demanded, the need for my acceptance coursing through him like blood. I sensed it, could feel that need in the air between us.

"I understand."

"You'll try to let me in?"

"I'll try."

"Thank you," he said before bringing my hand to his lips and kissing my knuckles.

I stared at him, unable to believe this amazing man was thanking me as if I were the one doing him a favor, like he hadn't just offered to sweep into my world and save it from falling apart. My heart filled with gratitude, I closed my eyes and lowered my head, blinking hard against threatening tears.

"Thank you, Ryan. For caring and for being there. And for wanting to do this with me."

He grasped my shoulders and shook me lightly until I lifted my head, then he stared at me like I was insane for even uttering the words. "Don't thank me for that. Any guy in his right mind would do the same," he said, then stopped short. "No, wait. Scratch that. No other guy on earth would do this for you, Sofia. Just me. Only me. I'm the only one for you."

I choked out a laugh, loving when he wasn't entirely sure of himself and needed confirmation. "Only you," I repeated, glad when the tension drained from his features.

"I know you need to go, but one last thing." He looked away and shifted his weight, making we wonder what could possibly come next.

"What is it?"

Ryan's voice tightened. "I'd be lying if I didn't tell you that I was a little worried about your safety. Derek could be watching us right now. He could show up wherever you are. He could scare you. Scare Matson."

I shivered as I glanced around the neighborhood, horrified at the possibility that Derek might be watching us here... now. My throat felt like it might close up entirely and rob me of air.

Ryan grasped my chin again, forcing me to focus. "I know this sounds possessive, and I'd never in a million years ask you this if we weren't in this situation right now, but will you please download that phone tracking app and let me have access to it?"

My heart beat out a conflicting rhythm. Track my cell phone? "Why?"

"My brothers and I all have the app on our phones, and we have access to each other's. I can also see Jess and Claudia's phones in an emergency if I need to. It's just a precaution in case something happens, but I don't trust Derek, and I don't put anything past him. He showed up at your work and he came here tonight. What's next? If something happens to you and I don't know how to find you, I'll go out of my fucking mind."

Ryan was so honest and vulnerable, my heart ached for him a little. His suggestion came from a good-hearted place, that much I knew. He didn't come off like some sort of jealous boyfriend.

How had I gone from feeling free and happy to feeling like I lived in a prison and under constant watch? I hated that Derek had this kind of impact on my life, but Ryan was right. Derek couldn't be trusted, and neither of us knew what he was capable of or what he wanted. And his actions tonight really unnerved me.

When I didn't answer right away, Ryan said, "I promise

I'll only use it if I think you're in trouble. I know it sounds over the top, but I feel like I need to have some kind of control. I don't know why the app makes me feel like I'm protecting you somehow, but it does."

"Okay."

"Okay?" His tone lightened instantly. "I'll give you access to mine too."

"All right. But I really need to go get Matson."

Ryan's lips met mine. "Go get your boy, and text me when you get home. Thanks again for dinner." He turned and opened his car door, and when he was in the driver's seat, his image all but disappeared behind the cracked glass.

"Can you even see?" I called out, and he gave me a thumbs-up.

I got into my own car, anxious to get my son and torn about whether to tell my parents everything. On the quick drive over, I decided that I wouldn't tell them yet. The fewer people who worried about me, the less guilty I'd feel.

When I imagined telling my mom, I could see exactly how she'd react. She'd go out of her mind with worry, constantly calling me, checking in nonstop, stopping by the house unannounced, demanding that I spend more time at her house than usual.

It might sound stupid, but I didn't want to live my life like that, under the parental microscope again like a teenager, and feeling like I had no say. I also didn't want to give Derek that kind of control over me, the power to change my life and how I lived it, so I decided to keep his actions to myself.

Now that Ryan was in the picture, I prayed that things wouldn't get out of hand.

I should have known that Ryan would be the match that started the fire in this scenario instead of the water that extinguished it. I should have known that adding him to the mix was like slipping a bullet into an otherwise empty chamber.

I should have known.

But I didn't.

UNWANTED GUEST
Sofia

THE NEXT COUPLE of weeks were quiet on the Derek front. When I didn't see him again for a while, my nerves settled down, even though both my gut instincts and Ryan warned me otherwise. "Don't get too comfortable," he kept saying, as if he knew something I didn't.

Unfortunately, Ryan and I hadn't been able to see each other due to my request that we hold off for a while, and our conflicting work schedules didn't help. Before I knew it, the self-imposed break I'd only intended to last a few days had somehow stretched to thirteen.

Ryan respected my wishes, only asking me to lunch four times during the first week. It didn't take long before he realized that I wasn't trying to push him away, I was just genuinely worried about my son.

Matson was having issues with his schoolwork, especially math. He hadn't been turning in his homework, and he'd failed his last two tests. I kept trying to help him with his homework, but I was completely lost. The new math my son was being taught at school wasn't at all like the math I'd learned, and I ended up confusing him even more rather than helping him.

When he broke out into tears of frustration, I FaceTimed with Sarin, who was a self-proclaimed math wizard. She ended up helping him understand the concepts in less time than I'd taken all week.

I assumed that Matson was affected negatively by my blossoming relationship with Ryan, so I pulled back, telling him that I couldn't see him again until I had Matson on track again. Being in a relationship was new to me, and I strived for balance, trying to be sure Matson wasn't being left out or neglected.

But no matter what I did, I felt like a crappy mom. I tried to give my son my undivided attention, but pushing a man like Ryan Fisher out of your head proved to be difficult. I daydreamed about him when I should have been working. I fantasized about his naked body when I should have been reading bedtime stories. Ryan burrowed his way into my heart before I even realized it was happening.

And if I was being honest with myself, I think it started long before I'd ever agreed to go on a date with him. I could almost pinpoint the exact moment in the hospital when my facade had started to crack. I lied to myself back then about my interest in Ryan, but I wasn't lying to myself anymore.

Even Matson noticed my change of heart, saying I had a silly look on my face whenever Ryan called or texted. He would point and giggle and tell me I was *in looooove* the way only kids could say it, making me feel like I was ten years old and on the playground again. I knew the dopey smile I wore, could feel it spread across my face, but I couldn't stop it. No matter how hard I tried, it wouldn't go away. So I accepted the teasing from my kid and reminded him that one day he'd like a girl and would get the same look on his face.

"Gross." Matson did an exaggerated full-body shudder. "I'll only ever like you, Mama," he said, going back to his homework. I laughed.

During those thirteen days, Ryan and I talked on the phone every night, and our relationship grew in ways I hadn't expected. When you removed the physical aspects and depended solely on oral and written communication, things seemed to happen on a completely different level.

It wasn't something that I was used to, not that I was used to much of anything in the relationship department, to be honest, but this was different. We compared the last two weeks to what we assumed being in a long-distance relationship must be like, never seeing each other in person and only communicating through devices.

I hated to admit that I enjoyed it, because I really liked looking at Ryan, but there was something special about getting to know each other better in this way. Emotions took over and everything else fell to the wayside, because that was the only place for it to go. We talked about our days, our families, our hopes, our pasts, and he ended each call asking when he could see me again. And I had given him the same answer of *I don't know* each time until tonight.

"I was thinking this weekend might work. But Matson would have to be with us," I said, knowing full well Ryan wouldn't object. I'd talked to Matson earlier about spending time with Ryan, and he had pumped his fist in the air like he'd won some kind of award.

"Really? This weekend? Thank God, angel. I was about to go insane if you kept me from you any longer."

"Did you hear me about Matson coming along?" I asked.

"Of course I heard you. I'm excited. That just makes it better."

Makes it better, huh? "In what way?"

"In the serious *you're going to fall in love with me* kind of way."

He might have said it in a teasing voice, but there was truth hiding there. Ryan never kept his feelings or intentions a secret, least of all from me. He was so committed, so certain, so willing to give this relationship his all, that he erased nearly all my lingering doubts. But some walls refused to crumble to dust overnight.

"So, Saturday afternoon then?" I asked, giving him a formal invitation into my life and Matson's.

Ryan cleared his throat. "I was thinking Saturday morning."

Disappointment coursed through me, although I wasn't exactly sure why. "The morning instead? Okay," I said, taking whatever I could get. As much as I adored our phone calls and video chats, I missed seeing Ryan in person, and I was excited about him and Matson spending time together, even if I was a little nervous too.

"Not instead. As well. Morning and afternoon, until I have to leave for work. If that's okay with you, and Matson doesn't want to kick me in the shins by then." Ryan laughed, and I smiled as my disappointment was replaced with elation and a willing heart.

"Yes," I said quickly, and we laughed together, giddy with anticipation.

*

SATURDAY TOOK AN eternity to arrive. My mom failed at calming me down, reminding me how good-looking Ryan was, and how sweet and rare guys like him were.

"You're not helping," I whined over the phone.

"I know. Sorry. Have fun, *mija*. You deserve this. Matson does too. Call me after he leaves and tell me everything," she said, her tone excited before she cleared her throat. "If you want, I mean. You don't have to."

"I will, Mom," I promised. Of course she'd be the first person I'd want to call and share my day with.

The doorbell rang, and I hung up quickly as Matson bounded down the hall.

"I'll get it!" he shouted, and before I could stop him, he had the door open and was looking up at the man who made my heart skip a beat just from his presence.

Ryan looked gorgeous, dressed in jeans and a T-shirt, the fabric stretched across his chest and shoulders. The backward baseball cap on his head was perfect. No one else on earth had ever looked as good to me as he did right now.

"Hey, buddy. Remember me?" Ryan crouched down to his eye level, and Matson put his fist out. Ryan bumped his knuckles, and my heart warmed at their exchange.

"I remember. Want to see my toys?" Matson said before pulling Ryan by the hand through the door.

Ryan's blue eyes met mine from across the room. "Can I say hi to your mom first?" he asked politely before waiting for Matson's response.

"She's in the kitchen. I'll show you where it is."

I ducked back behind the wall and pretended to wash a dish as Matson led Ryan into the kitchen.

"Mama, Ryan's here."

I turned around and smiled, but hesitated. *Should I give Ryan a hug?*

It was such a simple gesture, but Matson had never seen me be affectionate with anyone other than him or my dad. Before I could react, though, Ryan made the choice for me, pulling me into his arms and hugging me tight. When he let go, Matson stood there staring at us.

Ryan released me and looked at my son. "Hope that was okay with you, buddy. I guess I should have asked."

Matson shrugged. "Nah, I think she liked it. It's fine with me."

I covered my mouth with my hand, pursing my lips to stop the laughter from bubbling out, but Matson didn't notice.

"Can I show you my room now?"

"Sure." Ryan gave me a wink and let Matson lead him away. That man was going to be the death of me.

When they disappeared, I finished getting ready, packing a few snacks and drinks in case we were gone longer than expected. The mom in me never left the house unprepared.

"Can we go to the park now?" Matson ran back into the kitchen, and I looked up to see Ryan following close behind him.

"I guess we're done playing," he said with a shrug.

Matson turned around to look at Ryan. "We're not done. I just want to go outside for a little while. Get some fresh air. Mama says fresh air is good for growing boys. Don't you like fresh air, Ryan? We can play in my room later."

"I love fresh air, and your mom's right. We should definitely go to the park. Is it the same one as before?" Ryan asked, and I nodded.

"It's his favorite."

"Monkey bars on the beach. What's not to love?"

"You're really good with him," I told Ryan, wanting him to know his efforts didn't go unnoticed, and that I appreciated them.

"He makes it easy. He's a great kid, Sofia," Ryan said with a grin, and I melted more inside.

As we walked outside, Matson's face lit up at the sight of Ryan's car.

"I'll drive," Ryan said, and the second I went to protest, Matson jumped in.

"Yes! Your car is awesome, Ryan."

"Thanks."

"Can I sit in front?" Matson asked, and Ryan's gaze immediately met mine.

Shaking my head, I told Matson, "No, you have to sit in the back of this car too. You know the rules."

Matson's face fell, and he muttered, "Okay."

"Are you sure you want to drive?" I asked, and Ryan looked at me like I had grown two heads.

"Why wouldn't I? Get in the car, woman," he said, and Matson copied him.

"Yeah, Mama. Get in the car, woman!"

During the drive to the park, Matson kept talking about Ryan's car, pointing out all the features in the backseat, from the white stitching in the leather seats to the control panel he had only for his seat. Ryan nudged me and I glanced at him, smiling, but my smile faded as I noted his somber expression and the nod of his head.

I looked in my side mirror and noted the truck behind us following a little too closely. The black truck had tinted windows, and even though we couldn't see the driver clearly, I knew we both jumped to the same conclusion—that it was Derek following us.

"How long?" I asked, knowing Ryan would pick up on my meaning without my having to explain further. The last thing I wanted was to alert Matson that anything could be wrong.

"Since we left your house," Ryan said in a low voice.

"Since we left?"

He nodded. "Do you know what he drives?"

"I have no idea."

"What are you guys looking at?" Matson tried to crane his neck, but thankfully he was too little to see over the backseat and out the rear window.

Ryan and I exchanged glances.

"Just a funny guy riding a bike," I said lightly, completely lying.

Matson laughed, believing me without question. "Was he naked like that other guy?" His head cocked to the side and his blue eyes sparkled as he referred to the afternoon on Venice Beach when we'd seen a guy streaking while the cops chased him.

"Almost," I lied again.

Matson couldn't contain his laughter, which made me laugh too.

Before I knew it, the car was filled with uncontrolled giggling, Ryan included. I'd almost forgotten we were being followed until Ryan pulled his car into the paid parking lot and craned his neck to watch the truck continue down the road past us.

"Maybe we're just being paranoid? I haven't heard from him since the windshield night."

"It was him," Ryan said firmly.

"How do you know?"

His jaw tightened. "I just do."

I pulled Matson's backpack filled with beach toys from the trunk and helped him out of Ryan's car. The three of us walked to the playground before Matson said he wanted to build a sandcastle first.

"Have you ever caught sand crabs?" Ryan asked.

Matson's face lit up. "No. Do they hurt? Are they big? Can we catch them? Can we, Mama?" He looked at me, and I nodded.

"Come on. I'll show you how to find them." Ryan reached for his hand, and they walked toward the water's edge.

I snapped a couple of pictures on my phone as I followed behind, my heart nearly bursting at the sweet sight.

"Okay, first we wait for the wave to come in," he said, still holding Matson's hand. "And as soon as the wave goes out, we look for little holes in the sand."

"Holes?" Matson squinted up at him.

"Like that. See?" Ryan pointed at the wet sand where a tiny hole appeared. "It's an air bubble, and it means they're in there. Hurry. We have to dig before the wave comes back."

Ryan fell to his knees and thrust both hands into the wet sand. Matson followed suit, having no idea what he was looking for until Ryan laughed.

"I have one!"

Pulling his hands out of the small hole he'd dug, Ryan showed Matson a fistful of wet sand before shaking it away. The tiny gray sand crab appeared and quickly tried to bury itself back into the sand, but found only his hand instead. The crab kept trying to burrow with all its might, but it was no use.

Matson stared at Ryan's open palm. "Does it hurt?"

"No, it tickles."

When Ryan put the tiny crab in Matson's hand, he giggled before quickly dropping it and watching it disappear into the mud.

"I dropped him."

"It's okay, there's more." Ryan's eyes met mine, and I smiled at him. He was so natural with my son, it was like he'd always been in our lives.

"Let's build a castle first," Matson exclaimed before running away from the water and toward the playground.

I stared at Ryan until he noticed and stopped walking.

"What?" he asked with a smirk.

"It's just . . ." I shook my head. "You're so much more than I expected."

"You are too." He leaned down and planted a quick kiss on my cheek.

"Ryan, Mama, come on!" Matson shouted as he plopped down in the sand.

I could tell that Ryan was on edge even as he pretended to be calm. Every so often, he'd stop his work on the sandcastle we were building with Matson and scan all around us.

"Shoot," Matson said as our third attempt collapsed.

"The sand's too dry. We need more wet sand," Ryan said

with a smile, and my heart warmed at their interaction.

"I'll get it!" Matson jumped up, bucket in hand, and ran toward the water.

I watched him closely, unwilling to tear my gaze from him until he was back with us, carrying the bucket with both hands.

Ryan peeked inside. "That looks perfect."

"It's so heavy," Matson said before dropping it to the sand with a thud.

As we poured, shaped, and patted the walls, I marveled that this was my life. I never realized how alone I'd been until Ryan showed up. I'd convinced myself that Matson and I were perfectly fine, didn't need anyone, and now I sat in the sand questioning every lie I'd told myself.

Ryan jumped up and wiped his hands on his jeans, spraying sand everywhere. When I shot him a questioning look, he nodded toward the street. Derek was standing across the street, leaning against the very truck that had been following us earlier.

So it had been him.

"Hey, bud, why don't you go play on the playground while your mom and I go talk to someone real quick."

Matson stopped digging and looked up at Ryan. "What about the castle?"

"We'll finish it after."

Matson seemed to consider Ryan's offer, but I could tell he wasn't convinced. "What if someone knocks it down?"

"Then we'll build a new one. A better one." Ryan smiled and extended his hand. Matson reached for it, and Ryan helped him up. "Your mom and I will be right over there." He pointed toward the street.

"Don't leave the playground, Matson. And make sure that I can see you at all times. If you can't see me . . ." I paused, waiting for him to finish our safety motto.

"Then I can't see you. I know, Mama." He ran over to the monkey bars and started climbing.

As Ryan and I turned toward Derek, I thought he might get in his truck and leave. Maybe he only wanted us to see him watching, I hoped.

But he did the exact opposite. Derek stalked across the street toward us, walking through oncoming traffic without even looking. Horns honked, brakes squealed, but he didn't stop.

I wanted to get closer to Derek before he reached us, needing to keep space between him and Matson, but Derek's pace was quicker than ours, his steps hurried. He reached us first.

"Isn't this cute? You two playing house now? With my son." He looked right at Matson, who was fortunately not paying attention.

"What do you want, Derek?" I demanded, and Ryan pulled me to his side, his grip tight on my waist as he asked Derek, "Why are you here?"

Derek's eyes narrowed. "Why are *you* here, Ryan? If anyone doesn't belong in this picture, it's you."

My eyes flew open wide. "No, Derek. You don't belong here."

"I'm his dad. Of course I belong here."

"Then where have you been the last eight years?" I fired back, stepping away from Ryan's protective hold and into Derek's personal space. "You might be his biological father, but you're not his dad."

"You think I'm going to let this kind of person raise my son? A fucking bartender?" He spat out the last word like it was laced with poison.

"I actually own the bar," Ryan said calmly, sounding almost bored, and his reluctance to engage pushed Derek's buttons more.

"You think I don't know that?" Derek rolled his eyes. "You think I don't know every single thing about your brothers and their girlfriends?"

I gasped, wishing it had been internal instead of out loud. Derek always enjoyed getting a reaction out of me.

"Your family business is a bar," Derek said with a snarl. "It's a trashy, piece-of-shit occupation that no sane person would stay in for any length of time."

"As opposed to your family business? In what universe does defending the guiltiest scumbags of the world, who only get off because they have more money than God, make you a better person than me?"

Derek laughed. "In every universe. Especially this one. Ask anyone which job they think is the more respectable one—lawyer or bartender. Lawyer wins ten times out of ten, and you know it. People look up to me. They look down on you."

Ryan shook his head. "I bring joy to people's lives, Derek. You bring pain. I help people, but you hurt them. I go to sleep with a clear conscience. I can't imagine you doing the same."

"Matson's not yours!" Derek yelled, his tone and demeanor shifting quicker than the weather.

"Lower your voice!" I pleaded.

"Why?" Derek's lip curled and he turned to yell toward

the playground. "Hey, Matson! Do you know who I am, son?"

Matson's head turned toward us, his eyes wide and confused.

Ryan stepped closer to Derek. "Don't call him son."

Thank God he could get the words out before I could. I was too busy watching in horror as Matson ran in our direction.

Before I could stop him, Matson was at my side, staring at Derek. "Did you call my name?"

"Do you know who I am?"

Derek's tone sounded menacing instead of kind, and Matson reacted by edging behind Ryan and wrapping his arms around Ryan's waist for protection. Ryan reached back and patted Matson's shoulder, reassuring my son that he would handle things and it would all be okay.

"I think you should leave," Ryan said, never taking his eyes from Derek's infuriated gaze.

"I'll be back." Derek pointed at me before trying to make eye contact with Matson, who had squeezed his eyes shut and buried his face into Ryan's back. "See you later, son," he said before stalking away.

I knelt next to Matson and tried to pull his arms from Ryan's waist, but they wouldn't budge.

"Is he gone?" Matson asked, holding on even tighter.

"He's gone," I said as calmly as I could, even though I was unraveling on the inside.

"Who was that man, Mama?" Matson's eyes met mine, and I didn't know what to tell him.

Ryan maneuvered his body so that Matson released his grip and he could kneel down with us. "He's someone your mom used to know. A long time ago," he said slowly, and I was so grateful in that moment for the help.

"Like when you were in third grade like me?" Matson's head tilted back as he looked up at me.

"Not that little, but still littler than now."

"Oh," he said as if it all made sense. "I'm hungry."

"Me too." Ryan grinned. "Pizza or In-N-Out?"

"Pizza!" Matson shouted, and the somber mood instantly shifted.

"I know the perfect place," Ryan said, and reached for Matson's hand.

As we all walked to the car, I looked at Ryan and mouthed *thank you* as I fought back tears.

How could I have ever thought that Ryan would be a bad role model for my son? How could I have ever thought that he wouldn't be good enough for us?

THREATS AND PROMISES
Ryan

ASIDE FROM THE whole Derek fiasco, the day spent with Sofia and Matson was damn near perfect. Being with the two of them was easy and effortless. The way they communicated with each other and made decisions was as if they had their own language. Yet I found myself merging into their little circle, my presence not disruptive, but welcome.

Matson was such a great kid. Even though he adored his mom, it was obvious he missed having a male presence in his life. He clung to me, wanting my attention, and asked me a million questions about my car and work.

It felt so natural being with them that when I left their house to go to work, I told them both I'd see them later, even though I wouldn't. It had been so natural to say, it came out of my mouth before I realized it.

I was still on a high when I walked into Sam's to find Jess and Claudia sitting side by side at the bar, both impatiently tapping their nails against it.

"Finally," Jess said when she caught sight of me.

Glancing at the time on my phone, I said, "I'm not late."

Jess smiled. "I know, but I've been waiting for you to make me a drink since I got here," she said, bouncing in her seat.

Pointing my chin toward Nick, I asked, "Why didn't you have your boyfriend make you one?"

She leaned her elbows on the bar, propping her chin on her laced fingers before batting her eyelashes at me. "Because I want something new."

Damn, I adored this girl. In my mind, she was already family. I never knew I wanted a little sister before Nick brought Jess home.

"Okay then. Something new, it is. Give me a minute to get situated, and then I'll fix you right up."

I placed my cell phone and keys in a drawer and locked it, then headed into the office to grab a few bottles we were running low on. Noticing a few more things we should order, I stopped to make a list for Frank, and placed the note on his keyboard so he'd see it.

Fifteen minutes stretched to thirty, and I forced myself to step out of the office and back into the bar.

I reached for a few mixers and grinned at the girls. "Sorry that took so long. All right, Jess, something new. What about you, Claudia?"

"Sure. It's been months since I tried anything new."

"Months? That's embarrassing. Where's the support?" I teased before getting to work creating something that wasn't on the menu and I had only experimented with recently.

"How's Sofia?" Claudia asked while I measured and poured.

"When do we get to meet her?" Jess added.

Claudia's eyes sparkled. "And her son."

When I frowned, their hopeful expressions faded. "It's hard for her to come in here, you know? But I really do want you to meet her, so hopefully soon. Maybe we'll have to plan something away from the bar."

Jess laughed. "Well, obviously. She can't bring her son here."

"We can have everyone over to our place." Claudia glanced at Frank, and he smiled at her suggestion before agreeing.

"I'll see what I can do." I handed each of the girls a cocktail fashioned from tequila, falernum, and aperitivo, the glasses garnished with lime.

I crossed my arms over my chest, annoyed when they sniffed at their glasses as if they didn't trust me. Seriously? Ten minutes ago they were begging me to make them something new.

Wanting them to just try it already, I huffed out a sigh. "Just drink it. You'll like it."

They sipped carefully, and then Claudia smiled at me, her eyes wide. "This is so good." She glanced at Jess and took another sip.

Jess nodded. "I don't normally like tequila, but this is so refreshing." She downed the entire drink and pushed her empty glass at me. "I'll have another."

I laughed and grabbed Nick by the shoulder. "Better watch her tonight. She's a lush."

"Wait," Jess said, holding up a hand. "What are you naming it? This has to be on the menu."

I racked my brain for only a second. "Committed," I said without another thought, and both girls grinned the way only females could as they read between the lines.

"I like it," Claudia said. "It should come with a ring pop."

The girls giggled, but I pretended I didn't hear them as I

made them another round of drinks, then wrote down the recipe so my brothers could make them on their own.

"I need to talk to you."

A loud male voice raised above the conversations along the bar, and I looked up to find myself staring into eyes that looked so much like Matson's, the sight actually made my heart hurt.

Both Nick and Frank's heads swiveled at the angry tone, and without a word, they dropped what they were doing and moved to stand behind me, obviously presenting a united front.

"Why are you here?" I pretended to sound bored as Derek's gaze bounced between me and my brothers.

"You again?" Frank's mouth tightened into a straight line. "Didn't think you had that much fun last time."

"I need to talk to you, Fisher," Derek demanded. "Now."

I wanted to ask him who the hell he thought he was, but knew there would be no point. The man was a loose cannon, and ignoring him wasn't going to work.

The girls looked at him, both assessing the situation, but thankfully stayed quiet. I didn't want them involved or saying anything that might set him off.

"First of all, calm down. You don't tell me what to do or when to do it. Understand?" I folded my arms over my chest and could sense Nick and Frank tensing up behind me, wary of the situation escalating.

Derek laughed as he looked between us. "You're all looks and no brains, aren't you? Figures. We need to talk, and it can't wait." Without another word, he turned around and walked out the front door, obviously expecting me to follow him.

"Want me to come with you," Frank asked, and I shook my head. "He seems a little crazy, man."

I agreed, but I wasn't concerned. I was more annoyed than anything.

"I'll be right back." I tossed down my notebook and headed toward that asshole outside. Part of me hated that he'd made a demand, and it looked like I was following orders like an obedient dog.

I pushed the door open, on guard for any sneak attack that might come my way. But Derek leaned against the wall of the bar, his foot propped up like a cowboy in an old Western movie. All he needed was a Stetson and a toothpick to complete the picture.

"Wasn't sure you'd listen," he said without looking my way.

"What is it this time?" I stood in front of him, hoping to get this over with sooner rather than later.

"I want you to back off."

"Back off?" I repeated his words as if I had no idea what he was saying.

He pushed away from the wall and squared his body with mine, even though I towered over him. "Yeah, back off. Go away. Leave Sofia and Matson alone."

"What are you talking about? Why would I do that?" Derek sounded insane, making a demand like my relationship with them was something he had a say in.

"I need you out of the picture." He spoke with confidence as if it would change everything, when in fact it changed nothing.

"Why?" I asked, hoping for a little clarity into his otherwise fucked-up mind. What did he want, and why couldn't he let it go?

"To get what I want. I need you out of the picture in order to get it. Think you can do that, pretty boy?" His lips formed a snarl I wanted to smack right off his smug face.

Struggling to stay calm, I forced myself to shrug. "Probably not."

"You're not listening to me, Ryan." He sounded like I was an annoying tick he couldn't get off his back. "Do you want me to stop showing up and scaring Sofia?"

My blood instantly boiled inside my veins, and my self-control slipped a notch. I hated hearing him say her name, would banish it from his vocabulary forever if I could.

"Yes," I ground out.

"Then disappear."

He said the words slowly, as if he wasn't asking me to do something as impossible as stopping the sun from shining in the sky. Disappearing from Sofia's life now that I was a part of it wasn't an option. I wouldn't leave her side, especially not while this psycho was running around threatening her.

"No."

"No?" He let out a disbelieving grunt.

"You heard me."

"You really are as stupid as you look." He pushed past me, his shoulder deliberately clipping me as he passed. "Watch your back, Ryan. And, remember, you did this to yourself."

"Fuck off." I flipped him the bird. Yeah, it was immature, I should have thought of something more intelligent to say, but it was all I had at the moment.

Anger fueled me as Derek got into a different car than he had been driving earlier today, and sped off into traffic without looking, almost causing an accident.

I stayed outside a few minutes longer, willing myself to calm down before I headed back in.

Our bouncer hadn't arrived for his shift yet, so no one had been nearby to hear Derek's threats. Derek knew exactly what he was doing, making sure there were no witnesses, and that only aggravated me more.

The familiar sounds of a busy bar hit me as soon as I walked back inside. Frank and Nick's eyes immediately met mine, their curious expressions begging me to fill them in on everything that had happened so far.

"What was that?" Frank asked as soon as I rounded the bar.

I joined the girls and waved my brothers over so the five of us could form a tight circle at the end of the bar. I didn't have secrets from my brothers, and they would tell their girlfriends anyway, so I figured everyone might as well hear my side of the story from me.

"He told me to stay away from Sofia."

Nick closed our circle, his jaw tight. "We should call the cops, right? At least file some kind of report? This is the second time he's come in here threatening you."

"I've already talked to them. They said there's nothing they can do unless I want to file a restraining order. Technically, he's done nothing wrong that I can prove."

"But you have witnesses," Jess said.

Nick nodded. "You should get the restraining order."

"I think it would only push him over the edge," I said.

"He seems unbalanced."

Claudia gave me a confused look. "Why does he want you to stay away from her? Is he still in love with her?"

"I don't know why. He said it was to get something he wanted."

"What could he possibly want?" Nick asked, looking as perplexed as everyone else.

"I'm going to sound like a dick," Frank said, finally weighing in, "but I have to ask you."

Everyone turned their heads to stare at him, waiting to hear his question.

"What?" I asked.

"Is she worth it?"

"Yes," I said without a millisecond of hesitation.

Frank cocked an eyebrow. "You're sure?"

When he asked again, I couldn't help but get defensive at the insinuation that Sofia was anything less than worthy. This drama wasn't her fault. She hadn't caused it, started it, or wanted it. I couldn't blame her for something she had no control over. And I didn't.

"I'm sure," I said again.

Nick reached up to squeeze my shoulder. "He just doesn't want you to get caught up in this kind of craziness for no reason. We both know how badly you want to fall in love," he added, which told me they'd already talked about this when I wasn't around.

"It's not about falling in love. I wouldn't do this with anyone else. I wouldn't go anywhere near a situation like this if it wasn't for Sofia."

"I'm just looking out for you," Frank said.

I nodded, understanding his worry, but this was my life.

I pointed at Frank. "You knew right away when it came to Claudia. And you," I pointed at Nick, "you knew when it came to Jess. Why can't I know when it comes to Sofia?"

"You can," Nick said.

"Well, I do."

Jess held up a hand to interrupt. "It's always intrigued me that we accept without question when someone says that they knew right away that a person was wrong for them. You know what I mean?"

Although I struggled to keep up, Claudia apparently was following along easily. "Like if I went on a date and said he wasn't the one, you'd agree and tell me the right guy was still out there?"

Jess nodded. "Exactly. But why don't we accept it when someone says they've found the right one? Why aren't we allowed to know they're the one for us, the way we're allowed to know that they're not?" Her green eyes searched each of our faces. "Am I making any sense? It makes sense in my head."

"It makes perfect sense to me. I get what you're saying," Claudia said to reassure her, and Jess seemed to relax with relief.

Nick pulled her close. "I get it, babe."

As my younger brother exchanged a loving look with his girlfriend, I realized that the longing I used to feel was gone. I didn't find myself envying what my brothers had the way I used to. I had something of my own that fulfilled me. Something good. Something I would damn sure fight for, and I'd do just that if it came down to it.

"I need to make a quick call. I'll be right back." I unlocked the drawer and pulled my cell phone out before walking into the office and closing the door behind me. Pulling up Sofia's contact, I dialed and waited for her to answer.

"Hey. Everything okay?" she asked, knowing that I normally never called her this early while I was at work.

"Yeah, but can I stop by tonight after I get off? I know it'll be late, but it's important." I tried to sound calm, not wanting to worry her.

"Of course," she said, and I could tell she was smiling. "Just call me when you're on your way so I can get up."

"Perfect. See you later, angel." I smiled too before pressing END and getting back to work.

*

AROUND THREE IN the morning, I called Sofia and let her know I was on my way. It was a shit thing to do, but I didn't want to keep Derek's visit from her any longer, and I wanted to tell her in person.

And seeing her answer the door wearing only a T-shirt that barely covered her ass was an added bonus.

"If it isn't Mister Good-bye Pants." She propped the door open and gave me a kiss on the cheek.

"The pants stayed on tonight, sweetheart. Unlike yours." I pointed at her bare legs, and she tugged at the hem of her shirt, trying to make it longer. "Don't do that. I like it just the way it is." I reached for it and started to tug it up, but she swatted my hand away.

"Stop it. What about the shirt? Did it stay on?" Her eyebrows raised in question, and I knew what answer she expected.

"It did," I said, remembering how I'd hidden in the office during last call to avoid the whole shirt thing. I decided that I'd quietly disappear during last call from here on out until people stopped asking for it. Either that, or one of our other bartenders could take his shirt off if they insisted on continuing the tradition, but I was officially done being a plaything for strangers.

"Really? You didn't take it off?"

"Nope, I didn't."

"I'm impressed." Sofia gave me a proud smile as she went into the kitchen and poured a glass of water.

"I'm impressive."

"So I've heard. Do you want a glass?" She held up her water, and I nodded.

"That would be great, thanks." I didn't move to sit on the couch, even though I should have. What I wanted was to lie in bed and hold her in my arms while I told her about Derek.

She handed me a glass of water. "So, what happened tonight?"

"Can we go to your room?" I knew I was being a bit forward, but hoped she wouldn't mind.

Sofia's eyes narrowed. "Are you trying to seduce me, Ryan Fisher?"

"Not yet," I teased, and she led me down the hallway by my hand, the curve of her ass taunting me the entire way there.

As we passed Matson's room, I couldn't help but stop and peek in on him. A small nightlight lit up his ceiling with stars, and I found myself grinning at how blissfully unaware he was.

"Come on." She pulled my hand and led me through her

doorway. A light was already on in her room, and I stared at her queen-sized bed.

"I need to lay down, but don't let me fall asleep," I warned, knowing that if her bed was half as comfortable as it looked, I might not get two words out before I started snoring and she wanted to plot my murder.

Just kidding. I didn't snore.

Sofia tilted her head, studying me. "I think you're strong enough to stay awake and tell me why you had to come over."

"Won't we wake him up if we talk?"

"No," she said with a laugh. "He sleeps through everything. I could vacuum next to his head and he wouldn't move an inch."

"Lucky kid." Actually, I was a little envious of that. I was a light sleeper, so damn near every sound woke me up.

I hopped onto her bed and propped two pillows behind my back, then leaned against them. Patting the spot next to me, I signaled for Sofia to sit beside me, where I could touch her. She did as I asked, snuggling into me as I played with her soft hair.

"Derek stopped by the bar," I said, barely having a moment to enjoy her closeness before she stiffened and pulled away, sitting up to face me, her legs crossed Indian-style.

"What? What did he want?"

"He wants me to keep my distance."

"From me or from Matson?" Her brows drew together, confusion written all over her face.

I sighed. "I got the impression he meant both of you."

Sofia stared at me with a stunned expression. "Why is he doing this?"

"He said he wanted something. And he needed me out of the picture in order to get it," I told her, hating the way the news was upsetting her.

"Do you think he wants Matson? Like sole custody or something?"

Her eyes welled up with tears, and I pulled her against me and held her close.

"I don't think so. And no judge in their right mind would give him that. He's been absent for the last eight years," I said, trying to get her to look at it logically, but her emotions took over.

"But his family knows judges. They know people, important people. If he wants to take Matson from me, Ryan, I bet he could do it," she cried out, getting more upset by the second.

I felt horrible for putting this on her. My coming over tonight was only to fill her in, not to upset her. "Sofia, we don't know what he wants. Let's not jump to any conclusions, okay?"

I pulled her close again, tucking her under my arm, and rubbed soothing circles on her skin. She wrapped an arm around me and held tight, and after a few moments, her panicked breathing slowed.

"Okay," she said, her words muffled against my chest. "You're right. So, what did you tell him?"

"Huh?"

"When he told you to keep your distance. What did you say?" She pulled out of my grip again so she could look at me. It was funny how she used to avoid making eye contact, but right now it was all she seemed to do.

"I told him no."

Sofia let out a laugh. "You said no?"

"Yeah," I said, hoping I sounded as tough and manly as I felt.

"And?"

"He didn't like my answer."

A smile spread as she closed her eyes for a moment before cupping my chin. "Well, I loved your answer."

The words fell from her lips so softly that I couldn't help but stare. I wanted those lips all to myself. I craved them, desired them. I wanted to taste every inch of her skin, if she'd let me, and I hoped to God she would.

"So you don't want me to keep my distance?" I asked, wanting her to admit she was falling as hard and as fast as I was.

Her smile dropped. "Not even a little bit," she said almost sheepishly, as if it was hard for her to say out it loud.

"Good. Because I don't plan on going anywhere."

There. More truth and more feelings for her to process. Sofia knew she wasn't a fling, but she needed to hear it from me. So I planned to tell her everything she needed to hear, as often as she needed to hear it, until she believed me.

"I don't think I'll ever want you to," she said softly.

I lifted her chin until she met my eyes again, wanting to be very clear. "This isn't temporary, Sofia."

Her gaze dropped to my lips, and when it rose again, it was filled with heat. "I don't want it to be."

When the words I needed to hear left her lips, I cut her off with a hard kiss. There were too many emotions in the room, too many feelings hanging in the air, and I was only so strong.

I needed to feel her, needed to taste her, and when her head dipped back, giving me access to her neck, I knew she was granting me permission to much more—to her body and her heart. I wanted all of it, every single bit of her that she'd allow me.

I planned to be gentle . . . tried so hard to be. But things don't always go as planned.

NOT GOING ANYWHERE
Sofia

RYAN GRABBED MY ass, now covered only by my silky panties since my nightshirt had ridden up to my waist. My heart pounding, I moved my body on top of his and rubbed myself against him. I wasn't above dry-humping like a fifteen-year-old, and from the way his hard-on bulged and shifted beneath his jeans, he wasn't either.

It had been far too long since anyone had touched me the way Ryan was doing, his fingers digging into my back as I rolled my hips, pressing myself against his groin.

When he ground out, "You're killing me, angel," I continued my movements, afraid that if I stopped it all might end. The last thing in the world I wanted right now was for that to happen.

I'd never been the type of woman to care about sex. I'd gone lengths of time without a man inside me that made most women shudder in horror. They never understood how I kept it all together when I wasn't allowing myself to come apart. Matson had always been my priority, and an orgasm seemed like a distant second . . . or fifth to my vibrator, if I was being completely honest.

But in this moment with Ryan, his hands all over me,

lifting me higher so he could press kisses against my bare stomach, I wondered how I'd survived so long without it. My body ached to be filled with him, the need building between my legs before spreading through my entire body.

"I want you," I whispered.

Ryan froze and stared at me. "You sure? Because I'm only asking once. It's taking every ounce of willpower I have not to take you. I'm so turned on, Sofia."

"Take me then," I said breathlessly, and it was all the permission he needed before his grip on me tightened and he flipped us over in one movement.

"You have any idea what you do to me?"

He kissed me before I could answer, and the feel of his weight on me made me moan out loud. Ryan's muscles were hard, but his skin was soft. His body was chiseled in all the right places, yet his touches were sensitive. He was a contradiction of the best kind, and I found myself craving more of him . . . all of him. My need for him consumed me.

Ryan let out a ragged breath. "God, I want to take things slow, but I'm not sure I can."

"Then don't. I need you in me. Now," I said, surprising myself with how forward I was being.

He leaned back, his lower half still pressed to mine before he hopped up and unbuttoned his jeans. I wanted to be sexy, to take control and tell him I'd undress him, but I didn't say a word. I lay there, a little breathless as I watched him get undressed, then pull out his wallet and remove a condom from it.

Thank God he didn't make me ask whether he had one. The last thing I wanted to admit was I wasn't on birth control since I hadn't had sex in a hundred years.

He stood there in his fitted boxer briefs, the muscles in his thighs bulging like his crotch. My lips parted as he pulled his briefs to his feet and kicked them off, not a care in the world about where they landed.

"You still okay?" he asked, the condom gripped between his fingers.

"Oh yeah," I said, staring directly at his cock.

"Enjoying the view?"

He sounded like he was teasing me, but I could tell he was a little self-conscious.

"Hell yes, I am," I said with as much reverence as I could. It was one hell of a view.

He grinned before moving back to where I waited. I hadn't moved an inch. Reaching for my shirt, he pulled it over my head and gasped as he looked down at me. I wanted to cross my arms and cover myself until his words hit me.

"You're so beautiful."

He kissed my stomach and hips, tracing the faint white lines of my stretch marks with his fingertips. His eyes drank me in, making me want to drown in this man. Reaching for his head, I ran my fingers through his hair, scratching his scalp lightly, and he dipped his head between my legs.

"I have to taste you."

He gave me no choice as he pulled my panties down and tossed them aside before his tongue teased my inner thigh. Moving closer to my core, he breathed me in before stroking my folds with his tongue.

A moan escaped me, my hands still firmly gripping his head. "Oh God, Ryan."

He groaned in response, taking his tongue deeper, lapping at me with quick, feverish licks. It darted in and out of me before he moved to my clit, and licked it up and down like he couldn't get enough. God, this man knew what he was doing, and I felt like I was going to explode. My vibrator paled in comparison to Ryan's tongue.

I wriggled beneath his mouth, pulling at his hair in an attempt to get him to stop. "In me. Please. Ryan, get inside me now," I begged, not caring how desperate I sounded.

The sound of the condom tearing open made me grin as his head moved from between my thighs and back toward me. His face glistened with my juices, and a primal need swept over me. He wiped at his scruff with the back of his hand before coming down to kiss me, the taste of me all over his tongue. I'd never done that before, kissed a man after he'd gone down on me, but I was so turned on that all it did was fuel my desire for him more.

My fingertips dug into his back as I spread my legs open for him. Ryan didn't take his time, and he wasn't gentle like I'd expected. He plunged into me all at once without warning, as deep as my body allowed. The sound that escaped me was part pleasure, part pain.

"Sofia, you feel so good. So perfect," he said as he drove into me over and over again.

His shoulder muscles flexed as he moved above me, making my eyes close in response to all the delicious, mind-blowing sensations he was creating. Ryan filled me, reaching places inside me I'd never known existed before.

"What are you hitting," I asked with a pleasured moan.

"Am I hurting you?" He slowed his pace a little but didn't

stop moving.

"No, it feels amazing. I've just never felt it before."

He smiled at that but didn't answer. I decided that I no longer cared as he continued to pump his length in and out of me, hitting whatever the hell it was he was hitting.

"Oh God, Ryan, I'm going to . . ."

His mouth cut off my words as he kissed me, speeding up his pace as he gripped my headboard for leverage. He breathed out my name with each push inside me.

"Sofia . . ."

He groaned out my name again, his thrusts hard and rough. It was amazing, and not at all what I'd expected. Ryan owned my body, and it obeyed his every nonverbal command.

When my release hit, it felt like a wave of energy and emotion exploding all at once. Ryan still gripped the headboard as he used it to push into me with all his strength. Three pumps later and he came, his dick pulsing inside me, his hips still working in and out of me so slowly that I thought he might never stop. And I wasn't sure I would have minded.

He collapsed on top of me, the weight of him practically crushing me as we breathed hard, our chests moving in and out in sync. "That was—"

"Amazing," I finished for him as he rolled over and pulled me against him.

"I didn't mean to be so rough. I mean, not for our first time, but I couldn't help myself. You felt so good, and I was so turned on."

His apology was sweet, but not necessary.

"I needed it. Just the way you gave it. That's what I needed," I confessed, because it was true. I hadn't realized it before, but I didn't need sweet and soft tonight. I craved a rough release to let go of all the stress and tension that had been building. "It was perfect."

We lay on my bed, the sheet tossed to the floor, both of us still breathing hard as we floated down from our mutual high. My head lay on Ryan's chest, still slick with sweat, and thoughts of Matson walking in and seeing us like this flashed in my mind.

"You'd better go before Matson gets up," I said softly, drawing lazy circles with my fingers across his abs.

"You kicking me out after having your way with me? That's cold." His stomach bounced up and down with his laughter.

"I know. It's just that I don't want to confuse him," I said, starting to overexplain before he kissed the top of my head and I stopped talking.

"I was only teasing. Of course I'll go," he said.

"But not forever, right?"

Suddenly, I found myself second-guessing having sex with him so quickly. Maybe I should have made him wait longer, or work harder? As women, we were taught—whether subliminally or not—that our body was our greatest weapon, and withholding sex was the surest way to keep a man coming around. But now that Ryan had gotten the proverbial milk for free without buying the cow, what if that was all he wanted?

My brain knew I sounded crazy, but my heart still worried, the poor thing fragile and vulnerable.

Ryan squeezed me tighter. "Not forever. I'm not going anywhere, remember?" When I didn't respond right away, he pushed up, cradling my head as he pulled away to look at me.

"Do you believe me?"

I avoided looking into his eyes, feeling ridiculous as my heart whined and my mind willed it to pull itself together.

He gave me a worried look. "Sofia?"

"I believe you," I said, looking into those blue eyes that weakened my resolve. "Or I'm trying to." I winced, thinking that he would hate my response.

"I'll take it."

"But what if Derek gets too crazy and you can't handle it anymore?" I found myself asking.

My doubts and fears were eating me up inside, roiling around in my mind and making me worry. If Ryan thought he couldn't eventually handle this, I needed to know now. I had to mentally prepare myself for the possibility that he might walk away at some point. And if he did, I wouldn't blame him. No one needed drama like this in their life.

"I'm not leaving, Sofia." He brushed his fingers along my cheek. "Do you hear me?"

I nodded, and he turned my face to look at him.

"Say it."

In a small voice, I said, "I hear you."

"Derek can't do anything to make me want to give this up, okay? Whatever happens, we handle it together. It's you and me now. We're a team."

God, what have I done to deserve this man? Please tell me. I want to be sure to keep doing it so I never lose him.

"A team," I repeated, but it came out sounding like a question.

"Yup. Partners. Teammates."

Ryan pushed up off the bed and reached for my hand. He pulled me to my feet and began to get dressed, finding his clothes strewn all over the floor. I pulled on my nightshirt and walked Ryan to the front door.

"Thank you for letting me come over tonight," he said. "I promise I didn't plan on letting you take advantage of me, but I'm not complaining."

I laughed. "Oh, so I took advantage of you, huh?"

"You threw me on my back and started dry-humping me like we could win a gold medal for it," he teased, making my face burn. "I'm kidding. I loved it. You can do that anytime you want."

"Go away now," I said, practically shoving him out the front door.

"I'll call you later." He leaned down and gave me a sweet kiss, his tongue exploring my mouth.

My body tingled all over again. Trying to ignore it, I said, "Text me when you get home so I know you're safe."

"I think that's my line." Ryan winked before walking away.

I watched him swagger toward his car, enjoying every second of the view.

YOU'RE NOT LISTENING
Sofia

SINCE I'D KEPT Ryan up until almost sunrise, he slept most of Sunday before he had to go to work.

As much as I wanted to see him, especially after sleeping together, I needed to ease him into our lives carefully. The last thing I wanted was for Matson to feel like some guy had shown up out of nowhere and never left. Even though he asked no less than five times on Sunday where Ryan was and if he was coming over, I felt like the preservation of our mother-son relationship was important and vital.

When I dropped Matson off at school on Monday morning, I thought I noticed Derek's truck parked across the street, but I couldn't be sure. Convinced that I was being paranoid, I tried to let it go. But when I mentioned it to Sarin, she convinced me to call his school, just to be safe.

After talking to the vice principal and ensuring that the only people on Matson's approved pickup list were my parents and me, I hung up feeling somewhat better. Derek showing up at Ryan's work or mine was one thing, but the idea of him showing up at Matson's school was a horrible prospect that took my breath away.

I planned to see Ryan during my lunch break, but my

boss's meetings ran over and I couldn't leave. Being forced to eat lunch at my desk happened sometimes, but I never complained because it meant overtime pay.

I typed out a quick text to Ryan.

SOFIA: *Sorry I can't make it. Maybe tomorrow?*

He immediately responded, making my heart race.

RYAN: *It's okay, angel. But just for the record, I miss you terribly.*
SOFIA: *I miss you too.*

"Texting with lover-boy?" Sarin teased as she passed by my desk.

"Shut up," I said, knowing that stupid smile I couldn't control was plastered on my face.

She stopped, turning around to come back and lean on my cubicle's wall. "Sofia, in all honesty, you deserve to be happy. You know that, right?"

"I do." I believed that everyone deserved to be happy. I was no exception to that, but I wasn't sure it was meant for me before Ryan came along.

"Good. Because happiness looks good on you. I bet Ryan looks good on you too." She laughed before tapping my cubicle and hurrying off.

After work, I was on edge as I walked out of the building and to my car in the parking garage. When Derek was nowhere to be seen, I thanked God as I got into the driver's seat.

Derek seemed to be growing more and more confrontational, and fear of what he might do next weighed heavily on me. I found myself constantly looking over my shoulder, expecting him to be around every corner. It was exhausting.

When I pulled up to my parents' house to pick up Matson, I thanked God again that Derek wasn't lurking. The same gratitude returned as I parked my car at home and we walked safely through the back door.

"Mama?" Matson tugged at my shirtsleeve.

"Yes?"

"Can we go see Ryan at his work?"

I choked on a small laugh. "Why do you want to go see Ryan at work?"

"Because he hasn't been here in forever, and I drew a picture at school today. I wanted to give it to him and you said he's always at work, so I thought we could go there."

Matson dug through his backpack and pulled out a purple folder. I watched as he opened it, clearly searching for his drawing.

"Here it is!" He sounded so excited as he retrieved the drawing and pulled me toward the kitchen table.

I sat down and he sat next to me, placing his picture on the table and pointing things out.

"That's Ryan," he said, pointing at a stick drawing he'd made with big arm muscles, a giant smile, and blue eyes. "Ryan has blue eyes just like mine. And he has a cape on because he's a superhero. He fights the bad guys. Remember the bad guy from the beach?" He pointed at a stick drawing that had a frowning face.

"I remember," I said, my heart breaking at the fact that Matson's villain was his father, and he had no idea.

"That's you." He pointed at a stick figure of me smiling with long brown hair. "And that's me." He'd drawn himself holding on to Ryan's waist, the same way he had that day. "Do you think he'll like it?" His head cocked to the side as he waited for my answer.

"I think he'll love it. Especially the muscles," I said with a smile as I pointed at them.

"I think he'll like the cape best." Matson rolled his eyes at me before hopping away from the table.

"You might be right."

"Probably. Because I know what boys like." He grabbed a magnet off the fridge and used it to anchor his drawing. "It can stay here until we give it to him, okay?"

"Sounds perfect." I smiled, my heart warming. "Hey, I have an idea."

"What?"

"How about you hold up your drawing, and I'll take a picture of it and text it to Ryan so he can see it right now."

"Okay!" Matson immediately took the drawing down and held it in front of his chest, a huge grin on his face.

I snapped the picture with my phone and sent it to Ryan, wondering how my life had changed so quickly. My phone pinged out a notification, and Matson reached for it.

"Is it Ryan? What did he say? Did he like my drawing?"

I read the message out loud. "He says that's the coolest drawing he's ever seen. He loves the cape."

"Told you he'd like the cape best."

Matson sounded satisfied, so I kept the rest of his message to myself. Ryan had also said that I made one hell of a sexy stick figure.

About an hour after Matson had gone to bed, I sat on the couch catching up on my shows, and jerked with surprise when someone knocked on my door. I wondered who could be here this late, and hoped it was Ryan, showing up to collect his drawing in person.

My smile dropped when I opened the door to see Derek standing there, looking shifty. His tie was loosened, his shirt unbuttoned at his neck and wrinkled. Although he always maintained appearances, Derek looked uncharacteristically disheveled, his eyes wild.

"We need to talk."

"You can't be here," I said, but there would be no point. Arguing with an irrational person was like banging your head against a wall.

I started to close the door when his words stopped me.

"Since your boyfriend is too stupid to listen, maybe you will. I know he was here last night. Stop seeing him, Sofia, or he stops breathing."

Pulling the door back open, I stared at Derek, standing in the glow of my porch light. His normally clean-cut face was unshaven, his hair scraggly and uneven.

"What?" I shook my head, knowing there was no way he could have said what I thought he had.

"You heard me." His eyes were wild again.

"Why are you doing this? What do you want?"

I stepped outside and closed the door behind me in case Matson woke up. I didn't want him to see or hear Derek, especially not after seeing his drawing from earlier. Plus, whatever Derek wanted to say or do would have to be done out in the open. There I could scream bloody murder, if I needed to, and have a better chance that one of my neighbors would hear and come running.

"I need to have Matson in my life." He ran his hands down his face, his fingers raking his jaw.

"Need?" I pulled my head back at his word choice. Derek didn't say that he *wanted* Matson in his life . . . he said that he *needed* him. There had to be some ulterior motive behind his behavior, and I wanted to know what it was.

"Yes, Sofia. *Need*."

"Why?" I crossed my arms and stood on the porch step above him, making us almost eye level with each other.

"You really want to know?"

"You show up here after eight years, demanding to be a part of Matson's life, acting crazy and threatening my boyfriend. Of course I want to know."

"My father's been trying to get me to make amends with you for years."

At his disgusted tone, any part of my body that had relaxed instantly tensed again. "He has? Why?"

"Because you gave me an heir."

I swayed a little, feeling light-headed. Derek seriously considered Matson his heir?

"And he says I've shamed the Huntington name."

"An heir? You can't be serious." I scoffed at him with as much disdain as I could summon. My head spun as I tried to wrap my mind around how asinine this all sounded.

Derek glared at me. "One day Matson will be the rightful CEO of the Huntington firm. You know that all the men in the family work in the company. My father took over for his father. I'll take over for mine. And one day, Matson will take over for me."

I stopped myself from spitting in his face. "Matson will

never be a part of that world."

"He won't have a choice."

"My son will always have a choice," I cried out, feeling my insides burn with the fierce protectiveness only a mother could feel.

"No, he won't. And he's my son too."

"Since when?"

"Since my dad said that I can't have the company if I don't fix this shit between us," Derek said, the confession spilling from his lips without apology.

My mouth dropped open. "So this is all about the company?"

"It's about money, Sofia. Money and power."

"You don't really care about getting to know Matson?"

My stomach twisted as the sound of his sick laughter filled the night air.

"Care about getting to know him? No. I never want to know him."

"Can't we just tell your dad you've made amends without actually doing it? I'll send him an email, call him, whatever he wants." I was practically begging, but I'd agree to almost anything if it meant Derek would get the hell out of our lives and leave us alone forever.

"You know he'd never take me at my word. And he wouldn't believe you either. He's probably having me followed right now." He glanced around, scanning the street behind him.

I huffed out a sound of disgust. "The apple doesn't fall far from the tree."

"I know he's having you followed. He probably always has.

He knows about Ryan. It was actually his idea to get rid of him, said it would help you see who you really belonged with . . ."

Derek continued to talk, but my shock and disbelief drowned out his words.

"Stop," I whispered, then raised my voice. "Stop. Stop!" When Derek's mouth snapped shut, I looked directly into his cold, dead eyes. "This is insane. Madness. I don't belong with you. I never did."

"Well, dear old Dad doesn't see it that way."

"What does he want? For us to be some big happy family?"

"In a nutshell."

"How are we supposed to do that?"

"We'll have to convince him. Together."

I shook my head, refusing to believe this was happening. "No."

Derek leaned toward me, his posture threatening. "He's going to give the company to my cousin, Sofia. My worthless fucking cousin who couldn't count out a hundred pennies if his life depended on it. I'll be the laughingstock of the firm. The first Huntington son who didn't take over for his father in sixty years."

"I don't care," I said, my tone cruel. If Derek thought for even a second that he'd have my sympathy, he was batshit crazy. "I'm not doing this for you."

"If you take away my future, I'll take away yours." He looked me dead in the eye, his expression cold.

My body chilled with his threat. Stunned, I stood there with my head swimming, my eyes watering, as I wondered what to do. Would he really hurt Ryan?

Derek gave me a sly look. "Remember what happened to that boy in high school? What was his name again?"

I searched my memory, and Joseph Bray's image appeared in my mind. I was surprised I could still stand upright once I connected the dots with the memories that flooded through me.

"Joseph," I said in a whisper, and Derek nodded.

"That's right. Joseph. Shame what happened to him. Ended his football career, didn't it?"

I refused to move, or answer the questions he clearly remembered the answers to. After all this time, I finally knew the truth.

Part of me had always suspected that Derek had either caused Joseph's car accident or was involved in it. I had heard the whispers in the hallway and seen the stares from my classmates, but I never knew for sure, and no one was brave enough to tell me what they also suspected. Over time, the whispers stopped and the suspicion seemed to die down.

Derek had become distant from me a few days before the crash, and I remembered asking him what was wrong. We'd only been dating a few months, and I thought he'd grown tired of me already and was planning to break up with me. I continued to ask him but he blew me off, insisting that I was being paranoid. But after Joseph's accident, Derek walked around school like he was untouchable, his arm wrapped possessively around my waist, everything between us back to normal.

Guilt flooded my veins, as if the accident had happened yesterday rather than almost a decade ago. It killed me knowing it was my fault that Joseph's legs were broken and he would never play football again. If Derek hadn't found out about Joseph asking me out during lunch one day, the crash never would have happened. Joseph would have had a completely different life than the one he ended up living.

How could I ever forgive myself?

"I know what you're thinking, Sofia, but I didn't do it because of you." Derek sounded disgusted that I could even contemplate being the reason for his actions.

"Then why did you?"

Derek glared at me. "He embarrassed me in front of the whole school. He disrespected me by asking you out. Joseph knew you belonged to me. Everyone knew. I was humiliated, and had to teach him a lesson."

"But he always blamed himself for that crash. You know how much he hated himself for it. He said he never knew why he fell asleep at the wheel that night," I said, trying to put together all the pieces from that night so long ago. "That he didn't remember even being tired before he got into the car."

Derek smirked. "That's what happens when something gets slipped into your post-workout drink. Knocked him out cold in less than ten minutes."

My mouth dropped open. "You drugged him? He could have died that night, or killed someone else!"

I couldn't believe what I was hearing. How could Derek have been this unhinged when we were dating, and I had no clue? How had I ever loved someone so manipulative, someone with such a cold heart? And how could I make sure that Matson turned out nothing like him?

Derek pointed a finger in my face. "Stay away from Ryan until my father gives me the company, or else his blood is on your hands. You know I follow through with my threats, Sofia," he warned before he started to walk away.

Stopping abruptly, he turned back toward me. "And don't even think about going to the cops. I have a solid alibi, and they'd never believe you anyway. I've already told them that you're a scorned ex-girlfriend who had my baby when we were kids, and you've never gotten over my decision to leave you. I've filed a report saying you've been trying to extort money from me for years. And that I've refused to pay you a dime until you provided me with a test proving paternity, which you never have."

He scanned my face, his expression smug at the shock that must have been plastered there. My face had turned cold, probably because all the blood had drained from it.

Smirking at me, he said, "Don't push me," and turned to stride off into the darkness.

I stood there alone with my thoughts, now as dark as the night's sky.

Derek meant everything he said, every word. That much I was sure of. If he was crazy enough to hurt Joseph back in high school because of his ego and pride, then he was certainly crazy enough to hurt Ryan now if he thought his inheritance and family name were at stake.

I knew what I had to do, and I hoped with all my heart that Ryan would be able to hear me out rationally. His life literally depended on it.

*

STEPPING INTO THE protective warmth of my house, which

suddenly felt a little less of each, I walked toward my room, stopping to check on Matson first. He was sleeping peacefully in his bed, and I took a few moments to stand there and watch him, my heart full of so much love and protectiveness for him.

After pulling his door closed a little, I headed into my bedroom and pulled my cell phone from its charger. I'd missed a call from Ryan.

Perfect.

Sitting down on the edge of my bed where Ryan had been inside me only a couple of nights earlier, I dialed his number. I had to call him before I lost my nerve, before Derek's threats settled somewhere into the recesses of my mind where I could wish them away and pretend they weren't real. The memory of Joseph's accident replayed in my head as I pressed CALL and waited, knowing Ryan might not be able to pick up if the bar was busy.

"Hey, angel," he answered, sounding so happy that a lump formed in my throat.

"I need to talk to you," I said, getting straight to the point. I couldn't delay or pretend everything was fine when it was anything but.

I heard a door close in the background, muting the background noise, then Ryan said, "What's up? You okay? You don't sound okay."

Dear God, please help me do this. I know it's something I have to do, but I need your strength and your guidance right now. And please, please, please, help Ryan understand.

"We have to stop seeing each other." I forced the words out matter-of-factly, stripping the emotion from them, and Ryan cut me off before another word could leave my lips.

"Don't move. I'll be right there."

"No, Ryan, don't. It won't change anything, and you'll only make it harder." I gripped the phone so tightly in my hand, I thought I might crack the screen.

His voice dropped, sounding so defeated. "Tell me what's going on. I know you can't possibly want this."

I couldn't tell Ryan the whole truth, but I could tell him parts of it. I refused to be the girl who fed him lies about my heart, telling him things like *I don't really want you* or that *I have no feelings for you* in order to get him to stay away. Especially when none of that was true, and he knew it.

However we ended our situation tonight, I didn't want it to be because of miscommunication. If anything, I wanted it to be the opposite. Part of me knew that the only way to get Ryan to accept what I was about to ask of him was to be forthcoming.

"Derek was just here."

"He came to your house?" Ryan's tone sharpened.

"Yes."

"Did he tell you the same things he'd told me the other night?"

"Basically. He knows you were here, though. After he told you to stay away from me, he knows you came here that night anyway."

"So what?" Ryan said, not understanding what was truly at stake.

"So he's pissed. And he's unstable. And capable of anything," I reluctantly admitted.

A crash like a fist slamming into something reverberated through the phone.

"Did he hurt you?" Ryan asked.

"No."

"Are you lying?"

His question made my heart ache. "No. He didn't hurt me." *But he wants to hurt you*, I stopped myself from saying.

"How did he convince you to end things? What hold does he have over you? Please tell me something that makes sense, Sofia, because right now, nothing does."

"He threatened to fight me for custody of Matson."

I hadn't planned on lying to him, but it slipped so effortlessly from my lips that I couldn't have stopped it if I tried. Ryan would never do anything that would hurt my son, and I knew it. It was a low blow, but I felt like I needed the help it gave me.

"He'll take Matson from you if you don't stop seeing me? Why? What does he gain from that?"

I fidgeted on the bed before standing and pacing back and forth. What else could I say? "He needs you out of the picture, or else his dad won't give him the company."

"Why? I know I keep asking you why, but I don't understand."

I pictured Ryan in my head, pulling at the strands of his hair, his eyes tired, his heart aching.

"I know this all sounds crazy, but his family is insane. And until things settle down and Derek goes away for good, we have to stop seeing each other. I don't want to fuel his anger, and I'm afraid that something will happen to hurt Matson. I have to make sure my son's okay. I have to give him all my attention right now, and if I'm worried about you or about us, then I won't be worrying about Matson. You're too distracting, Ryan."

I thought he was going to say something, but when he didn't, I continued. "You're distracting in the best possible way, but it's still a distraction I can't afford to have right now. Matson has to be my first and only priority."

"How can I argue with that?" Ryan's voice was so sad, it nearly broke my heart.

I knew that he couldn't argue, knew he wouldn't fight me on this. "I need you to know that this has nothing to do with the way I feel about you and what I want." I stopped pacing and held my breath as I waited for him to say something.

"I know that. I wouldn't have believed you if you tried to tell me otherwise." His tone softened. "I want to be with you, and I hate agreeing to this. I feel like I'm walking away and leaving you to fight alone when it's the last thing I want."

"This is a fight I have to handle by myself. Having you by my side will only make it worse. I know that doesn't make any sense," I said, and it didn't. "But we're not dealing with a rational person here."

"It doesn't feel right, and I need you to know that this goes against everything I believe in and everything I feel. It's killing me to even think about agreeing to this."

The pain in Ryan's voice ripped through me, tearing my heart to pieces. But I convinced myself to stay strong, because anything less could end up with him getting hurt. *Really* hurt.

"It's just until his dad gives him the company," I reminded Ryan, hoping he would see that as the silver lining in this crappy situation.

"I'm not going anywhere. I'll be right here when this is all done. You just make sure you come back to me."

My eyes instantly welled up with tears. What if Derek's

dad never gave him the company? Or what if it took years? Was I supposed to stay away from Ryan for that long? Who in their right mind could expect me to do that?

"I don't know how long it will take."

"It doesn't matter."

"I don't deserve you."

"Yes, you do. We both do. We deserve each other. What you don't deserve is this drama, and this asshole having any say in your life."

"I feel like all I do is bring you pain." Suddenly, I felt unworthy of Ryan's adoration or respect. All I'd done since meeting him was judge him, avoid him, and bring a level of drama into his life worthy of a television series. It was embarrassing.

"That's not true. You bring so much joy to my life. You and Matson both," Ryan said, his words aiming straight for my heart and hitting their mark.

"I'll be back, Ryan. I promise I'll be back for you." I swallowed my emotions and wiped at my falling tears.

"You know I'd never let you stay away," he said, but I could hear the smile in his voice.

I moved to end the call, but pressed the phone back to my ear instead. "One more thing."

"I'm listening."

"You can't contact me. You can't come over or call or show up somewhere, okay?" I needed him to agree to this because I knew that Derek would be watching. "I need you to promise me. It's important."

"How will he know if I do?"

"Derek thinks his dad is having me followed, so he'd know

if we saw each other. And knowing him, he probably has access to my cell phone logs, so he'd know if we talked."

"So I really do need to disappear?" Ryan's voice cracked, a lot like my heart was doing right now.

"For now, yes. I can't lose Matson. That would kill me."

"Literally breaking my heart here, angel, but you know I'd never do anything to mess up your custody with Matson. I wouldn't fucking allow it to happen either. I need you to know I'd do everything in my power to stop him from taking your son. Derek's dad might be powerful, but my dad is too." He paused before adding, "In his own way."

Ryan's words were a reminder that I knew very little about his parents or what they did. But that part of getting to know each other would have to wait.

"I can't even think about that right now. But thank you. And please know how much I hate all of this. I promise it won't be for forever, and I'll make it up to you."

"You and Matson coming back is all the making up I need. Just make sure you do that," he said, and it sounded like he was fighting off tears. I prayed that he didn't cry, because if Ryan broke down on me now, I'd never recover.

"'Bye, Ryan." I pressed END before he could say anything else.

Everything that needed to be said had been, and if I stayed on the line with him any longer, I couldn't trust myself not to take it all back and beg for his forgiveness. I'd promised him that we'd work through this and fight Derek together, but I knew that we couldn't. At least, not yet.

So I told him good-bye and left the pieces of my heart dangling somewhere between his house and mine. And I prayed to God that Ryan would know they were there so he could pick them up and keep them safe. I'd been so difficult with him for so long, and now that I was ready to be with him, we were being torn apart. It wasn't fair.

But then again, life so rarely was.

DEADLY DESPERATION
Sofia

OVER THREE WEEKS had passed, and Ryan had made good on the promise I'd forced him to make. He remained quiet, leaving me alone.

Even though I knew he was only doing what I'd asked of him, it hurt that he could. Every day, it killed me to not reach out to him in some way, but the potential consequences stopped me cold.

It had shocked me at first how quickly I'd gotten used to Ryan being a part of my life. And how his being gone was what now felt wrong, instead of the opposite. His absence had a presence; his silence, a heartbeat.

I hated that he listened to my pleas to stay away, but I loved that he stayed true to his word.

My heart was a constant contradiction, beating out pained thumps inside my chest, feeding me lies and questions that only inflicted more hurt.

Maybe he's forgotten about us, it thumped.
We told him to disappear, it beat back.
He's glad we're gone, it pounded.
We told him to leave, it drummed against my rib cage.

This continued day after day, until the only peace I found

was while I slept.

It took Matson almost two weeks to stop asking about Ryan. At first, he wondered when he was going to be able to give Ryan the picture he drew. It still hung on our fridge, held in place by a cheerful Hawaii magnet. I couldn't bring myself to take it down, and it would have only confused Matson more if I had.

Each day when I picked him up from my mom's house, he would ask if Ryan was coming over. And each time I told him *not tonight, sweetheart*, his smile would drop and he'd stare at his feet until I pulled into our driveway, what was left of my broken heart breaking even more.

Eventually, I had to tell Matson that Ryan was out of town for work, and that we'd see him as soon as he got back. But even that hadn't stopped his questions entirely. Matson was too smart for his own good, asking to talk to Ryan on the phone, or video chat the next time he called. And when I couldn't give him either of those things, I expanded my lie, telling him that Ryan was far away. That it was daytime when we were sleeping, and when we were awake, it was nighttime where Ryan was.

Matson huffed out a breath, the way kids do when they don't like the answer but know they have to accept it. Frowning, he said he hoped Ryan hurried up and came home soon, because he missed him. I wrapped my little boy in a hug and told him that I did too, but that Ryan wasn't gone forever.

I really hoped that part wasn't a lie.

*

I STEPPED INTO the empty elevator and pulled up my personal email on my phone for the first time that day. I'd been slammed with back-to-back meetings and scheduling issues for my boss, so I hadn't had time to check it. The doors closed as my inbox loaded and a message from Ryan appeared that he'd sent before noon.

I couldn't click on it fast enough, but being inside the elevator made my wireless connection slower than usual. Tapping at my screen as if that would get it to load faster, I felt my stomach flip-flop with anticipation.

The spinning circle stopped, and his message finally loaded as the doors to the basement garage opened. I stepped out, pausing so I could process whatever he'd said to me without the distraction of walking.

I know this breaks all the rules, but I thought you should know that Derek's dad is really sick. I've been researching his family for weeks now, and I came across an article that said he was in the hospital recently. It makes sense why Derek's shown up after all this time. Figured you'd want to know. I miss you so much it hurts.

My knees buckled and I leaned back against the concrete wall for support. Derek's dad being sick made sense, too much sense, but what got to me the most was Ryan saying he missed me so much it hurt.

I was relieved. I was sad. I was pissed. I was joyful. But mostly, I was mad, thoroughly pissed off.

I hated that Derek was keeping this man from my life and Matson's. I hated that I felt powerless over my own life. I hated everything. But mostly, I hated the fact that I was allowing it to happen instead of figuring out a way to fight back.

Letting my anger fuel me, I regained my strength and pushed off from the wall. Heading toward where I'd parked my car, I nearly stumbled when I spotted Derek pacing behind the rear bumper. My anger quickly dissipated into unsettled emotions.

Did he know that Ryan had emailed me? Was that why he was here? Had he hurt him or come to warn me?

Nervous energy pumped through me as I wondered if he did know, and if he'd buy whatever lie I could feed him to gain us some time. Ryan always knew when I was lying to him, but Derek didn't know me at all anymore, so maybe he wouldn't catch on.

As I approached him, I slowed my pace, noticing that Derek still looked unkempt. It was an odd thing to focus on, but the scruff looked so out of place on his face. Maybe he still hadn't set things right with his dad. Or maybe his dad was really sick like Ryan had suggested.

"Derek?" I said his name as calmly as I could. I needed to know what he wanted without tipping his scales over to crazy town. "What are you doing here?"

His bloodshot eyes met mine. "I need you to go with me to an event honoring my father." He crossed his arms over his chest and stepped between me and my car, blocking my door.

So he didn't know about the email. My relief flitted away as anger worked back into my veins, giving me strength.

"No."

"You have to," he insisted, sounding unnerved.

"No," I repeated, my tone as cold as ice.

"You have to come, Sofia." He slammed his fist on the hood of my car, leaving a dent.

"No, I don't."

Every single atom inside me refused to allow me to give in to him. I'd never forgive myself if something happened to Ryan, but I was tired of feeling like a puppet with Derek pulling my strings. I decided that second that I'd talk to Ryan later and tell him everything so we could figure out a solution together.

Derek pushed away from my car and raked his hands through his hair as he paced back and forth. "My father needs to see us together. He doesn't believe that we're happy," he shouted, and I realized he'd given me enough space to get into my car, but I'd have to be quick.

"We're not happy." I looked at him like he was a freaking lunatic.

"He thinks you're still with Ryan, and even though he has no proof, he won't let the idea go. He's ruining everything."

As Derek continued to pace back and forth, I darted toward my door but he got there first, slamming it closed with one hand as I tried to yank it open.

"You'll come with me to this party, or you'll regret it." He pulled his jacket back, revealing the silver handle of a gun sticking out of his waistband.

All my strength evaporated like a popped balloon, the puppet strings firmly back in place. My head spun as I fought to keep control of my balance.

Derek lunged toward me and gripped my arms, but I was frozen in place. I tried to command my arms to move, but they were stuck to my sides like they were superglued there.

"I told you that if you ruined my future, I'd ruin yours," he shouted, spraying spittle on my face.

"Derek, let go. You're hurting me, and I need to go pick up Matson."

He squeezed tighter before abruptly letting me go. "You're coming with me to that party." He pointed a shaky finger at me, poking me painfully in the forehead twice.

I didn't respond, just thankful my body was finally cooperating again. I hopped into my car and quickly locked the doors, but when I looked in my mirrors, Derek was nowhere to be found. It was like he'd never been there at all.

Once I pulled out of my parking space, I'd just stepped on the gas when the sound of tires squealing behind me got my attention. In my rearview mirror, I could see Derek's black truck riding my ass. He was so close, I was afraid he was going to hit me.

Making a right out of the lot, I intentionally sped up to see what Derek would do. He stayed right on my tail. And when I jerked my car across two lanes of traffic without warning, I watched in my mirrors as he did the same.

Derek continued to aggressively follow me as I navigated the streets of Santa Monica, too scared to drive to my parents' house. I refused to pick up Matson while Derek was this reckless. And my poor parents . . . they had no idea any of this had been going on, and it seemed too late to try to explain it all to them now.

Terrified, I drove erratically, making turns at the last second without using my blinker, and going in circles around blocks. But Derek refused to let up, flashing his brights and honking his horn like a maniac. When he tapped my bumper,

I almost lost control and crashed into a parked car on the side of the road.

My nerves were shot, fear fueling my adrenaline, and I knew there was only one place I could go. Racing into the employee lot of Sam's bar, I turned off my engine and sprinted through the back door, praying that Ryan was inside.

Desperate, I searched for him, my heart nearly pounding out of my chest. When I spotted him near the back of the bar, wiping off a table, I ran to him.

"I'm so sorry, I didn't know where else to go. He's chasing me, and he's crazy," I said through shaky breaths.

Ryan pulled me into his arms and held me tight. "It's okay, it's okay. Who's chasing you? Derek?"

"Yes," I said, but my emotions caused me to get choked up. Seeing Ryan and being in his arms after these past few weeks, coupled with being pursued by Derek, left me feeling overwhelmed.

"Is he here?" Ryan tensed, his body stiffening beneath my palms.

"I think so. He followed me."

When I pointed toward the back entrance, Ryan released his hold on me and took off, slamming the door hard against the building as he bolted outside. I'd never seen him so angry, so determined, so protective.

He was back inside the bar within seconds. "He sped off as soon as he saw me. What happened?"

The ping of a text message alert stopped me from answering Ryan's question.

> UNKNOWN NUMBER: *I told you his blood would be on your hands. Remember that you caused this.*

I almost dropped the phone when Ryan tried to read the message. Terrified that Derek might storm in and start shooting up the place, I panicked.

"I'm sorry. I'm so sorry. Don't follow me, Ryan. I mean it. I shouldn't have come here. I won't make that mistake again."

"It wasn't a mistake. Sofia, it wasn't a mistake," he shouted.

But I was already running out the back door for my car so I could lead Derek away from Ryan and any innocent bystanders. My thoughts instantly went to Matson. If I didn't show up soon to pick him up, he'd worry. It was my job to protect and worry about him, not the other way around.

As soon as I exited the parking lot, Derek's truck came into view. He'd been waiting for me.

When I got stuck at a red light, he pulled up next to me and yelled out his window, "You couldn't just stay away from him, could you? You've ruined everything!"

When the light turned green, I floored it like a hero in an action movie, foolishly thinking that I could outrun him this time.

Allowing Derek to get behind me again was my first mistake.

Calling Ryan after I'd just stormed out on him was my second.

I wouldn't get the chance to make a third.

CRASH INTO ME
Ryan

I WAS GOING out of my damn mind. Sofia had run into my arms and just as quickly run away again, telling me it had been a mistake.

I stood outside and watched her drive off, noticing as Derek's truck followed soon after. She'd said she shouldn't have come here, but the gnawing feeling in my gut told me otherwise. Here was exactly where she was supposed to be.

I couldn't shake the bad feeling. She'd been gone for less than five minutes, and I still didn't know what the hell to do. My phone was firmly gripped in my hand, my finger poised to open the app I could use to track her phone.

"I gotta go after her," I said to Frank, who nonchalantly waved a hand toward the door.

"Then go."

"I mean it," I said, hoping he'd tell me I was overreacting. But then again, Frank hadn't seen Sofia when she came running in here, tears streaming down her face. He'd been in the office with the door closed, and only came out once he heard me shouting and running after her.

"So do I," he said.

Torn, I started pacing, practically wearing a hole in the

floor with my indecision. If I chased her and I was wrong, she could lose Matson, or at least have to gear up for one hell of a custody battle. She'd never forgive me if I was the one who made that happen and it didn't go her way.

Sofia hadn't exaggerated about the Huntington family's power and reach. I'd learned as much during my research I started on them after the night she broke up with me. She was right to be worried. It was part of the reason why I'd stayed away instead of showing up at her house every night like I wanted to.

Aside from the email I'd sent this morning, I hadn't contacted her at all these past weeks. It killed me that she didn't write back. I hadn't expected her to, but I still thought she might. Or maybe I just hoped that she would? Wondering if she missed me the way I missed her was absolute torture.

Not having answers to the questions that plagued my mind was maddening. And disappearing from her life and Matson's these past three weeks with no communication at all was tearing me apart.

I missed them, both of them, and drove myself crazy wondering what she'd told Matson in my absence. Had he asked about me? Did he think I abandoned him? Questions like those kept me up at night, tossing and turning in my bed.

My cell phone vibrated, and Sofia's contact info flashed on my screen.

"Sofia? Are you okay?"

"He won't stop chasing me, Ryan. I'm driving so fast, but I can't lose him. I'm scared."

She sounded terrified, and I hated myself for letting her get in the car and drive away tonight instead of stopping her. I should have confronted Derek and made him end this charade once and for all.

"I'll be right there, Sofia. Sofia?" I yelled, but the call had already ended. "Sofia!" I shouted into the void.

Pressing START on the tracking app, I watched as the red dot that represented her car appeared. I held my breath, waiting to see if it would move or not. When it did, I glanced at Frank, who looked more worried than I'd ever seen before.

"What is it?"

"He's chasing her. I have to go." I held up my phone.

His eyes widened when he recognized the app. "Go! Be careful, and call me as soon as you're safe."

I ran from the bar, my eyes locked on my phone's screen. I jumped in my car and started it quickly, cursing at the navigation system to hurry up and sync with my phone. Finally, the red dot that represented Sofia's location appeared on my much larger dashboard screen.

Seeing it move as I tore out of the parking lot stressed me out. How the hell was I going to reach her before Derek did? What if he hurt her? I raced in their direction, my stomach knotted with fear, my mind racing with more *what if*s than I could process. I refused to think the worst. I couldn't.

But when her dot stopped moving, a whole new level of stress filled me.

Why had it stopped? Was she at a stop sign? Did she throw her phone out the window? Was she at a red light?

I pressed on the gas, my instincts screaming at me that something was terribly wrong. I sensed it, knew it. I *felt* the danger radiating through me, tearing me up inside.

As I sped toward her location, her dot remained stationary.

I pressed another button to overlay a satellite map, which revealed she wasn't near any structures—no houses, no schools, no businesses. Sofia was on a two-lane road near the coast, her dot still motionless.

Panic unlike anything I'd ever known before crashed over me from head to toe. I closed in on her location, agonizing over what would be waiting for me. What would I see when I reached her?

One last curve and the glow of taillights caught my eye. Speeding closer, I saw smoke pouring from an engine, the front of a car crushed against the base of a massive oak tree.

Sofia's car!

When I made out her silhouette slouched over the steering wheel, I couldn't get to her fast enough. I slammed on my brakes and my car skidded to a stop right behind hers, the tires kicking up gravel from the road's shoulder. Frantic, I unbuckled my seatbelt and jumped out, my feet almost slipping in the gravel the same way my tires had. Pounding on her driver's side window, I screamed her name, begging her to come to, but she didn't move.

Adrenaline flooded through me as I yanked on her door handle, trying to pull it open, but it wouldn't budge. *Locked.* I pulled and pulled, as if I could somehow will it to unlock and let me in.

I shouted her name again and again, my throat already raw, but she remained still, slumped over the steering wheel. *This can't be happening* repeated in my head as shock turned me ice-cold.

I pounded on the window again, praying it would break.

It didn't.

And she still hadn't moved.

Tears slid down my face, and at first, I had no idea where the moisture was coming from. It blurred my vision, and I desperately needed to see. I couldn't help her if I couldn't see her.

"Sofia," I yelled again, but it was no use.

Desperate, I ran back to my car and called 911 from the console, and gave the dispatcher my location, ignoring her as she begged me to stay on the line until help arrived. I didn't have time to waste staying on the phone with strangers when the girl I was falling in love with was hurt, unconscious, and I couldn't fucking get to her. So I left the line open and ran back to Sofia's car.

"Sofia, please." My voice strangled out a hoarse cry as sirens blared in the distance. I couldn't tell how close or far they were, but that seemed quick—too quick, I'd only called them seconds ago—and nothing made sense.

"Turn around, Ryan."

Derek's voice yanked my attention away from my angel. In all the chaos, I'd completely forgotten about him.

How could I have forgotten that he was the reason we were in this mess in the first place?

"I said turn around."

His voice was low but deadly, angrier than I'd heard before. Wary, I slowly turned to face him, wondering what the hell he wanted now. Hadn't he done enough?

My gaze instantly homed in on his hand and the gun he had pointed straight at me.

Had he planned on shooting Sofia? I looked back at her, and for the first time felt thankful that she still hadn't woken up. I didn't want her to see any of this.

"You were going to shoot her?" I asked, completely shocked. This guy was seriously fucking deranged.

He laughed, taking a menacing step toward me like I'd done to him all those times before. "Her? No, Ryan. I was never going to shoot Sofia."

My head swam. Nothing made sense. Nothing added up. "Then why do you have a gun?"

He sneered at me. "You just can't stay away, can you? I warned her. Told her if she destroyed my future, I'd destroy hers."

"I know. She told me you want custody," I said, focusing on his finger hovering over the trigger.

"Custody?" He let out a sick laugh. "That's what she told you? Genius."

"She said you were going to take Matson from her." I shook my head, more confused than ever.

It was funny how you reacted when something unimaginable happened to you—like having a loaded gun pointed in your direction. My ears picked up every sound—the sirens getting closer by the second, an owl hooting nearby. My eyes noticed every detail—the way the wind blew Derek's hair into his eyes but he refused to brush it out of the way, how his beard looked rough and unkempt, and the way his roughly loosened tie hung crooked. But my brain—my brain couldn't process the words he said and make them make sense. My senses were heightened, but my mind seemed dulled.

Derek scoffed at me. "I would never take Matson from her. What would I do with a kid?"

My brain raced, spinning in circles but still unable to figure shit out. If he hadn't threatened to take Matson from her, then what exactly had he threatened her with?

"Still confused, huh? All looks and no brains? Let me spell it out for you." He raised the weapon higher, aiming for my head. "I told her I'd kill you. She knew I meant it after I told her what I'd done to one of our classmates back in high school."

"Why?"

"Guess you'll never know," he said, smirking like this was the most enjoyable thing he'd done all day.

Sirens blared, but Derek remained unconcerned. I wondered if he even heard them or not. Maybe his brain was on point, but his senses were dulled like mine.

"The cops are getting closer."

"You think I don't hear them?" he shouted before lowering the gun and kicking at the dirt. He started hitting his own head with his free hand the way someone who was at their wit's end would do. "Why did you have to be around? None of this would be happening if you had just gone away like you were supposed to!"

Although tires skidded and screeched to a stop nearby, Derek continued ranting, blaming me for all his problems and saying everything was all my fault.

I held up my hands. "If you shoot me, you'll go to jail. You can't get whatever it is you want from behind bars." It was a reach, but I had to try something. Otherwise, this guy was going to kill me, and I really didn't want to die.

He laughed again, the sick smirk back on his face. "You think I'd go to jail? You really don't know anything, do you, Ryan? My father would never allow that to happen. Huntingtons don't go to jail."

"Put down the gun," a voice boomed over a megaphone, but Derek's wild eyes stayed fixed on mine.

He was going to shoot me. I was going to die. They say your life flashes before your eyes just before you die, and they were right. In that moment, it happened for me.

It was more like a movie montage, scenes of my childhood with Frank and my parents mixing with my present day. I saw both my brothers, their girlfriends, my mom and dad, Grant—and, of course, Sofia and Matson. They whipped through my mind's eye in a flash, each image filled with smiles and happiness. I was thankful for having the chance to have experienced that, the joy and the love.

"Put it down!" the voice demanded again, and my blood ran cold.

Derek's finger tightened on the trigger in slow motion as shots rang out. I covered my ears with my hands, the sounds so fucking loud around me as I bent over, convinced I could duck and avoid any flying bullets or shrapnel. Dirt kicked up, gravel hit me in the shin, but otherwise I was unhurt.

Derek's body recoiled three times in rapid succession before his footing gave way and he fell to the ground. Blood poured from his chest, his body unmoving, but his eyes remained open. It was the first time I'd ever seen a dead body, and I hoped it would be my last.

Blood pooled around him, thicker and darker than I'd imagined it would be. Blood doesn't flow like Kool-Aid the way they show it on TV and in the movies. Real blood is thick and moves slowly like molasses as it leaves your body.

Police surrounded me, demanding I get on my knees with my hands behind my head.

I yelled at them to get Sofia out, desperately pointing toward her car before I followed their directions. I had no idea how much time had passed, but my girl still hadn't moved.

FAMILY
Ryan

O<small>NCE THE POLICE</small> had determined I wasn't a threat, I bolted toward the ambulance where the paramedics already had Sofia strapped in and were preparing to take her to the hospital.

"Where are you taking her?" I asked the paramedic.

"General," he said.

"Is she going to be okay?" I was frantic. She looked so pale, already hooked up to an IV, machines reporting her vitals with annoying beeps. But what bothered me most was that her eyes were still closed.

"She's stable. I gave her something for the pain."

"She was awake?" How much she had seen and heard?

"Only for a minute. We gotta go," the paramedic said, then climbed into the back of the ambulance and shut the doors.

I ran toward my car, determined to follow them, but a police officer stepped in front of me, blocking my path.

"Not so fast, Mr. Fisher. We need your statement."

I shook my head wildly. "I have to go with her," I pleaded, but he refused, his hand still in the air.

"It's either now or later."

"Then later. Please. I have to go. I need to go." I felt like I was going to go crazy as the ambulance pulled away, sirens screaming, my girl in the back.

"You'll be at the hospital?" the policeman asked as he surveyed our surroundings, and I did the same.

Derek's body was being processed. The coroner had just arrived, a police photographer was taking pictures of the body, and yellow evidence markers dotted the scene.

"I'll be at General," I told the cop. "I won't leave. Unless she's released, and then I'll be at her house. Meet me there. I'll come to you. Either way, I don't care. just let me go, please." I was desperate, not making any sense, but he finally relented and stepped aside.

"Drive the speed limit," he yelled as I closed my door and pulled onto the road, spitting out gravel behind me.

Nothing had sunk in yet—not Derek having a gun on me, not him almost shooting me, not him being shot and killed. The only thing I could think about was Sofia in the back of that ambulance . . . all alone.

I called the bar and told Frank briefly what had happened and where I was headed. Contacting Sofia's parents entered my mind, but I had no way to reach them. I had no idea where they lived, and I didn't have their phone number. They had to be worried since she never arrived to pick up Matson after work.

It hurt my heart to imagine how scared Matson must be. The two of them were so close, and Sofia told me how he hated having his routine changed. And her not showing up to pick him up was one hell of a change.

I decided to make one last call before I pulled into the

hospital parking lot, and dialed Grant's number. He would want to know what happened. He'd never let me forget it if he read about in the paper or learned about it online instead of from me. And since he had no other life aside from butting into mine, I knew he'd meet me at the hospital and keep me company while I waited. Our conversation was brief; I cut it short when I reached the hospital.

After parking in the first space I found, I ran into the emergency entrance and headed straight for the woman sitting behind the check-in desk.

"Can I help you?" she asked with a smile.

"Sofia Richards. They just brought her in?"

"She's here, but she can't see anyone yet. Are you family?"

"No."

"Husband?"

"No."

"You'll have to have a seat then. I'll let the on-call nurse know you're waiting for her. In the meantime, I've called her emergency contacts, so they should be here soon." She dismissed me after that, her eyes focused on the computer screen in front of her.

When I hadn't moved after a few seconds, she glanced back up at me and frowned as she pointed at the empty chairs in the waiting room.

Feeling defeated, I headed toward the ugly fabric chairs and plopped into one. And I waited. I would waited all night, all week if I had to.

Thankfully, I didn't have to wait alone for long.

A woman walked into the waiting room holding Matson's hand. As soon as he spotted me, his eyes lit up.

"Ryan! You're back!"

He ran over to me, and I opened my arms to scoop him up.

"Hey, buddy. I missed you."

The woman gave us a curious look, probably thinking our reunion seemed over the top.

"I missed you too. Mama said you were someplace far away, and that's why I couldn't give you your drawing yet. You liked the cape best, though, right? I told her you would."

I propped him on my hip as he talked a mile a minute, filling me in on what had happened in his life lately. My heart swelled with so much emotion, I was afraid it would fucking burst.

"Matson, who's your friend?" The woman who looked way too much like my Sofia focused her gaze on me.

"This is Ryan. Mama's boyfriend. You know." Matson shrugged, completely unaware of why he was here at the hospital.

I placed Matson on his feet and extended a hand to Sofia's mom. "It's nice to meet you. Is she okay?"

"You too, Ryan. I've heard a lot about you. I'm Mira," she said before glancing over her shoulder. "And that's my husband, Craig." She pointed at the burly man hovering around the check-in desk, looking as anxious and worried as I felt. "We're waiting to find out. They said she's still being examined. Do you know what happened?"

I glanced down at Matson, who watched me with rapt attention. "I do, but—" I stopped myself from saying anything, not wanting Matson to hear this.

"Is Mama okay?" He looked up at his grandmother with

big eyes.

She gave him a reassuring smile and kissed the top of his head. "We'll know soon."

The kid was smart, I'd give him that. He saw right through her. Within seconds, his eyes welled with tears.

"Hey, hey," I said, crouching in front of him to focus his attention on me. "The guys in the ambulance told me she'd be okay. She just didn't feel good, so they gave her something to help her sleep."

"Okay," he said before leaning his head against my shoulder and yawning.

Sofia's mom stared at me. "You two kind of look alike," she said with a grin, and Matson's head shot up.

"It's the eyes. Mine are blue just like Ryan's."

"You're right. They are." She smiled at him before looking back at me. "I need to know what happened," she whispered, and I nodded.

"Not here." I nodded toward Matson, and she understood.

The hospital doors slid open, and a bunch of people walked in all at once. It took me a minute before I realized that it was my brothers, their girlfriends, and Grant.

"Ryan!" Nick called out as I pushed up from the chair and hugged my younger brother. "Are you okay?" he asked, and I nodded.

Frank grabbed me next, pulling me into a tight hug. "I'm glad you're okay."

"Who's watching the bar?" I asked, suddenly realizing that if they were all here, then no one was there.

"I closed it," Frank said, and when I asked him how, Nick laughed.

"He went old school. Just wrote a note and taped it on the door. It probably blew off the second you walked away."

Frank shrugged. "I don't care."

"Glad you're okay." Grant stepped forward and patted me on the back. "Is our angel all right?"

"They said she would be, but we haven't heard anything yet."

A look passed between us, and I knew exactly what he was thinking. The last time we were in a hospital together, it was for him. Who would have thought we'd be back so soon, and for Sofia this time?

"Oh my gosh, is this Matson? Are you Matson?"

Claudia bypassed me and headed straight for the cutest boy in the room. He clung shyly to his grandmother for only a second before putting out his hand for her to shake.

She took it and said, "I'm Claudia. I'm, um . . . Frank's girlfriend."

"Who's Frank?" Matson asked, and we all laughed.

"Frank is Ryan's brother," Claudia said as Jess walked over.

"Hi, Matson. I'm Jess. I'm Nick's girlfriend."

Matson's face scrunched up. "Who's Nick?"

More laughter. "Nick is Ryan's other brother."

"You sure have a lot of brothers," Matson said, giving me a disgruntled look. "I don't have any."

Honest to God, I had to bite my tongue. It took everything in me to not tell him that I could fix that.

Sofia's dad joined us and I made quick introductions. Everyone started chatting at once as if they were old friends. And just when I thought my heart couldn't expand any more, my parents walked through the doors.

Frank saw my surprise. "I called them."

Dad grabbed me first and tried to squeeze the life out of me. "I'm so glad you're okay. I don't know what we'd do if we lost any of you boys." His voice broke, which surprised me. I'd rarely seen him so choked up.

The second he let go of me, my mom swooped in. "Ryan, are you okay? Frank told us what happened. You almost died?"

Mom's voice was loud and I tried to shush her, but it was too late. Sofia's mom was at our side in an instant.

"Almost died? Ryan, I need to know everything that happened. Right now." Mira's fierce expression softened and she stopped to look at my mom. "Hi, I'm Mira. Sofia's mom."

"I've heard all about your daughter, but I haven't had the pleasure yet, I'm sorry to say," my mom said with a genuine smile, and Mira smiled in return.

"Well, I only met Ryan for the first time about," Mira looked at her watch, "ten minutes ago?"

"Kids these days." Mom rolled her eyes, and Mira chuckled.

"Ryan, can I steal you?" Mira glanced at Matson, who was currently bouncing between Claudia and Jess's laps, eating up all the attention and looking like he was having the time of his life.

We walked outside, and once the doors closed behind us, I filled Sofia's mom in on everything that I knew, all the way up until Sofia's accident and Derek's shooting. She didn't interrupt, taking in every one of my words, her hand firmly placed over her mouth the entire time.

By the time I'd finished, her eyes were wide with horror. "I can't believe I didn't know any of this was going on."

"She didn't want to worry you," I said, standing up for my sweet girl.

"She could have been killed. You could have been killed."

Mira started to cry, and even though I wanted to comfort her by insisting that wasn't true, I couldn't lie to her. Instead, I patted her shoulder awkwardly until she sniffed back her tears and tried to smile at me.

"Thank you, Ryan. Thank you for saving my baby girl."

"She saved me too."

I meant it in more ways than one. Aside from selflessly dumping me to keep me alive, Sofia had saved me from myself, from the lonely life I was living before she and Matson became a part of it.

She gave me things I never knew I needed, things I now refused to live without.

NURSE RYAN
Sofia

MY EYES REFUSED to open. My brain gave the orders to do so, yet they refused, feeling like they were glued shut. Forcing myself to relax, I sucked in a few calming breaths before I attempted to open them again.

This time they did, and my blurred vision slowly cleared. Ryan sat sleeping in a chair I didn't recognize with Matson asleep in his arms. I focused on that scene, wondering if I was dreaming. *No, this isn't a dream*, I told myself as I stared at the man I wanted to share my heart with as he held the little boy who already owned it.

Groggy, I took in my surroundings and noticed a second chair, where Grant sat with his chin on his chest, snoring. He looked so comfortable, even though I knew there was no way that he could be.

Suddenly, the puzzle pieces inside my head connected, and I realized I was in a hospital. I lay my head back on the pillow, searching for the reason why, but I had no memory of what happened to land me here.

Afraid to close my eyes again in case they decided not to open, I stared up at the ceiling and tried harder to remember. Why was I here, and where were my parents?

Think Sofia, think, I chastised myself, knowing the answers were in my head somewhere. Bits and pieces flashed in my mind, but all I saw was Derek and me taking a curve way too fast.

Parched, I looked at the table near my bed, hoping to find a glass of water and thankful to see one there. But when I moved to grab it, I knocked it over, sending the plastic cup bouncing to the floor. Liquid splashed all over the white tile, and I cursed under my breath as Ryan's eyes shot open and Grant startled awake.

"Angel." Ryan sounded so relieved as our eyes met across the room. He struggled to move, but with Matson sleeping in his arms, he was momentarily stuck.

"She's *my* angel, pipsqueak," Grant said in a low voice, his tone teasing. He pushed himself awkwardly out of his chair, avoiding the spilled water on the floor as he came to my side. "Hey there, sweet girl. How are you feeling?"

"A little groggy," I answered honestly before being struck with an odd thought. "This is how we all started." I looked between Grant and Ryan and tried to smile.

"Come again?" Grant tilted his head.

"In a hospital. The three of us," I said, trying to explain, but was afraid I wasn't making any sense.

"Don't tell me you forgot, old man," Ryan whispered from the chair, where he still hadn't figured out how to get up without waking up Matson.

Grant flipped him off. "I didn't forget; I just didn't know what was she was talking about. She did hit her head, you know."

I reached for my head and pressed my hand against it,

wincing with the pain. *Ow.* Deciding to ask more about that later, I moved my hand back to my stomach.

"I'm sorry I woke you both. I really wanted that water." I almost started crying, but I had no idea why. I was really confused. And thirsty.

"I'll get you some." Ryan finally maneuvered Matson out of his arms and placed him gently on the chair before shaking his arm out.

"Asleep?" I asked.

His arm had to be. Every time Matson fell asleep with me on the couch, it always made my arm fall dead asleep. But I refused to move it, because holding him was worth the pain. One day he wouldn't want to snuggle with me anymore, so all the pins-and-needles discomfort was worth it.

"Killing me." Ryan walked over to me, giving Grant a little shove before leaning down to give me a kiss. "I'm so glad you're okay. Let me get you that water, and then we'll talk."

"All right."

Ryan returned in seconds with a nurse in tow. She smiled when she saw I was awake.

"How are you feeling?"

"Fine, I think. Just thirsty." *And foggy and confused*, but I kept that part to myself.

"Ryan mentioned that."

The nurse cast him a flirty glance, and instead of being annoyed, I was amused by it. That man wanted to be with *me*. He held *my* son in his arms. I had nothing to worry about when it came to him and other women.

She bent down to clean up the water I'd spilled, and filled a clean cup before handing it to me. "How's your head?" she asked, and I didn't make the mistake of touching it again.

"Sore, but manageable."

"Just press that button if it starts to hurt." She lifted a handheld controller and placed it in my hand.

"Thanks." I dropped it beside me, wishing she would leave so I could figure out what happened, how long I'd been here, and where my parents were.

She took her sweet time as she checked my vitals and fussed over me, no doubt wanting attention from Ryan. But he refused to even make eye contact with her as he walked to my bed and sat on the edge of it, reaching for my hand and bringing it to his lips.

"Okay," she finally said. "I'm going now."

"'Bye," I said, my humor clearly shifting back to annoyance. Hospital Sofia was moody. When the nurse left and closed the door behind her, I huffed out a breath. "Thought she'd never leave."

Ryan laughed. "She was here for less than two minutes."

"I wanted her to stay." Grant waggled his eyebrows.

I let out a soft laugh that hurt my chest and rib cage. Was my whole body sore?

"Angel," Grant said gruffly, "I'm really glad you're all right. I'm gonna go home and let you and this big oaf have some alone time."

"Thank you for being here." My eyes pricked with unexpected tears, and he let out a huff.

"I refused to leave."

"Really?"

"They tried to kick the old man out, but your parents said he could stay." Ryan looked at Grant like he was crazy, but in a good way.

"I wouldn't have left anyway. I would have camped right outside your door." Grant was stubborn, but that was part of his charm. "Take care of *my* angel." He gave Ryan a finger poke to the chest before leaning down to give me a kiss on my cheek. "I'll be in touch."

"Thank you again."

"I plan on being just as annoying as you were to me," he said as he headed toward the door.

"Deal," I responded with a grin as he disappeared.

With my attention back on Ryan, I launched into all the questions on the tip of my tongue.

"I'm dying here, Ryan. What happened? Where are my parents? Is Matson okay? I mean, is he worried? Scared? Are you okay?"

Ryan had started counting my questions on his fingers, but stopped. "Your parents and mine left to get some dinner."

He said it like it was no big deal, and I blinked twice.

"Together?" I asked, unable to picture it. "They went to get dinner together?"

"Yes. It was the only way I could get them to leave. But I should probably text them and let them know you're awake."

"Not yet. Just wait a second. How do they even know each other?" A terrible thought ripped through me and I placed a hand over my heart. "Oh my gosh, Ryan, how long have I been here? Tell me it hasn't been weeks or months."

I craned my neck to stare at Matson, taking in his each and every feature. He looked the same, not like I'd missed any significant time in his growth.

Ryan intertwined his fingers with mine, his thumb caressing my skin, the touch instantly calming me. "You've been here since last night. You've woken up a few times, but your head always hurt, so they gave you stuff for the pain that made you sleepy."

"Okay, so our parents have met. Sounds like they like each other, yeah?" I was hopeful.

He grinned. "They like each other. They like each other a lot." He said it like a mischievous boy, which made me laugh.

"Really?" I asked, needing more clarification.

"They're acting like they're old friends instead of people who just met yesterday. Your mom and my mom are already lining up 'play dates' with Matson and each other." He gave me a silly look as he used his fingers to make air quotes.

I smiled because it sounded so perfect. I wouldn't have wanted their eventual meeting to go any other way. "That's actually really nice. It makes me happy."

"It is really nice," he said with a chuckle. "Wait until you see them together. I'm afraid we're never going to get them apart again."

There were so many horror stories when it came to your significant other's mom, and the idea that it wouldn't be like that for us filled my heart with gratitude. I knew as I looked at this man that he was my future, and I didn't have to ask him to know that he felt the same way about me.

But I still needed answers about how I got here. There was so much I didn't remember.

"Ryan, what happened?"

His amused expression turned solemn. "What do you remember?"

Frowning, I looked at the ceiling, thinking. "Just bits and

pieces, mostly. Derek. You. I lost control of my car, I think." I met his amazing blue eyes, which winced with pain when I said those words. "Is that right? Did I crash into something?"

"Yeah, you hit a tree. The force of the impact sent your head back, and you slammed into your headrest before you crashed into your steering wheel. Knocked you out cold."

"The airbag didn't deploy?" I had no idea why I even thought of that question when I should have been thinking of a million others.

"No, it must be faulty. We need to get that checked while they're doing the repairs. What if Matson had been in the car?" Ryan asked.

I shuddered at that, shaking my head to chase away the thought. "I can't go there."

"Me either," he said, and I couldn't believe the way this man cared about my son.

"Where's Derek?"

I asked the one question I'd been avoiding, afraid that Ryan would tell me he was still out there, waiting for us to leave so he could hurt us both. Ryan still didn't know the truth about why I asked him to stay away; he believed my reasons were all centered around Matson.

I needed to be completely honest with Ryan and apologize profusely for lying. I'd never felt good about the lie, but it had been the only way to get him to listen. Still, I hated myself a little for doing it.

"There's no easy way to say this . . ."

As Ryan struggled to find the words, I had no idea what was coming next. But I found myself comforting him, running my hand up and down his arm. "Just say it."

Ryan met my gaze, his forehead creased. "Derek's dead."

"What?" I looked at Ryan, finally taking in the worry I hadn't noticed until now. Apparently, he was concerned with how I'd react to the news. "He's dead? How? What happened?"

"You lost control of your car. You remember that, right?"

"Kind of, yeah."

"Well, when I got to you—" His voice broke with emotion, and I could tell how hard it was for him to relive those moments again. "When I got to you, you weren't moving. You were slumped over the steering wheel, and I couldn't get in. I tried so hard to get to you, but I couldn't."

A single tear rolled down his face, and my heart broke at the thought of all he must have gone through.

"Derek showed up with a gun. I thought he was going to shoot you, Sofia. I thought he wanted to kill you. But he wanted to shoot me."

Ryan's anguish brought tears to my own eyes. "Are you hurt? Did he hurt you?" I pawed at him like a madwoman, checking him over for bandages or injuries.

He grabbed my hands and held them tight. "I'm fine. When I left the bar to chase after you, Frank called the cops and had them follow me. If he hadn't done that, I don't know what would have happened. Probably would have been too late. But they weren't . . . they showed up just in time. They told Derek to drop the gun, but he didn't. He put his finger on the trigger, and they shot him."

I couldn't believe that I remembered none of this. Why hadn't the gunshots woken me up? I'd been passed out unconscious while chaos erupted around me, and I had no idea. Ryan could have been killed, and I wouldn't have even known.

"Are you okay?" Ryan cupped my cheek, his brows pinched with concern. It was so sweet, how worried he was about my reaction. But if our roles were reversed, I would have felt the exact same way.

"Is it wrong that I feel relieved more than anything?" I whispered.

He shook his head. "No. He told me he warned you to stay away from me or else he'd kill me."

My eyes flew open wide. "He told you that?"

Ryan nodded. "He got a lot of pleasure out of telling me that. But he wouldn't tell me why."

"I'm so sorry I lied to you about that."

He gave me a sympathetic look. "Don't be. I understand."

"I didn't think you'd really stay away if you knew the truth."

He gave me a lopsided grin. "You know I wouldn't have. So, tell me, why the threats? I haven't been able to figure it out on my own, and not knowing is driving me crazy."

I explained what Derek had told me, about his father's insistence on our getting back together, and his threats to leave the company to Derek's cousin.

Ryan's face turned grim. "That's one messed-up family, angel. We've gotta make sure Matson never goes anywhere near them." He squeezed my hand and looked at my son, and I squeezed back.

"I know."

*

THANK GOD, MY memory came back shortly after getting released from the hospital.

I remembered everything—from showing up at the bar, to calling Ryan from the car in hysterics, and right up until I crashed. I remembered seeing the huge tree and not being able to avoid it. But I didn't remember anything else until waking up at the hospital with Ryan and Grant, although I was told I'd woken up several times before then.

For the next few weeks, Ryan catered to me, even though it wasn't long before I was fine. He refused to leave my side, wanting to be sure that I was not only physically all right, but emotionally okay as well. Even after I went back to work, he made sure to be with me as much as possible.

It was sweet, being cared for like that. After having Matson, I'd never allowed anyone, aside from my parents, to do anything for me. I wasn't sure I knew how. But with Ryan, it felt nice to allow myself to depend on him . . . right, even. He did things for me that I would have wanted to do for him if our roles were reversed, so I reminded myself of that fact often. Ryan showed me day after day what the true meaning of a partner was, something I'd never known before him, something I hadn't been sure I was ever going to have.

He stayed at the house every night, sleeping on the couch so Matson wouldn't get confused or pushed aside. And no matter how many times I told him to go back to work, Ryan kept insisting he wasn't ready. He'd swapped shifts with one of their day bartenders so he was still at the bar while I was at work, but the second I got home with Matson in tow, Ryan was quickly behind.

I liked having him here. Actually, I loved having him here,

but I knew it couldn't last forever. Eventually, he needed to work the hours he was meant to, and would probably have to go back to sleeping at own place at night.

Secretly, I hated that he would probably go home soon. Ryan Fisher sure was easy to get used to.

"I want to be here for you until I know you're okay."

He assured me of that night after night, and part of me wondered if he needed to stay with me just as much as I needed him there. Ryan had gone through hell too. We both had.

Tragedy tended to bond the people who experienced it together, and no matter how badly others wanted to relate to our experience and understand it, they couldn't. Ryan and I needed each other in order to come out on the other side.

*

ONE NIGHT AS we were getting ready for bed, Matson told Ryan, "You should sleep in Mama's bed. It's way better than the couch."

"Would you be okay with me sleeping in her bed?" Ryan asked, trying not to make it a big deal, but it was clear he wasn't sure how to navigate this. When he looked at me for help, I made a face and forced him to take the lead.

Matson shrugged like he wasn't bothered in the least. "Why not? It has pillows and everything."

"It does sound nice," Ryan said, nodding seriously as if he were considering it for the first time, and I had to stop myself from laughing out loud.

Matson leaned close to whisper in his ear, but I still heard him anyway. "And that way when I sneak in, I can sleep between both of you instead of just with Mama. Her hands are always ice cold, and yours are always hot."

Ryan had always told me that my hands were made of ice, but he claimed to like it, placing them on any sore spots he had on his shoulders and back.

"Well, if your mom says it's okay," Ryan said, giving me a sly glance, "then I'll start sleeping in there with her."

Matson nodded. "She'll say okay. She likes you."

I cleared my throat, causing Matson to jump away from Ryan like he'd gotten caught stealing the last cookie. "Time for bed. Go brush your teeth, please." I only had to ask once, and Matson practically skipped down the hall after he stopped to give me a hug.

"Guess I'm sleeping with you now, ice pack," Ryan teased, and when I swatted at his arm, he grabbed my hand and pulled me hard against him. "Ice-pack angel? Angel ice pack?"

"Will you start the hashtag? I still like #CryinOverRyan the best."

His lips brushed mine. "You would."

Ryan was right. That particular hashtag started on social media after word got out that he had a girlfriend. A bigger person wouldn't have enjoyed it as much as I did, but apparently I liked the world knowing he was off the market.

Ryan had also been right about Derek's father being sick. Damian Huntington passed away a few days after Derek had been killed, and the company ended up going to his cousin, just like Derek had feared. It was the first time in the history of the firm that it didn't go to the Huntington heir, and I was actually grateful that the cycle had been broken. As far as I knew, no one from the company knew Matson even existed, and since I gave him my last name and Derek wasn't listed on his birth certificate, there would be no reason for anyone to suspect he had a son.

*

I WAITED ALMOST a full month after the accident to see if Mrs. Huntington would reach out to me after everything that happened. When she didn't, I decided to be the bigger person. As much as I disliked her family, I knew she was grieving and had lost her whole world within the span of a few days. I couldn't imagine what she was going through, or how alone she must have felt. She deserved to know she had a grandson.

I knew she still lived in the same house they'd lived in when Derek and I were in high school, so I dropped a condolence card in the mail to her, along with a recent school picture of Matson.

Mariana Huntington showed up on my doorstep the same day she got my card, expensively dressed, her shoulder-length brown hair perfectly styled, and tears in her eyes.

"Sofia, I had no idea. Derek and Damian said you were pregnant, but they told me you didn't have the baby. They said they paid you off, and I never questioned them or thought about it again. I'm so sorry."

"You didn't know?" I was bewildered how she couldn't have known. It also made me incredibly sad that I'd wasted so much time hating her for being able to stay away from us for so long when it hadn't even been true.

"No, I didn't. Can I come in?" she asked as she wiped her

eyes.

I held my front door open and allowed her inside before offering her some tea. We sat at my kitchen table and cried together over all the time we'd lost due to miscommunication.

She absolutely lost it when she learned what the men in her life had been up to behind her back. The poor woman had been completely left in the dark about the ugly inner workings of the Huntington men.

To be honest, I think she preferred it that way. Mrs. Huntington wasn't stupid, but I think staying blissfully unaware of her family's dirty dealings helped keep her sane and her conscience clear. She slept peacefully at night, and I couldn't—no, I *wouldn't*—blame her for that.

She left that day with the promise to keep in touch.

When I decided a few days later to tell Matson who she was, he was so excited.

"I'm going to have three grandmas? That's so cool!"

My heart swelled at his reaction, especially the fact that he'd included Ryan's mom as one of his grandmas already.

Ryan warned me that our moms had bonded while I was in the hospital, but I had no idea just how much. His mom accepted Matson and me like we were blood relatives, and my family did the same for Ryan. It never ceased to amaze me that family dynamics like this existed.

*

THREE QUICK KNOCKS sounded at my front door before the doorknob turned, alerting me to the fact that Jess and Claudia were here. They'd been stopping by without warning for days now, often enough that I'd learned to expect them.

"Did you miss us?" Jess asked as she walked in.

"It's like I don't know what to do without you two anymore," I teased back before giving them each a hug.

These women were both so welcoming, accepting, and nice, I understood completely why Frank and Nick loved them. I felt like I'd been initiated into a secret club that revolved around the Fisher brothers, and I never wanted to be out of it.

"Aunt Jess?" Matson yelled from his room before he careened down the hall and into her arms, giving her a big hug as she swung him around.

Matson had a huge crush on her. "I like her yellow hair," he would say every time she left, and would run to the kitchen table to draw a new picture of her. There were yellow-haired drawings all over my house.

"I'm starting to get a complex, little man," Claudia whined, and Matson dove into her arms next.

I stared at them, grinning from ear to ear, wondering how in the world my life had changed so drastically in such a short time. Our family had grown so big, and yet I hadn't realized we had such a small one before. I'd always thought that my heart and Matson's were full, our lives fulfilled and our family complete, but having all this love and these wonderful people around us made me see just how much we'd been missing.

We were the luckiest people in Santa Monica, and I hoped that never changed.

MY FUTURE
Ryan

Eight months later

TODAY WAS MATSON'S ninth birthday, and everyone was in our backyard eating before we headed to the bowling alley for his actual party. My parents, my brothers and their girlfriends, Sofia's parents, her friend Sarin, Grant, and even Mariana Huntington were all sitting around the tables I'd set up, chatting like old friends. On days like this, I almost couldn't believe this was our life. It seemed too good to be true—too easy, too fucking wonderful.

Sofia and Matson were my family now, my future, and I'd do anything to stay in their lives. I wasn't ever leaving their sides again, which was why I insisted on moving in with them at the end of Matson's school year.

Okay, insisted might be too strong a word, but I strongly suggested the idea, and both Sofia and Matson had enthusiastically agreed.

We went out for ice cream to celebrate that night. I wanted to puke after eating all that sugar, but I promised to punish myself at the gym the next day. We went out for ice cream again when the owners of Sofia's rental house said they weren't planning on moving back to the States, and sold us their house at a fraction of what it was worth. Clearly, I never learned my lesson on celebrating good news with ice cream.

I tried to pay the owners more money, considering that I could afford it with the success of the bar, but they wouldn't have it. They said they didn't need it, and told us to save it for all the other babies we planned on having in the future.

Sofia's face had paled a little when she heard that, and mine had done the complete opposite. There was nothing I wanted more than to have a few dozen little Sofias and Ryans running around our yard, but I knew that no matter how much I wanted to knock her up, that would have to wait.

"Hey, loser," Grant grumped as he came up next to me in the doorway. "Why are you over here? We're all out there."

"I was just watching," I said with a smile I couldn't erase if I'd tried.

Sofia happened to look over at that moment, and she looked so damn happy, it almost made my heart burst. Her smile was just for me, but I knew Grant was going to claim it was for him. I was in too good a mood to fight him over it.

"She's your angel now," he said, and I swung my head around at him in shock.

"Say what?" I cupped a hand around my ear and leaned toward him, not believing what I was hearing.

"You heard me, jackass. Plus, I might have a new angel." He nodded toward Mariana Huntington, and I slapped him on the back.

"You dog. You sure move on quick."

"She's a nice lady," he said. "Sure got a raw deal with that marriage of hers."

I nodded because he was right. When Sofia had first told

me about Derek's mom, I was wary, distrustful, all my protective instincts flaring. Could she be trusted?

But after I met Mariana, all my fears disappeared. She was a good person, truly kindhearted. I had no idea how someone like her could have possibly raised someone as screwed up as Derek.

My admiration for her only grew when she told me she planned to pay for Matson's college expenses, and anything else we needed help with, since Sofia had done everything on her own for so long. Mariana had told me first because she knew I'd have to talk Sofia into accepting any help of that magnitude.

And she was right.

At first, Sofia put up a fight, but I eventually got her to see it was Mariana's way of apologizing, of trying to make amends in *her* own heart, not necessarily Sofia's. Mariana had a lot of guilt she needed to work through, and this was part of her way of doing that.

Sofia made her way toward me and gave me a hug, wrapping her arms around my waist as she nuzzled her head against my chest.

"I love you," I said against her hair.

She looked up at me, those hazel eyes shining. "I love you too."

"Where were you headed?" I asked as she pulled out of my arms.

"To pee." She laughed before hurrying away, and I swatted her ass.

Smiling, I looked around our yard at everyone who cared about us. Nick held on to Jess like she might run away at any moment, his fingers hooked through the belt loop on her shorts. He wasn't entirely wrong to be worried—Matson had been trying to steal her away for months now. Did I mention that my house is filled with crayon drawings of Jess? They're everywhere. I think I could wallpaper Matson's room with them if he asked.

Frank and Claudia stood arm in arm, both wearing black shirts and dark jeans, which I knew they hadn't planned. It was the family joke now how they always showed up in matching outfits without trying. They both claimed that when they got dressed, they usually picked out the same color shirts, and then they both refused to change. Nick was relentless in his teasing of them, but I thought it was sweet.

Grant currently had Mariana laughing hysterically at something he'd said, and I chuckled at the idea of him hitting on her. Maybe they'd be just what the other needed—friendship, companionship, or even love? I had no idea, but I was glad they found each other.

As for me, I planned to propose when the time was right. The ring I bought a couple of months ago was sitting in the safe at the bar, next to the one Nick had bought for Jess ages ago. I couldn't wait to give Matson a little brother or sister.

Or five.

Or maybe twelve.

However many babies Sofia would let me put inside her belly, I planned on doing exactly that. I'd do it tomorrow if she let me. Hell, I'd do it right now.

I'd probably have to enlist Matson's help on the baby front since Sofia seemed a little skittish. Having your first child all by yourself probably wasn't the best memory for someone to have. But every day, I remembered how excited Matson got when he met my brothers that night at the hospital, and all I'd wanted since then was to give him siblings of his own.

Our future was crystal clear in my head, and waiting for it to start was sheer torture.

"I just want to start our life," I complained to Sofia almost daily.

"It's already started, babe," she'd tell me every time. "We're in it. This is our life. It's begun."

And I knew she was right, but it was the rest of it that I wanted—the wedding, the babies, being husband and wife. All the other things that I envisioned and planned for in the future, I wanted them right now.

No one said I was a patient man.

"Uh, Ryan?" Sofia said in a strained voice.

I spun around, and when I saw how pale she looked, I rushed to her side. "What's the matter? Are you sick? You don't look okay."

She shoved a white stick at me, and I stared down at it. PREGNANT showed in the tiny oval screen.

My breath left my body as my heart thumped. All rational thoughts exited my head before coming back. I picked her up and swung her around, planting kisses all over her face before gently placing her back down.

"You're happy?" she asked, sounding absolutely terrified.

"Happy? I'm ecstatic, angel!"

"Really?"

"Hell yes! If I would've known you could get pregnant despite your birth control, I would've tried a lot harder."

Sofia swatted at me, her worry flitting away, leaving a huge smile on her face.

I guessed I wouldn't have to wait for our future to begin, after all. Sofia was right . . . we were in it. It was happening. And it was happening exactly how I wanted it to.

Right *now*.

The End

Thank you so much for reading Ryan and Sofia's story. I hope you enjoyed reading it as much as I enjoyed writing it. Have you met the rest of the Fisher brothers? Make sure you read Nick's story, *No Bad Days*, and Frank's, *Guy Hater*.

And please join my mailing list to be notified of any new releases or sales!
http://tinyurl.com/pf6al6u

AUTHOR'S NOTE

This story was quite personal to me. I say that every time, but I've never written about a single mom before. Which is crazy because I am one, and I always write what I know. Maybe I avoided it for some reason until now, maybe I wasn't ready to go there . . . and yet here we are.

Writing Sofia's story was as cathartic as it was painful. I really do hope you loved it. I hope I gave you a little insight into the inner workings of a mom's heart and mind—not just a single mom, but moms in general. I hope I made you proud.

Thank you so much for reading my books, for giving them a chance to touch your heart . . . and I hope they do. If you'd be so kind as to leave a review before you head on to your next book adventure, I'd really appreciate it.

Thank you again.

ACKNOWLEDGMENTS

My books don't happen by themselves. Michelle Warren makes my covers beautiful so you want to buy the books. Pam Berehulke edits my books, prettying up my words so you want to read them. And my beta readers Krista Arnold and Emma Mack make the story better, so you'll hopefully love it as much as they did. Thank you all so much for helping me tell Ryan's. I appreciate you. :)

Thank you to all the Kittens in my reader group on Facebook—you make the whole internet a better place to be. I've never met a more amazing group of women (and couple of men) than you all. Thank you for reading my books and for supporting my heart the way you do (you girls know what I'm talking about).

Thank you to Blake—who made me a mom. Who's the best thing to ever happen to my life, and who makes every day exciting and fun.

Thank you to my mom for her plot ideas on this story while we sat in her sewing room talking about it. Let's do it again sometime, Lady! It was fun.

Thanks to my man—for showing up in every story I tell. For letting me hear you in the dialogue that I write. For being everything I never knew I needed and wanted in life. You inspire me daily. Don't ever change.

And thank you to Mario & John's in Petaluma—especially Danny, who helped with all the drinks that Ryan creates.

Danny is one of the most talented craftsmen around and introduced me to the world of incredible cocktails. If you're ever in the area, make sure you stop by and tell the guys hi!

OTHER BOOKS BY J. STERLING

In Dreams
Chance Encounters
10 Years Later – A Second Chance Romance
Daniel Alexander
Dear Heart, I Hate You

THE GAME SERIES
The Perfect Game – Book One
The Game Changer – Book Two
The Sweetest Game – Book Three
The Other Game (Dean Carter) – Book Four

THE CELEBRITY SERIES
Seeing Stars – Madison & Walker
Breaking Stars – Paige & Tatum
Losing Stars – Quinn & Ryson (Coming Soon)

THE FISHER BROTHERS SERIES
No Bad Days – Nick Fisher
Guy Hater – Frank Fisher
Adios Pantalones – Ryan Fisher

ABOUT THE AUTHOR

Jenn Sterling is a Southern California native who loves writing stories from the heart. Every story she tells has pieces of her truth in it, as well as her life experience. She has her bachelor's degree in Radio/TV/Film and has worked in the entertainment industry the majority of her life.

Jenn loves hearing from her readers and can be found online at:

Blog & Website:
www.j-sterling.com

Twitter:
www.twitter.com/RealJSterling

Facebook:
facebook.com/TheRealJSterling

Private Facebook Reader Group:
facebook.com/groups/ThePerfectGameChangerGroup

Instagram:
www.instagram.com/RealJSterling

If you enjoyed this book, please consider writing a spoiler-free review on the site from which you purchased it. And thank you so much for helping me spread the word about my books, and for allowing me to continue telling the stories I love to tell. I appreciate you so much. :)

27530731R00186

Printed in Poland
by Amazon Fulfillment
Poland Sp. z o.o., Wrocław